T0279232

WE ARE HUNTED

Tomi Oyemakinde

FEIWEL AND FRIENDS
New York

For my father and my brother:
I am beyond grateful for the relationship we have.
It is unlike the worst parts of this story while
embodying the best parts.

For Alex and Naomi. Happy anniversary.

A Feiwel and Friends Book
An imprint of Macmillan Publishing Group, LLC
120 Broadway, New York, NY 10271 • fiercereads.com

Copyright © 2024 by Tomi Oyemakinde. All rights reserved.

Our books may be purchased in bulk for promotional, educational,
or business use. Please contact your local bookseller or the Macmillan Corporate
and Premium Sales Department at (800) 221-7945 ext. 5442 or by email at
MacmillanSpecialMarkets@macmillan.com.

Library of Congress Cataloging-in-Publication Data

Names: Oyemakinde, Tomi, author.
Title: We are hunted / Tomi Oyemakinde.
Description: First edition. | New York : Feiwel and Friends, 2024. | Audience:
Ages 14–18. | Audience: Grades 10–12. | Summary: Expecting paradise on
a remote island vacation, seventeen-year-old Femi and fellow guests are
instead met with terror when the animals on the island turn feral.
Identifiers: LCCN 2024010853 | ISBN 9781250868169 (hardcover)
Subjects: CYAC: Resorts—Fiction. | Islands—Fiction. | Feral animals—
Fiction. | Extortion—Fiction. | Black people—Fiction.
Classification: LCC PZ7.1.O8985 We 2024 | DDC [Fic]—dc23
LC record available at https://lccn.loc.gov/2024010853

First edition, 2024
Book design by Michelle Gengaro-Kokmen
Feiwel and Friends logo designed by Filomena Tuosto
All emojis designed by OpenMoji—the open-source emoji and icon project.
License: CC BY-SA 4.0
Printed in the United States of America

ISBN 978-1-250-86816-9
1 3 5 7 9 10 8 6 4 2

I
POETIC
JUSTICE

"It is such an uncomfortable feeling
to know one is a fool."

—L. Frank Baum, *The Wonderful Wizard of Oz*

"My magnum opus will never come! That is to
say, my heights will continue to rise as long
as there is wonder left in the world,
and breath in my bones."

—Richard Jenkins, *Vanity Fair* interview

CHAPTER 1

DEPARTURE

THE SHADOW FROM THE MOUTH OF THE FERRY SHROUDS our car in fuzzy darkness. Up ahead are fierce-looking headlights belonging to the car in front of us. We creep forward and dim, overhead light emerges to soften the darkness.

I stretch my arms wide, yawning until my eyes water. "Finally," I mutter.

We left home for the Port of Dover at six in the morning and were on the road for just shy of four hours. I'd spent most of that time thinking about how to get through this holiday: Dad and I keep butting heads over my future, while Dapo and I are in the middle of a cold war.

Nothing a week on a tropical island resort won't fix, I think, with a wry smile. *I'll just have to keep to myself as much as I can.* I purse my lips and roll my eyes. This whole trip was Mum's idea. All the top shareholders of Jenkins & Children were told to attend a mandatory conference on this tropical island or risk losing their shares. Dad was prepared to go alone until Mum intervened. "You and Dapo should go with your dad to this resort. It will be good for you to bond," she'd said, knowing full well things had shifted between her "three favorite men." Knowing she'd booked a girls' trip to Malta at the same time.

It's not all doom and gloom, though. The resort in question—on the island of Darlenia—is an enigma. Its official website is a black page with words, in white, that say: EXPERIENCE PARADISE, REIMAGINED.

Beneath them is the logo of Jenkins & Children—a pale face gazing at its reflection in the mirror. Everyone knows that five years ago, Richard Jenkins, the CEO, introduced the island he'd discovered to the world. The press coverage was extensive yet vague, and within the year he was *Time* magazine's Person of the Year. Since then, Richard Jenkins has been everywhere. Countless profiles, documentaries, and books.

The only people who know what the words *Experience paradise, reimagined* mean are those who have been to the island, and they're silenced by an NDA. The night before we signed *our* NDAs— with two witnesses present—I dried out my eyes googling everything and anything I could find on the island. Reddit threads, wiki pages, and video exposés all have their own theories. Some claim the island has an artificial climate, with manufactured clouds and rain and rainbows appearing on demand; another rumor is adamant the island is an immersive experience, populated with actors like those on *The Truman Show*; while a minority believe it's full of advanced androids and AI. Every theory is an outlandish derivative of the former. The one unifying thread I managed to find, that I'm sure is true, because it *has* to be, was that, on arrival, every expectation of the island is shattered.

My expectations are high. I'm thinking never-been-released technology, amazing scenery, and attractions that put Disney World to shame.

Craning my neck, I peer through the back windows and see the last bits of the land we're leaving behind. I deflate, but refuse to sink, shaking my head and taking a deep breath. I might not like the situation, but I'm going to enjoy myself by fire, by force. My toes scrunch in my shoes, and I turn over the phrase *Paradise, reimagined* in my head.

A sharp tap on my knee jolts me. Dapo twists around in his seat to hold out a couple of fancy-looking earplugs.

"Here, Femi. I got these for you. For your tinnitus."

I go to reach for them but hesitate. Dapo's been in the habit of keeping score and reminding me of his good deeds when we clash. "Thanks, but I'm fine," I say, focusing again on my phone screen. "No humming or buzzing for months."

"Sure. But I read that ferry terminals can be quite loud, and better safe than sorry. You don't want to be without them when your tinnitus inevitably spikes. Plus, I did a lot of research to make sure these would work a treat."

"Do you want a medal?" I regret the words immediately. There's no reason to escalate things when he's trying. "Sorry. I appreciate it, but I just don't need them."

Dapo sighs, then thrusts his hand into my eyeline. "I'd feel a lot better if you would just take them. I paid a fortune, and I can't take them back, so…"

Not my problem.

"Okay, how about this: If my tinnitus acts up, I'll come find you and claim them." His hand continues to hover and I frown. "Seriously, why can't you just—"

I catch Dad looking at me through the rearview mirror, his stare as intense as clashing cymbals. "Fine," I say under my breath, taking the earplugs from Dapo. "Cheers."

"They're high fidelity, which means you can reduce—"

"Reduce the sound levels without distorting it, I know. Not my first rodeo." I've been dealing with tinnitus for the past few years.

Dapo opens his mouth to say something, but instead he swallows his words and fiddles with the collar of his hideous polo shirt before turning back around.

I *told* Mum a boys' trip was a bad idea.

Dad stops the car and cranks the hand brake. A tall, rake-like man in a dark gray, military-style uniform stands waiting, the dim overhead lighting bouncing off his dark-brown skin. Shiny gold buttons wink as he takes a step toward the driver's side where Dad sits. There's a navy-blue acrylic nail on the man's index finger. Before he can tap it against the glass, Dad's already rolling down his window.

The man smiles and brings his hands together, revealing another acrylic nail—same color—on the pinkie finger of his other hand. "My name is Cuplow, and I am here to help you get situated. May I take your booking references, please?"

Dad reaches into his shirt pocket and *hmm*s. Then he reaches into both trouser pockets and mutters under his breath. Each second he can't find what he's looking for makes him more flustered. "Oh no, oh no, oh no. Where is it?"

I clear my throat. "Dad, it's all right. I thought this might happen. We can use the email you forwarded us. I've got—"

Dad grunts. "Hold on, Femi. Not now, please."

"There's no connection here, so your email won't load," Dapo states.

I sink my nails into the palm of my hand, not allowing my anger to boil over. Dad's always going on at me about contingencies and thinking ahead, and when I've done what he's suggested, he won't listen. No comment on Dapo.

"Where is it?" Dad almost growls. He flashes an apologetic grin at Cuplow whose smile is shrinking.

I take a deep breath and exercise self-control. "Dad, it's all right, I took a screenshot." I flash the QR codes on my screen to Dad and Dapo.

"Oh," Dad says.

Dapo says nothing as I hand my phone over to Cuplow, who scans them. His machine *beeps*.

"Splendid." Cuplow reaches into the darkness behind him, and when he turns back, he's brandishing three smartwatches, the straps navy blue in color.

"These are yours. Their color indicates the level of your guest package. Please do not lose them. They've been preloaded with relevant data, GPS, and varying degrees of access to parts of the resort. You may also use them to preorder and pay for items. And yes, you may keep your watch once you leave, though all data related to the island will be wiped, of course."

I take the watch offered to me and slide it onto my left wrist, noticing it has no buckle. There's a gentle buzz before it adjusts to hug the shape of my bony wrist. I'm transfixed. There's no other way to put it—this is the coolest thing I've had on my wrist ever.

Cuplow claps his hands. "Now then, on to formalities... yes, formalities." He takes a deep breath and turns to Dad. "The ferry is expected to reach the island tomorrow. Your designated parking spot on our ferry today is 1010—straight ahead, it'll be on your left—and your suite is in the east wing, room 237. Once parked, follow directions to the elevators. If you need anything, anything at all, tap your watch against the various help points and someone will assist. It is a pleasure to have you and your family with us, Mr. Fatona."

Dad smiles. "Where are you from? You look like you could be West African."

"My family originates from Senegal, sir."

"Yes. Very good." Dad tips Cuplow a fiver and drives off toward the designated bay.

The elevator doors open with a sigh onto an enormous lobby busy with guests motoring to and fro. They're wearing watches with different-colored straps—I spot navy blue, emerald green, and vivid orange—and I wonder how different the guest packages are.

Just as I step out of the elevator, I'm yanked back by Dapo. A group of staff in the same uniform as Cuplow's whiz by, carrying a wooden table, an aquarium, and two golf bags.

"Thanks," I say, smoothing out my clothes and stepping onto the plush carpet.

The forest of people clears enough for me to catch a glimpse of a tall, blond white man with ruddy cheeks. *Richard Jenkins. The one who discovered the island we're headed to.* Adjusting the scoop neck of his long-sleeved T-shirt, he yawns and scratches at his neat stubble. Two gym rats wearing earpieces and sunglasses stand on either side of him.

My eyes flicker back to Richard, who stands still as though he's the sun. *I want to feel like that*, I think. The thought is quick and intrusive and...inaccurate. *I don't want to be the center of attention—not like him.* I want to exist and have people understand me and what I'm about. I glance over at Dapo and Dad, who share a joke, then back at Richard.

A woman enters his orbit, a wry look on her face as she shows him something on a tablet. I can't lip-read, but his deep frown says enough.

"It's him," Dapo says, staring with his eyebrows pushed up by the sheer power of his admiration.

"It is," I say. "He's flesh and bone like you and me. Stop drooling."

Dapo laughs. "I'm not. But I don't think you understand. He's a risk-taker to his core—he gave up a high-powered job as an investment banker to pursue a start-up cargo transport business *during* a recession. And *he discovered a new island.* Sometimes I wish I could be like that. Take risks like him..."

I'd love to see that. In a blink, Richard and his security are gone, swept up in the hustle and bustle of the lobby.

"Our room's this way," Dad says, heading along the walkway. Dapo falls into stride with him.

I adjust the straps of my rucksack and follow. Dad's laugh

warbles through the air, and when he places an arm around Dapo's shoulder, a lump forms in my throat. I wonder what it would be like to walk a mile in Dapo's brogues. Would the metaphorical blisters be worth it?

Maybe.

Dapo unlocks the room with his watch. Before he disappears inside he gives me *the look*. When we were younger, I thought it was him showing solidarity in the wake of a brewing storm. But nah, now I know it was just him being glad he wasn't the one in trouble.

Dad stands in my way. There's a look of concern grooved onto his face. "Fems, can I talk with you?"

His rhetorical question grates like a synth being bashed by a toddler.

"Okay." I answer, keeping my hands rooted in my pockets.

"You had your meeting with that musician before we left, right? How did it go? Have you heard anything?"

"Yeah, with Xavier." I shrug. "We won't be making a song together, but it's fine. It is what it is. I've reflected and I think there will be more opportunities."

"Oh," Dad says, taking a step toward me the moment I try to squeeze past him. "I'm sorry. What happened? Did he say why?"

"He didn't get what I was trying to do, so we agreed it was better if we didn't work together." I don't bother mentioning the ultimatum I gave Xavier or the choice words he had for me before our call ended.

Dad tilts his head, his eyebrows bunching together. "Son, you don't do that. You don't turn down opportunities because they don't align with what you want."

"I said we agreed." I frown and hold back a scowl. "The decision was mutual and for the best."

"Sometimes you have to compromise. I compromised just the other day. Your mum wanted to watch a nature documentary. I find them boring, but I sat and watched with her because I wanted to spend time with her. And actually, I enjoyed the documentary."

"First, not the same. Second, you don't get it." My jaw clenches. *You never do.* I take a deep breath and loosen my curled fist. "He didn't want to compromise. He wanted to change everything I'd done. My whole sound."

"Well, uh, maybe he knew what he was doing. I, uh, I mean Xavier won an Oscar last year, didn't he?"

I close my eyes for a flutter of a second. "He won a *Grammy*, and that's not the point. You don't erase the details that make your sound *your* sound. That's like—I don't know…" I struggle to translate my thoughts into an example he'd understand. Instead I shake my head.

Dad puts a hand on my shoulder, and it takes everything in me to not shrug it off in frustration. "Son," he starts, "have you thought maybe this whole music thing isn't…meant to happen?"

Does he even care about me? I don't get it. He *knows* this is what I want. He wouldn't ask me that question if I were Dapo.

"It's…good to be open-minded," Dad continues, his cadence slower as he chooses each word. "When I was your age, I thought I'd make one significant breakthrough in the physics world by the time I left university. Then I thought by the time I turned thirty. Then I made it to forty and found my passion in organometallic chemistry."

"Why did you give up?" I ask. "If you want something, you should keep working for it. Isn't that what you've told us since we were little?"

"Yes, of course, but—I don't—I mean— Well, that's life. My point is, there are other things you could be working toward—passions you could be missing out on—instead of spending all day stuck in your room on your computer."

"Like what?"

"Like"—Dad looks away for a second—"applying to—"

"Applying to the sixth form Dapo went to?" I ask, talking over him. "We keep having this same conversation." I free my hands from my pockets. My voice is getting louder, but I don't care. "I'm fine with where I'm at. Can you please—just *please*—stop bringing it up? I don't need to take the same path your favorite son took."

"*Femi*. Fix your attitude. I only put it forward because they have lots of opportunities there as well as good music facilities. I only want the best for you. There's no need to get worked up."

"So wanting me to go to a school where they only cater to *classical* music students is the best for me? When you *know* I produce hip-hop and R & B?"

Dad's lips press together, and his nose wrinkles. "Son, I'm sorry if I upset you. At my age, you've seen a lot of things. Lived through a lot of mistakes. It gives you perspective. I don't want you to regret anything. Yeah?"

I feel a rush of disappointment. It's always the same, and in a week or so we'll be right back here again. "Yeah," I mumble.

"Good." Dad leans in for an awkward hug, and I let him. His

closeness sends warmth shooting up my neck and into my face. "Love you, son."

"You too," I whisper, backing out from the hug. I do love him; I just don't *feel* like loving him right in this moment. My mouth is dry and my hands are clammy. "I—I'm going to go walk around. Be back in a bit."

The ferry is bright and airy, with lots of potted plants and hanging abstract art. But I realize, I'm more interested in the guests. They're dressed as though their existence is an event in and of itself.

A family of four, the same shade of warm beige, walk with clockwork precision: mother and daughter at the front, father and son behind. Each pair is in a conversation of delicate laughs and shallow smiles. In contrast, the clothes they wear are loud. Their matching co-ord tracksuits shine like they're made from some sort of flexible metal, and when they pause to take a group selfie, the camera struggles to handle the shine.

"Souriez!" the daughter says.

"Je ne suis pas prêt," her brother complains.

Coming at the family is a girl dressed in all black: overalls, short-sleeved turtleneck, boots, and a black beret with some sort of mesh over it. Her eyebrows are bleached blond. They pop against her terra-cotta skin and pink lips. I wonder where she's from.

The display of color and style and air of *This is me and I don't care* energy gets my creativity firing. I start making a beat with my mouth, letting my wordless singing build into a melody. Before I know it I've got my headphones on and I'm recording wordless vocals as I walk. The melody loops, and as it plays I grimace. It's not as crisp as I'd like, but it is what it is. Can't stop now. I snap my fingers to the beat into the headphones' mic.

My melody layered with finger snaps plays back on a loop in my ears. I make another beat, this time with my breath. I feel energy rippling from the tips of my toes and fingers. Before a beatboxing rhythm can sprout from my lips, my attention is grabbed by—

"Deja," I mumble. Then, louder: "Deja!"

CHAPTER 2

AT SEA

DEJA TURNS. THERE'S A BEAMING SMILE ON HER FACE and when she waves, her slicked-back bun glistens as sunlight streams through the hallway windows. She strides toward me, swaying with a gentle grace. My heart stutters, reminding me of a sharp snare drum pattern. "Femi." She hugs me tight—she smells like vanilla. "I . . . I didn't know you'd be here. Guess your dad's dragged you along while he attends this conference, too?"

"Yep." *I'm so glad you're here.*

She pulls away, and I take her in: her round face, the dimple on her chin, and her deep brown eyes that lock with mine. I look away. Seeing her after so long is disorienting. Time hasn't dampened any of my unspoken feelings. The silence stretches between us.

"So, Femi. I know it's been a minute since we last talked. Or saw each other," she says.

Nearly two years since I last saw her. And just under three months since she left me on read.

"Honestly, I've been meaning to reach out and I kept . . .

forgetting," she continues. "I've been following your music, though. I even listen to some of your beats sometimes. You're killing it."

"That's okay, and thanks. Appreciate it." I swallow, unsure what to do or say or where to put my hands. "You look healthy. And by healthy, I mean—"

Deja laughs, cutting me off. "Thank you. I'm glad I look healthy. You always had a way with words ... need I remind you of your raps back in the day?"

I grin. "When are you going to let that go? It's been ages."

"Never. I mean, what was running through your mind? Your rap verses were such rip-offs of Xavier's!"

"I'm well aware I wasn't any good. I thought it was the best way to get my thoughts out there ... Everything changed when I first came across an instrumental." I straighten my posture and gaze past Deja, recalling the melody I heard. The way it set my heart thumping. "*That* was poetry. Instruments, sounds, and patterns all working together in perfect harmony to ... convey truth."

"You know, I've heard you talk about that before, and I still don't get it," Deja says. "But you've said the same about my love for justice and wanting to be a lawyer."

"I definitely have, because who wants to do all that studying?"

"We aren't having this conversation *again*. Listen, I'm glad you haven't changed a bit."

A part of me is glad because she's glad. Another part of me deflates. Because I thought she would get why I love music by now. I open my mouth to explain, but instead I say, "It's good to see you. I was worried this trip was going to be dry. Mum's on a girls' trip, so it's just me, Dad, and Dapo, and ... things are shaky."

16

"Ah, sorry to hear that. I can't imagine you and Dapo butting heads. You guys were inseparable back then," she reminds me. "Listen, I need to go find Dad, but maybe we can talk over dinner? Let me know."

She rushes off. When I try to get back into the flow with my beat, my thoughts are all over the place. Having Deja around can only be a good thing. Maybe we'll end up—

Deep breaths. I need a distraction, so I start to wander down hallways and through duty-free shops, soaking in as much as I can.

After a while, I find myself on one of the higher levels of the ferry. It's dim, with curtains drawn across the windows and bursts of lighting here and there. Several large paintings hang on the walls and I catch glimpses of them through guests. The paintings contain surreal elements like blueberry-blue bark on trees and strange-looking plants. Fragments of conversation reveal that the paintings are meant to depict the island we're heading to. An employee with ginger hair in an asymmetrical pixie cut stands in a corner, and after walking several steps past her, I turn back around and approach her.

"I had a question," I start. "Those paintings everyone's looking at. Are they accurate?"

"Would you like them to be?" she responds.

It's a simple yes or no, I think, bristling inside. But I mull her question over and say "Yes."

"There's your answer."

I blink, and once I realize she will not offer me anything else, I laugh and shake my head.

Instead, I wander the ferry some more until the familiar background music for *The Guests* game draws me toward the arcade.

The Guests is the hottest battle-royale game out right now and one I've spent a *lot* of time playing, especially when I've got a creative block. Or when I'm procrastinating.

I step into the arcade and, following the music, end up in front of a screen and controller. I choose my avatar, psychic powers, and vehicle, then press play.

The map flashes on the screen, and a countdown begins. "Okay, let's see." I pick my start point and get ready to confirm it.

"I wouldn't do that," a voice says from behind me.

My shoulders jerk upward, and I'm close to dropping the controller. I turn around. "The hell is—"

I'm face-to-face with a girl who can't be any older than eight. Her smile is wide and cheeky and brings into focus the faint freckles stretching across her warm beige skin. Her hair is jet black and in a messy ponytail. Standing on a chair, with her hands in her pockets, she giggles. "Hey."

"Hey?"

"On this map, you should go south." I blink at her, wondering who she is. She shrugs like I've asked her some sort of question. "All I know is that you'll get butchered over there. Unless you've got an ultra-flashbang grenade. Right, Ken?"

I follow her eyes to an empty space behind me. I turn back to her and quirk an eyebrow. "Ken?"

"My best friend. Anyway, he says you should go over there." She points at a spot on the far left of the screen. "It's safer. You won't last if you start where you are. You plan to snipe, right? You'll get cooked."

"How did you—" I shake my head. *Ignore her.* I confirm my choice and get ready to play.

"Uh-oh," the girl says, blowing out her cheeks and giving me a look not too far from Dad's I'm-disappointed-in-you look.

The loading screen dissolves to show my avatar on a futuristic speedbike. I waste no time using my powers to levitate. The first rule of *The Guests* is to always have the higher—

The controller buzzes, and I swear out loud because that's the buzz of doom. It means you've been locked on to as a target for someone with an ultra-fast psychic javelin. The only way to stop it is with the aegis shield. Which I don't have.

Seconds later my avatar is speared and explodes like a firework. The girl lets out a deep breath. I expect her to taunt me for not listening to her. Instead, in one motion she leaps off the chair, forward rolls, and jumps up onto her feet.

"Nice to meet you . . ."

"Femi," I finish, impressed.

"See you around, Femi. Ken and I need to go back to our room. You can call me Mui, by the way. Well, bye. Come on, Ken."

Mui scampers off, leaving me to wallow in my twenty-third place finish. The game shows me the other active players in my area of the map. My eyes grow wide as it becomes a bloodbath.

For my pride, I press play on another round, this time starting where Mui suggested. I finish in the top three.

Mui was right. I kiss my teeth, put the controller down, and decide to forget *The Guests*. As I leave the arcade, a text from Dapo comes through.

> Dad and I have gone to the restaurant in the upper west wing—feel free to drop by

Feel free to drop by. I stare at the words and turn them over in my mind before letting out a forceful breath. I'm always an afterthought. Another text appears. The words drill through my chest like a corkscrew.

> You should apologise to Dad.

> For what?

> I heard the two of you talking. He was just trying to encourage you. I get he puts his foot in his mouth . . . a lot, but you know this. No need to go off on him like that.

I laugh out loud. *Go off on him?* He must be joking. I stood my ground, like I've seen him do plenty of times. Leaving Dapo on read, I march on, and when I step inside our suite on the ferry for the first time, I'm blown away.

I'm used to five-star hotels and first-class lounges, and their idea of luxury always ends up being the same—solid and boring and dull.

Here, the luxury is liquid and strange. The kind of thing you'd come up with if you asked AI to generate hundreds of luxury rooms and then combine them all. The leather sofa is frameless without any sort of internal structure, looking like a mattress that's been folded in half. The lamps dotted around the room are bulbous and painted with garish patterns. From the dining room table to the kitchen appliances, it's an eyesore.

It doesn't work, and I know it's a ploy—ugly in every way until someone says it's cool, and you don't want to miss out. It grows on you like a rash.

I fall backward onto my bed and message Deja.

Yeah, I can do dinner.

Any of the many restaurants on this ferry catch your fancy?

Splendid! Already booked 😊

Skinny Pig, 7 p.m. It's a date.

In Deja's words I can see her smile—see the way her right cheek quirks—and feel the warmth of her confidence. Maybe this week won't be so unbearable.

Too tired to explore my room, I scroll through my socials until my eyelids start shutting. I set an alarm for 6:30 P.M. and give in.

My eyes fly open to my alarm, a pillowcase dampened by drool, and irritating high-pitched sounds. Usually my tinnitus is a buzz. This is different. A mix of sizzling and clicking. High in pitch, and sharp, they persist. My toes curl tight. The combo of sound and sensation pulses from deep within my ears. I try plugging my ears with my fingers, but that makes it worse.

I groan into my pillow. *Why now? I swear, if this ruins my trip...* The sizzling grows. Then I remember Dapo's gift. I stagger out of bed to my rucksack. Fumbling with the zipper, I pry it open and reach for the earplugs. I stuff them into my ears, and the sound muffles—instant relief.

Thirsty and groggy, I head to the kitchen and fill a glass with filtered water. The floor beneath my feet shifts. That's right, we're on a ferry headed to Darlenia.

After putting the glass in the dishwasher, I step toward the windows and open the curtains. There's not much to see in the vastness of the sea. The few clouds in the sky race by, not wanting to hang about. There is nothing visible for miles, and it unsettles me.

I spin around and lean against the windowsill. I still remember watching *Titanic* far too young. I'd spent the last hour of the movie sobbing and hiding behind the couch.

Movement captures my attention. A growing shadow appears before Dapo emerges, moving toward me. In his hand are pain meds, and I feel a twinge of guilt knowing I'm the reason he takes them in the first place. He blinks, eyes adjusting to the dim light.

"You all right?" he asks, cocking his head. He points at his ear. When I nod, he sighs. "Sorry, that sucks. Wanna watch a movie, like we used to?"

I raise my eyebrows. Before the two years between us were stretched by puberty, personality, and the mess last summer, we were close. "Can't. Seeing Deja. Speaking of, do you know how to use the GPS on the watch?"

Dapo beckons me over with his index finger. Then he fiddles and taps and overexplains until my watch is ready to navigate. "Have fun," he says as I step out the door.

CHAPTER 3

DINNER

I GET TO OUR TABLE AT SKINNY PIG EARLY SO I CAN order Cokes for myself and Deja, remembering to ask for one with a slice of lemon because I know that's her go-to drink. The restaurant is packed, and I'm underdressed in my T-shirt and ripped jeans. Oxfords and heels clack against the wooden floors. Shadows stretch under impressive chandelier lights. Tucked away in the corner, a staff member plays the grand piano with expert ease.

While waiting, I think about what food I'm going to pick, because this restaurant is abstract. Opaque. Pretentious. You don't have dishes to pick, but sensations, and flavors. According to the menu's footnotes, most of the ingredients are sourced from the island.

Mixing sweet and salty could be interesting. I steer clear of the sensations like numbness and popping, and settle on a combination of sweet, salty, and melt-in-mouth: honey mushrooms with raptor-egg curds, served with melt-in-your-mouth wild rice in aspic.

Once the pianist finishes and guests break out into scattered applause, warm hands cover my eyes.

"Guess who!"

"You need to tell me the secret to your soft hands. I have tried everything, and mine are as rough as sandpaper."

Deja removes her hands, and I watch her take her seat opposite me.

Did she do something new with her makeup? *She looks good.* *She looks radiant.* *Is she looking forward to this dinner like me?* *She's looking at me.* *Has she thought about me since the last time we met?* *Her smile is cute.* *Say something.* *Say something.* *Say something*

I clear my throat and gesture to the Coke I ordered for her. "How are you always late? Admit it, you made some sort of bargain with an ancient evil. In exchange for being the most unflappable person ever, you have no sense of time."

"Hey! Not sure I like your tone," Deja says, broad grin on her face.

We settle into another silence. This didn't used to happen to us, but I'm not sure what to say. Jumping straight into complaining about Dapo and Dad doesn't seem right. I wring my fingers. "This ferry's pretty cool."

"It is." She frowns. "You mentioned stuff with your fam was shaky. Care to share?"

"Yeah, a bit of a mess to be honest." I walk her through the dynamic between Dad, Dapo, and me in vivid detail, interrupted only when the waitress takes our order.

Deja studies me with a slight smile. Then she sighs. "Look,

Fems, I adore you, so don't take this the wrong way, but it goes both ways. I see where you're coming from, but...have you tried understanding where *they're* coming from?"

"Deja, didn't you hear what I said? They—"

"I heard what you said. But if you want things to be less shaky, you need to first know what it is they're saying—and then talk." She takes one of my hands. "Do you want to risk getting to forty—your relationship with your dad and brother in shambles—and thinking, 'If only I'd gotten over myself'?"

Her words sear. "But I know what they're saying. There's nothing else for me to understand."

Deja *hmm*s. "Cute. I know you'll figure it out. Anyway, on to important business: What did you want to tell me the last time we saw each other?"

"Ah, you know what, I—I don't remember," I say with an even smile. Except I do—the awkward memory of us sneaking out to the beach to stargaze is inked on my mind like a tattoo.

"You expect me to believe that?" Deja asks, raising an eyebrow.

"Huh?"

"Come on, Fems. You still remember what I *wore* the very first time we met. There's no way you forgot what you were going to say to me. Or is it that something's changed?"

"First of all, who would forget someone wearing a beret, a French flag–colored puffer jacket, different-colored shoes, and huge, square-hooped earrings? Second, nothing has changed." I meet her eyes with a resolute stare, even though my heart is banging against my chest. *She must know what I wanted to say.* Back then it would have been written on my face in Sharpie. Deja stares, her face unreadable. "Why now? What—"

"Deja?" the waitress asks, interjecting. "Sorry, I have a message from your father. He requires you in the lobby immediately."

Deja nods at the waitress, then turns to me, her smile wide and bright. "Fems, hold that thought." She rises from the table. "If I'm not back in fifteen minutes, assume I'm not returning."

She leaves me at the table alone, and I take a deep breath of relief. I'm here to *enjoy* myself. Excavating words I never said with no control over the outcome is terrifying, even if a part of me did want to blurt out how I feel and be done with it. It sounded like my feelings could be mutual? Why else would she push me to answer? Unless she…I shake away the start of my thought. Whatever reason Deja has for bringing this up now, it must be good.

Fifteen minutes comes and goes, and in that window my food arrives. I wolf down the strange meal while scrolling through my social media feeds. The wild rice in aspic melts over the raptor-egg curds—the taste is delectable. It's a shame the mushrooms are a miss.

Deja's opinion on my family rings through my mind. *Am I missing something?* My knee won't stop bouncing. *A word is enough for the wise*, Mum always says. Maybe there is some truth to what Deja's saying, but I've tried to see where Dad and Dapo are coming from. They're the ones who refuse to see me. I take a deep breath. Whatever uneven ground Dad, Dapo, and I are on, it's not going to ruin my holiday.

Once I'm done with dinner, I head back to my room. Along the way, I take a detour back to the mini art gallery everyone was crowding around. The space is less crowded, and I'm drawn to one painting in particular. *In search of Darlenia*, the title reads.

It's a naturalistic painting of a man—legs longer than his torso, blond bowl-cut hair, white shirt, and black boots—with his back to us. He gazes out at land that seems impossible: There's white mist, trees with blueberry-blue bark, leaves the shade of butternut squash skin, neon flowers, vast greenness, and countryside cottages.

Unreal. It makes the rumors about an artificial climate seem watered down. I'm desperate for the reality of the island to imitate this art. My mind races with possibilities—exploration, peace, inspiration. All the things you want in a holiday.

"In one word, what do you see?" The voice comes from beside me. It belongs to Cuplow, and he's out of uniform. "When you look at the painting."

"Uh, that's hard. If I had to choose one, then I'd choose... 'beauty.'"

Cuplow nods and offers a light smile. "Really? Whenever I see this painting, the only word that comes to mind is 'melancholic.' I think the colors are pretty, but that is surface level." His voice is warm, but I get the feeling I said the wrong thing. "It reminds me of change."

"Sometimes things change." I cross my arms. "Sometimes we need to accept that. Maybe change is both melancholic and beautiful. Maybe it should be encouraged."

And then the conversation I had with Dad flashes in my mind with new understanding. Dapo's about to leave home, I'm a lot less dependent on him than he'd like, and Mum's recent lupus diagnosis is a lot of change to process. *What if the melancholic outweighs the beautiful?*

"No, I disagree," Cuplow says, puncturing my thoughts and

giving the painting a flat look. "What about how things were before the island was discovered? I often wonder about what history has been lost..." He holds eye contact with me, intense and sharp. My scalp prickles. He looks away and smiles. "Look at me, a grumpy man rambling. If you'll excuse me, I have some business to attend to. Take care, Mr. Fatona."

I'm left soaking up the painting, wondering what history of this island had been lost. I hadn't thought about the before, only concerned with the now. My phone buzzes and derails my thoughts.

Dad: Hello son, it's not nice you didn't drop by.

Dad: I'm surprised by that.

Dad: I'm not angry, but I think I need to point out the reason we are here. We are supposed to be bonding.

Lord, give me strength. He may be here for his conference, and to bond with us, but *I'm* here to make sure I enjoy the island and survive my family.

CHAPTER 4

ARRIVAL

THE NEXT DAY, WHILE THE FERRY SAILS SMOOTHLY, what happens inside is turbulent. Dad and I trade more than a few tense words (this time on my inability to take his advice). Dapo has made a point to avoid me. If we lock eyes, he slips his gaze past mine. It's rude, and Mum would be appalled, but it's better than being at each other's throats.

I'm wrapping up my shower as the ferry prepares to dock. If things go on like this between me, Dad, and Dapo, the space between us will be vaster than a valley by the time our trip is over. I step out when my fingertips start to wrinkle, a sure sign I've spent too long soaking in the discomfort of my own mind.

On a much more positive note, I completed another beat—an angry trap sound with heavy bass and a haunting, gothic melody. Fitting.

I'm halfway through applying cream to my back before a muffled, electronic bell breaks my rhythm. And then a voice. I pull out my earplugs to hear better, wincing at the humming that swirls in my ears. It's worse—stronger again—like a small fly is trapped in each ear.

"Ladies and gentlemen, welcome to Darlenia Island. Local time is oh-seven-hundred and the temperature is thirty degrees Celsius."

I finish moisturizing.

"For your safety and comfort, please remain in your room until your watches vibrate. This will indicate that your nearest exit is open and that it is safe for you to disembark. Please ensure you've taken all your personal belongings brought on board with you."

I pull on my shorts and a T-shirt.

"If you require assistance, please indicate this using our app. One of our crew members will be pleased to assist you."

Socks and shoes.

"On behalf of the Grand Darlenia Resort and the entire crew, I'd like to thank you for joining us on this trip. We are looking forward to seeing you on board again in the near future. Have a nice stay!"

Dad and Dapo are in the living room packed and ready. They're wearing matching polo shirts. *Obviously.*

"Aren't you going to comb your hair?" Dapo asks with a frown.

I press in my earplugs. "That depends. Are you going to stop dressing like a middle-aged man?" I smirk. "Hi, Dad."

Dapo rolls his eyes, opens his mouth to say something, but then admits defeat.

It takes about fifteen minutes for our watches to buzz. During that time, I can't stop fidgeting. We take all our stuff and head for the exit where Cuplow awaits, a brilliant smile on his lips. He nods when he catches my eyes. The heat from outside forces its way onto the cool ferry, and my armpits dampen. We step off onto a redbrick harbor dusted in sand, and it takes a few seconds to adjust to the glaring sun. Dad's got his handkerchief out and is patting away the beads of sweat that threaten to slide down his forehead.

I stare and inhale a sharp breath. The painting I saw last night becomes a dull memory as I see a dense forest of flora, lush and vibrant, that seems to spill over the horizon. Buildings in odd shapes and iridescent colors stick out like shells on a beach. Bright flowers and plants I've never seen before are scattered all around the immediate area. I crouch down and rub faded blue petals, shaped like a hook between my thumb and fingertips to make sure they're real. Now my fingers smell like roasted cashews. The trees nearby have the same blueberry-blue bark from the painting. It's as if someone soaked them in ink.

Then there's the path beneath our feet, which I notice is made from red bricks speckled with what looks to be silver, gold, and bronze. I wouldn't be surprised if each brick was hand-laid.

Chatter rises among the guests. I hear more French, some Dutch, and what I think is Korean. Some people point downward and smile, some point up and around and gasp, and one guest laughs in a way that sounds like they're glugging water. Younger children are hoisted onto the shoulders of adults and point out what they see.

"*Christmas!*" one kid cries at the billowing, tall grass that looks like tinsel.

"*Bug!*" another cries as a bumbling insect hovers across the path with a scorpion-like purple tail.

"*What's that?*" a boy asks, pointing into the distance.

Turning in that direction, I see the forceful silhouette of a red roller coaster that bends this way and that like an earthworm with no sense of direction. It's planted next to a tall building that gets thinner the higher it climbs. According to the data on my watch, it's the resort's centerpiece: Richard's Residence, complete with a Michelin three-star restaurant and a viewing gallery with built-in augmented reality. I blink. From here the towering residence appears to twinkle. The outside is made of glass and metal. I've never been a fan of fairy tales or movies like *Alice in Wonderland*, but I know another world when I see one.

Even though I feel a warm breeze brush against my skin—and it's humid as hell—I shiver in excitement. Every expectation has already been shattered.

"Fems."

Dapo nudges my side. I twist toward him. His finger is on his lips. He points up and to the left, at a tree. Others notice too and bring out their phones.

I look up and swallow. Among the faded-orange leaves, a large bird is perched on one of the lower branches, haloed by the early morning sun. Broad and still, like a gargoyle, it has a hawk's beak and a stork's long neck and awkward legs; its beak is metallic-gold and its feathers are iridescent green.

"Amazing," I say in a breath that rolls into laughter. On its leg is an orange tag of some kind and a number. A conservation tag?

No wonder Richard and the resort are so secretive. No wonder we signed an NDA. If the whole world knew about the animals he had discovered here, I'd give it a year before we see them in some zoo—legal or illegal.

The bird swings its beak in the direction of our gawking

faces, and for a moment, I think I see something feral dance in its beady eyes. I feel dizzy as an irrational thought flashes through my mind of the bird rushing at me. Then it looks away, and I can breathe again.

In the pulse of a heartbeat, it spreads its iridescent wings, cranes its neck, and glides to the ground, where several guests congregate around it. Unlike the pigeons of London, this bird doesn't jump or hop away. It seems quite content with all the attention it's getting and even nuzzles into outstretched hands. If I were in its shoes, I'd spread my wings, push off, and soar toward the heart of the resort.

"Welcome to the Grand Darlenia Resort, esteemed guests," says a soft voice, drawing our attention. I would've thought it belonged to a British person, but for a few words that sound like someone from somewhere between Luxembourg and Germany spoke them. In fact, the voice belongs to a tall, white woman whose arms are crossed and whose face is a bit squashed as she smiles. Like she's uncomfortable. I recognize her as the one who gave Richard an update he wasn't happy with when we were on the ferry. "I'm Ellen Trossard, the resort manager. For those of you involved in the formalities of the Somerberg Conference, welcome, and thank you for coming from far and wide to be here. It's only a short ride in the resort vehicles to our conference center, with myself and the staff. Breakfast will be provided." Ellen plays with the pen in her hand, spinning it around her fingers. "For all others, please follow our very own Richard Jenkins to the monorail."

Dad and other conference attendees get whisked off with Ellen. Before he goes, Dad tells us to *play nice.*

Richard claps his hands to address those of us here for a good time. The sound reverberates through the mic clipped to his shirt. "Welcome to the best moment of your lives."

Unlike Ellen's, Richard's accent is consistent. I've never heard a thicker Minnesotan accent, and I know he would not be out of place in the *Fargo* movie or TV show. I picture Richard wearing a trapper hat as he continues.

"I've done several of these introductions over the years, and I always look forward to when I get to do it all over again. Before I begin, I'd like to address one thing. I couldn't help but notice a few of you took pictures. Please go ahead and delete those. Photography of any kind is forbidden. We will check your phones upon departure and prosecute to the full extent of the law, if need be. Good, thank you.

"Now then, every once in a while, opportunities come along that change everything. Not just for you, but for those around you, too. Not everyone gets to experience or even notice such opportunities. However, I have been most fortunate to have experienced three of these moments.

"First, my company produced a revolutionary streaming device that not only changed the way we stream content but also changed the entire streaming industry: MSS. Multisensory Streaming—immersion at home like never before. Second, we developed technology that not only changed the way we operated as a company, but also changed the computer industry: sustainable quantum hardware." Richard pauses and smiles. "And the third is Darlenia. The jewel in a suite of products Jenkins & Children offers. Named after my mother, Darlene. She said something to me when I was about eight that has always stuck with me: 'My love, show the world your potential knows no limits.' And I listened.

"But perhaps this *is* the limit. It is a groundbreaking venture, one that embodies the very essence of the innovation and elegance with which our company has become synonymous."

There are several claps and cheers, and Richard basks in them. I find myself clapping, too; Richard speaks well and his words excite me the way a great beat does. I can't take my eyes off him. I don't think any of us can as we wait on what he plans to say next. *He's him.*

"There are many rumors about what this island is. Today, dear guests, I tell you as much of the truth as I am allowed. I discovered this island over a decade ago." He gestures around us with his arms, and we look. "Please, take it in."

I soak it all up once again, feeling awe grip my insides and squeeze tight. My mouth is suddenly dry in anticipation at being one of those in the know. In being part of the secret. Stronger than that, though, is the urge to explore the island. I can't keep still, shifting on the balls of my feet.

"When I arrived, it was not like this. It was a derelict, forgotten place—but I saw the potential to forge a new way. In envisioning this resort, my aim was to create an unparalleled experience, where technology seamlessly integrates with the serene beauty of nature to uphold a sustainable future. I drew inspiration from the Jenkins & Children ecosystem of products that have transformed life as we know it. Like the bird you saw, you will be up close and personal with wildlife beyond comprehension. You will be in awe, but apprehensive—they are vicious-looking animals—but rest assured, they're docile. I'd like you to follow me, please."

Dapo and I, along with the rest of the guests, follow Richard down the brick path speckled with precious metals to a set of escalators that climb up to the monorail station—a glass building pulsing with light like a fairground ride. At the top sits a sign:

↑ 🏰 *FOR RESORT VILLAS*

We're led toward the metallic barriers where we tap our watches against the glowing blue pad. With a satisfying beep, the waist-high gates part and let us through one by one.

"Every element of this resort has been curated to meet your every comfort and delight," Richard says. "As I said, it marries cutting-edge tech with the majesty of an environment that seems impossible. Coexistence is possible, and reality is what we make it."

Heading up a small escalator, we emerge onto a platform where the monorail sits, waiting, its many doors open. Dapo and I head straight for the front so we can see everything. Deja is there already, and she's placed her phone and sunglasses on two seats. When she spots us, she waves us over, and I plaster on a smile. I'm glad there's no hint in her expression of wanting to pick up where we left off before she had to dip from dinner. With any luck, whatever urgency she had to know what I never told her has fizzled out.

Once everyone's on—with me sitting next to Deja—the monorail pulls away from the platform. Richard's monologue continues through the loudspeaker system.

"Our smartrooms will respond to your presence, ensuring a seamless and tailored experience throughout your stay . . ."

"Remember two summers ago when we were all together last?" Deja starts. "We had a lot of fun back then."

"We?" Dapo crosses his arms and smiles. "*I* remember being the responsible one and keeping us out of trouble."

"Ah yes," I say. "You were the fun police. A real drag on the rest of us. If it wasn't for you, I'd be a local Cornish legend."

"Not true, little bro. If it weren't for me, I fear you'd be at the bottom of the deep blue sea."

Deja giggles. "That's probably true—sorry, Femi."

"I guess I forgive you, Deja," I say.

She rolls her eyes. "We all need to hang out this week, all right? Who knows when we'll all be together like this again?"

"*. . . Resort will enhance the human experience, foster connections, and create cherished memories . . .*"

"As long as it's not beach-based." I flicker through my memories. "Days later and the sand was still falling out of odd places."

"Agreed," Deja says. "But yeah, I've been looking at the map of the island. It's wild. I don't think I could have guessed any of it." She pokes me in my side. "We should def hit up the intellectual property theme park—that's where the roller coaster is and it looks like loads of fun, exclusive homages to franchises. There's also the gardens that surround Ethereal Lake. According to the map, the lake's color ranges from emerald to a milky pink and vivid orange."

"*. . . Embark on a journey that pushes the boundaries of what is possible, redefining the very notion of luxury and hospitality . . .*"

"Listen," I say, huge grin on my face. "This place is unreal."

The rest of the ride is idle chat and making tentative plans for the week ahead. Plans for the three of us. Plans for Dad, Dapo, and me in the evenings when the conference is finished for the day. We're leaning toward spa treatments, a bowling–slash–crazy golf–fusion experience, and go-karting. Plans for once the conference is over in two days and our dads can join in more with the resort fun. The possibilities seem endless, and even though we don't cement anything, the thought at what might be seems to satisfy us for now. When we settle into a comfortable silence, it's charged with excitement.

"Welcome to the Grand Darlenia Resort—an island that will forever etch itself in the fabric of time..."

CHAPTER 5

AMBUSH

"VILLA 127," AN EMPLOYEE SAYS TO ME AND DAPO when we step off the monorail. Deja got off a stop earlier to check out the Waterstones. She's *sure* they'll have early copies of prominent human rights lawyer Tessa Murad's autobiography. Knowing Deja, if they don't, she'll still leave with at least three books.

The employee wears the same gray military-style uniform I've seen on the others, except it's about an inch too short at his wrists. "Follow the signs and you'll be good to go. May I recommend Café Central if you are feeling peckish? They serve the best chicken and waffles. To find it, you can use the GPS on your watches, or follow the redbrick road until you reach a fork. Take the pearl-colored path. Can't miss it. Have a nice stay!"

I prod a bony elbow into Dapo's arm. If we'll be hanging out with Deja, we need to be civil, otherwise it'll be plain awkward for all of us.

"What?" he grunts, not bothering to look at me.

"Fancy going straight to Café Central?" Painful silence hovers between us, and I clear my throat. "It's fine if—"

"Sure. I could eat."

Following the paths as instructed, we make our way to the café in awkward silence. When we arrive, I smile at a pair of meerkat-looking animals with white shadowed eyes perched on the canopy extending over the entrance. Orange tags are on their ankles.

The stone building captures the easy elegance of the resort. But the chipped window frames and the stained stones make me think this building isn't new.

Inside, the space is large. Guests tap touchscreen tables and observe the intricate but faded patterns painted overhead on the high ceilings. Below that, everything is hustle and bustle, packed tight. *If I were a waiter, this would be a nightmare.* It's alive with conversation bouncing off the wood-paneled walls. Flowers with large floppy petals that look like wet tongues hang down and rest on the dark wood furniture. Bioluminescent, they glow yellow. Bugs the size of a baby's fist, with bronze hairs covered in purple pollen, crawl and hop along the walls. When I point my watch in a bug's direction, the app on my phone pings with a message:

> **Bombus Terrorem**—One of the largest bee species on the island. They have corkscrew tongues that protrude as they approach a flower. You may see a variety of them on the island with different-colored hair. Most are bronze; quite a few are burgundy. Others are navy blue.

We find seating toward the back. I let Dapo sit in the booth because it faces into the room, and I know he prefers that. See? I'm trying.

I slide onto the stiff, wooden chair opposite him. The table is one big tablet, and after a few taps I'm looking at the menu and ordering food—eggs Darlenia (eggs Benedict but with ham from one of the island boars and eggs from a golden raptor) with a side of pancakes.

The awkardness between Dapo and me is palpable, and I remember Deja's words. *Have you tried understanding where* they're *coming from?* I guess I could try to bridge the gap. "So... how are..." My words trail off, and I sneeze a couple of times in quick succession, making Dapo jump. I laugh. "Sorry, the pollen count here must be high. I was saying, how are things?"

He looks up at me. "Things?"

His tone and raised eyebrow annoy me, but I get it. *It's a terrible way to start a conversation.* Truth is, most things about Dapo these days are vague. I can't remember the last time we had a meaningful conversation we enjoyed.

"Yeah," I say, sounding a bit more defensive than I'd like. "You were applying to a few internship programs, right? Any news?"

"Well, there is one I'm excited about. It's—"

Steps creak from behind me. I look down, over my shoulder, and see a hatch open. A waiter emerges like a jack-in-the-box carrying a tray of food. Pancakes for me, French toast for Dapo. He sets the plates on the table, smiles at each of us, and descends back down. Neither of us bat an eye at the over-the-top presentation.

"It's what?" I ask, using a knife and fork to cut into my pancakes.

Dapo clears his throat. "Huh?"

"You were saying about one of the internships. One you're excited about?"

"Oh yeah. Just some position at the Ministry of Inter—you know what, don't worry about it. Things are good." He plants his ashy elbows on the table. "What about you? Made a decision about sixth form?"

"Oh that? Yeah, I have."

"Something tells me I'm not going to like it."

I shift in my seat and take another mouthful of food, buying myself time. "It's complicated."

"Indulge me." Dapo puts down his cutlery and leans back. "I'm listening."

"Are you, though?"

Dapo nods.

"I decided I'm going to drop out." His eyes bulge in surprise, and I crack up. "Brighten up, someone's going to think I offended you with that face. I'm just taking a gap year."

I go on to explain why, for which I have several reasons—all of them centered on the time I need to focus on my music.

"You can't be serious," Dapo states. "For one, Dad's not going to let you get away with that. And two, isn't that a big gamble?"

"I *am* serious," I answer, mouth full of pancake. "I've thought about this long and hard. And the more I think about it, the more I feel like it's the right thing to do."

Dapo does his best to keep his face from betraying his obvious panic. "Why?"

"I'm starting to make a name for myself. Even though I said no, Xavier did want to work with me, and you know how big he is. If I want to be what I know I can be, then the music industry needs to be my classroom. Not a stuffy sixth-form building."

"But that's not a good enough reason. This about your future, Femi, and Dad and Mum are going to have a million questions. You could easily—"

I sigh. *Hard.* "Can we talk about this later? I promise we can, but I wanted to focus on you and how things were going for you. You were saying about a position you were excited about?"

"When is 'later,' Femi?"

"How about"—I shove some eggs Darlenia into my mouth and chew, unable to enjoy the taste—"not now."

Dapo's nostrils flare. "You always do this."

"I've already had a variation of this conversation with Dad yesterday, and I'm not looking to have it again. Why can't we talk about this later? And since when did you care so much about what I did for sixth form?"

"Since you asked *me* for advice a few weeks ago. *You're* the one who involved me."

I put my fork down. "Get over yourself. Asking you *one* question isn't an invitation to bug me about it forever."

Dapo pulls an indignant face. "Honestly, you're so . . . so stubborn. I wish I could get through to you. I'm trying to help you. You never listen, you—"

"I do listen," I say, forcing myself to take a steadying breath. "Maybe try saying something of value for once, instead of being so condescending all the time."

"There you go again. If you just expressed how you feel about things in a sensible way, then maybe we'd get somewhere."

Even though there's plenty of background chatter, the silence that settles between us is loud.

"You know what?" I stand up and wipe my mouth with a napkin. "Not so hungry anymore." Leaving my food half-eaten, I head for the door, ignoring Dapo as he calls after me. *Bun him and his dumb psychology assessment. Deja can't say I didn't try.*

The dimness of Café Central gives way to the blazing Darlenia sun. After only a few moments, I'm already sweating like a can pulled from the fridge on a summer's day.

There's a crackle of static, and the loudspeaker sounds: *Official Weather Service is tracking a tropical storm heading our way. Early indications suggest it will graze the island. We will keep you updated.*

A smile forms on my lips. I wish a storm would wash away Dapo's condescension.

I let my feet carry me wherever they want to go, and as they pound against the pearl-colored pathway, the shallow echo inspires a melody. It builds and builds and—

The island arcade. It's meant to be much more impressive than the one on the ferry. I'll stop by and blow off some steam. Using my watch, I set a course for the arcade and the watch face guides me to my destination with arrows.

The walkways are full of people going and coming, hemming and hawing.

"Ugh, Mum, I can't walk. Any. Farther," a young boy says, somehow walking and throwing a tantrum at the same time.

The way he said the last bit of his sentence would have made the perfect sample for a beat.

"Oh really, honey?" asks his mum. "That's a shame, since

there's no wait time at the roller coaster right now. Guess we'll turn back."

At once the young boy stands to attention and shakes his head with so much vim, I have to stifle my laughter.

"I'm fine," he declares. "Let's goooo." He races forward.

My mind conjures a memory—nostalgic and amusing: me and Dapo when he had to take me to school one time. I was dragging the journey out until he promised he'd get me a hot chocolate before school if we got there early. I won't forget the way I ran. The memory fades and I'm left with a cold feeling.

I shake it off. Word to T. Swift.

The winding path my watch suggests takes me through a pocket of huge villas and up an incline. It gives me a view over some of the resort and into the distance. Unobstructed by the taller trees, there again is Richard's Residence looming large, side by side with the twisting roller coaster. I take it all in for a moment—this new island—thinking about what it must be like to have the support to bring your vision to life.

On the way back down, I'm drawn toward deep, cherry-red flowers blooming on a cluster of squat trees with purple-orange leaves. I lean toward them and inhale. They smell like matches that have just been blown out, but with a hint of peach. Movement by my feet catches my eye. The moment I home in on it, I jump backward and barely stop myself from stumbling into a heap. A centipede-like bug with butterfly wings ambles along, its legs moving in perfect harmony. My skin crawls.

I stare as it weaves in and out and over pebbles, fallen leaves, and sticks. I'm so mesmerized that I don't notice one of those golden-beaked birds arrive on the scene at first, staring at the creepy-crawly. When I look up, the bird cocks its head.

In a blink, it spears its beak downward, then back up. Half of the bug—the part with the wings—is writhing on the ground, trying to fly off. The other half slides down the bird's throat. Then the bird looks in my direction, a smidgen of blue blood on its beak.

I swallow nervously.

The bird breaks eye contact to collect the other half of the bug, swallows, and then lets out a hoarse screech that sends a shiver through me before it turns and waddles off. Composing myself, I take a few deep breaths and continue on my odyssey to the arcade.

When I arrive, it's being guarded by a broad man in shades, his face mean-mugging.

"The arcade is occupied," he says, looking past me. "Try again later."

"By who?" I ask. "I wasn't aware you could book the whole arcade." The broad man in shades shrugs, and while my blood was bubbling before, it's boiling now. "I asked you a question."

Nothing. *All right.* "Oy, whoever's in there and got this mug guarding the door, who do you think you are?" I shout.

The broad man steps toward me but stops when a voice says, "Clyde." Emerging from behind the man is—

"Richard Jenkins." He smiles, revealing teeth that are too white, and holds out a hand.

I regard him and, up close, I decide I don't like him. It's the smile and how practiced it looks. It makes me wonder if his smooth, wrinkle-free skin and well-matched eyebrows are natural or by design.

"I know who you are," I answer, shaking his hand. His grip is firm and he laughs. "I, uh, I'm Femi Fatona."

"Apologies for Clyde, Femi. He's perhaps a bit too zealous." Richard looks me up and down. "You strike me as a determined boy, and I've got some time to kill. Fancy a game of *FIFA*? Play for money?"

I nod. Winning money off Richard will put me in a much better mood. Stepping inside, I'm met with an elite VR setup, flashy arcade games, pinball machines, and pool tables. The walls are wood paneled, the lights are dim—so you lose track of time, I guess—and the chairs are top of the range. This is a gamer's dream.

We pick our teams and tweak our lineups. Well, *I* do. Richard tinkers and takes forever, moving individual players into specific positions. Tactics are important, I get that, but he's taking the piss. I'd tell him exactly that, if he didn't own the floor beneath my feet and everything I can see.

"Ready?" Richard asks with a smile. "Once we start, no changes till halftime."

I nod. "Let's play."

"Bullshit," Richard huffs when I score another goal. That's four goals for me, one for him. "They're not doing what I told them to do."

Yes, because these players have minds of their own. Come off it, man. I score one more before the final whistle and go to shake Richard's hand.

"Seems like it wasn't my day. I certainly wasn't expecting this." His smile is tight and grip extra firm. "Well done."

As much as I want to rub salt in the wound, I'm not going to do that. So I shrug. "Got lucky, I guess. How will you transfer the five hundred pou—"

"Again."

"Huh? Nah, I'm—"

"Ten thousand pounds on the table this time."

Is he mad? I blink at him. "If I lost, there's no way I could pay that. I don't have that kind of money."

And even if I did, I wouldn't offer that. Mum and Dad drummed it into Dapo and my heads: Money comes and goes, so use it wisely. Focus on needs and not wants. It's why we both got savings accounts instead of allowances growing up.

There's a hunger in his eyes. "Well, then, how about something personal? Something you'd hate to lose."

My mind arrows straight for my laptop. Well, the hard drive inside my laptop that's storing all my beats. The possibility is extinguished in milliseconds. There's no way. Before I can refuse, the woman who was speaking to Richard on the ferry rushes into the arcade gasping for breath.

"Rich," she rasps.

"Ellen. I thought I said I only wanted to hear from you if—"

"I know, sir. It's why I came here myself." Her words are windshield wipers, swiping away Richard's easygoing smile in one go. He glares through her, smoothing out his clothes.

"What was it this time?" he asks, each word sharp and sour.

Ellen glances at me before looking back at Richard. *Not here.*

Richard sighs. "Very well. Let's walk and talk. Femi, it's been a pleasure. I'll be ready for you next time."

Richard and his entourage exit and I stand in the arcade alone for a moment.

My money. I rush out of the arcade after Richard, but at the last moment decide not to burst into his conversation. I'm curious about what could have him annoyed. I linger far enough behind that they don't notice me while they walk, but it means I can't hear more than fragments of their frantic conversation.

"... you had two weeks to make sure this didn't happen ..."

What didn't happen?

"... Rich, you don't know how condescending you are ..."

No wonder Dapo likes him.

"... Do your jobs, how about that? And I'll do mine ..."

From out of nowhere, another bodyguard appears and steps in my way. His eyes are bloodshot as he chews with vigor on gum that's colored his tongue blue. "Piss off," he says in a voice that could give an ice cube frostbite.

"Richard owes me money."

"Now."

Like Clyde, I can tell Blue Tongue has no capacity for thought other than being an arse. "Tell him I want my money," I say, turning around and walking off, heading back in the general direction of our villa.

It isn't until about five minutes later, when I look around, that I realize I'm lost. I don't remember coming this way—the path is narrow and the trees are hemming me in. I try the GPS on my watch to set me straight for our villa. It pulses to life, and then I'm on my way. The fifteen minutes it'll take to get there gives me time to think about what I overheard. Or didn't hear. I'm not sure what wasn't supposed to happen, but it seems not everything that glitters is gold. Whatever it is will probably be fine. We'll be leaving the island before we know it, and I want to soak up as much as I can until then.

My watch pulses, and when I glance down the arrow says make a right... which can't be correct.

There's no path there.

I frown and decide to keep going straight and let it reorient itself. Which it does. Another pulse. This time my watch tells me to take a right, and though it's not super worn, there *is* a path. I step off the pearl walkway and head deeper into the woodland.

A flash of iridescence catches my eye, high above the trees. Then there's this strange smell: rusted metal interspersed with rotten meat. My mouth is dry, and before I know it, I'm pulling and twisting at my top out of discomfort, while covering my nose with my other hand.

My watch chimes with a message: You've arrived at your destination.

Be for real, I think to myself, glaring at it.

Beneath my feet is dirt. Above, dappled sunlight shifts as a gentle wind rustles the trees. I try again to set a course back to the villas, but my GPS keeps saying I've arrived. Frustration builds, and I spin around, trying to find the way back, but nothing looks familiar. My heart leaps in my chest.

Suddenly I'm face-to-face with an animal that comes up to my waist while it's on all fours. It's lizard-like with a translucent but iridescent body.

The lizard's golden claws rake at the dirt while its dull eyes stare in my direction. There's no orange tag to be seen as its forked, sickly-gray tongue slips out and back in a mouth smothered in dull red. *Dried blood.* The ground beneath my feet wobbles when it takes a step toward me.

My head whips around at the sound of a snapping branch behind me. Another lizard-like animal. This one is even larger, with chunks of flesh and fur caught in bared teeth. My heart beats like two hands are in my chest squeezing tight. Squinting, I make out the silhouettes of more of them lurking behind the second one. I force myself to breathe when I understand what is happening.

An ambush.

The eruption of sudden hissing rusts the joints in my knees, narrowing my hopes of survival. I know I'd crumble if I attempt a mad dash to safety. I touch-type Dapo an SOS message on my phone and press send, but when I glance down, I see that there's a clock icon next to my message.

No signal.

It's over.

A sudden, shrill noise cuts through the hisses. For a moment I mistake it for my tinnitus, but as the sound gets louder and clearer, I know it isn't. My tinnitus doesn't have a melody or a rhythm. The sound—singing—belongs to a person, and whoever they are, they don't realize they're headed toward a gang of mean-looking lizards. If I keep still, maybe they'll go after the singing person?

But I wouldn't be able to live with myself.

"Turn around!" I shout. *Act now, deal with the consequences later.* "Turn around!"

The person carries on, getting louder and louder until they appear on my right. I frown at the girl now at my side. *What is the point in drawing attention to myself if we're both going to—*

Her wicked smile cuts the thought short, and I take her in. Her skin is several shades darker than mine, and her tight curls are bunched into a puff on the top of her head. My gaze slides from her hair to her face to her eyes: deep pools of brown-ringed amber.

When I try to speak, words evaporate in my throat. *What is with that smile?* I swallow, confused. "Who—"

"I'm the person saving your life. Now keep quiet." She raises a finger to her lips and steps in front of me. "Glass dragons aren't to be played with. Not here, anyway." She reaches into her pocket and pulls out a plum-like fruit and a small pocket-knife. Slicing into the fruit with surgical precision, juice drips from her hands and an aroma of sweaty feet assaults me. I hold back the urge to gag.

The glass dragons, gathered together in front of us, perk up. Their tongues are coated in thick saliva as they drool.

Waiting.   *Watching.*
      Watching.   *Waiting.*

The girl launches the fruit deep into the bowels of the forest. There's a moment of stillness before the glass dragons go scuttling after it. Satisfied, the girl turns to me with a deep frown etched on her face. "Nice to meet you, Femi. Follow me."

CHAPTER 6

BLACKMAIL

HOW THE HELL DOES SHE KNOW MY NAME? I BLINK, fixated on the way she strides ahead as if this is her forest. Then I notice how quiet it is here. In my head, I mean. When I pull out my earplugs, there's no high-pitched humming anymore.

"You must be wondering how I know your name," the girl asks in a distinct accent. It reminds me of my Spanish teacher from back home, except this girl's accent is softer and more earnest. "Yes?"

"Uh, yeah." Blood rushes to my face and my scalp prickles. "Who are you?"

"Who are you?" she mocks. "Yos myo. What is the saying? No need to spill over cried milk?"

My nostrils flare. "Yes, who are you?"

She steps closer and stares into my eyes, forcing me to look away. Her laugh is sharp and mocking. "Hello, my name—" Her stomach grumbles and she mutters under her breath before starting again. "Hello, my name is Valoisa Ruiz, and usually people say thank you when someone saves their life."

"Yeah, well, it's not like I asked you to." The moment the words are out my mouth, I regret them. "Sorry. Th-thank you. Are you also a guest?"

"You're annoying." Valoisa looks around as she walks through the woodland, carefully avoiding a patch of mushrooms. Perched on top of a large, flat mushroom is a blue frog.

"Hey, wait. Where are you going? Can you at least tell me where we are going?" She keeps walking without a word. But then my phone rings, playing one of Xavier's old songs from his mixtape days. No matter our disagreements, the guy is brilliant.

"'I ain't never been the same, since I saw those green eyes behind your glasses frame. This is not a game,'" Valoisa sings along. She turns around. "Yos myo, I haven't heard that song since like . . . forever."

I decline the incoming call from Dapo. "You're a fan of Xavier?" *To be honest, who isn't these days?* "Have you heard any of his newer music?" A moment passes. "Want to hear more of his stuff?"

"I feel a connection to him. But no." She tilts her head as if considering something. "Tell me about yourself."

I hate these types of questions, because I never know where to begin. But today—gazing at Valoisa—I don't mind. I think for a moment and say, "I, uh, love music. That's the most interesting thing about me." She says nothing, but her soft smile and intense stare keeps me talking. It's nice to feel listened to for once. "I, uh . . . I feel I was born to do this. I put my hands, my brain, and my heart into the music I create." I take a moment and blow air out my nostrils. "I guess, unlike my family, music doesn't misunderstand me. I dunno if that makes sense or not. Music is communication. It's universal."

A couple of heartbeats go by before Valoisa nods. "No, that makes total sense. I love this island for the same reason—it understands me completely, and I, it. There's something special about being understood."

"Yeah," I say, leaning toward her and smiling. *She gets it.* "I wish my family understood me more. They think my music's some sort of ... hobby."

"Ah, family. We don't get to choose them. But I know how you feel. My dad thinks my love of art is a distraction. Anyway, you shouldn't let them discourage you. There's some wisdom to be gleaned, but you should pursue your passions."

Her words are gentle and settle in my heart. Her loving art is unsurprising given how encouraging she is. Then I'm thinking about my decision to take a gap year. My decision to turn Xavier down after one of my producer friends referred me. I don't have it all figured out, but sometimes it's enough to just "pursue." I say none of what I'm thinking. All I can say is "Thanks."

Valoisa leads us deeper into the forest to a log covered in dark-purple moss with small shoots of grass sprouting around. It's quiet here, except for the faint squawks of birds and rustle of leaves above. We sit down and settle into a conversation that turns into show-and-tell of some recent beats I've come up with. I explain how I produced them, the inspirations, and the way she nods to my music radiates warmth throughout my body.

"This is a beat you say your friend inspired?" Valoisa asks. I nod, ignoring the way my stomach twists when her question conjures an image of Deja. "Wow, it's beautiful. You must thank your friend."

"Yeah," I murmur, taking a moment to collect myself. When it comes to Deja, I feel unsteady. As though I'm walking across a rickety bridge, and at any moment, I'll step through a rotten plank and plunge into the abyss.

"Hey," Valoisa says, interrupting my thoughts by prodding me in my ribs. "You need to do something for me."

"Uh, what?" I press pause on the music and edge away. The air between us frosts. "I don't *need* to do anything."

"Yes, you do." Her voice is stony. "I *saved* your life."

I snicker. "Thank you, but you saved my life because it's human decency. I don't owe you anything." I look down at my watch and try to set a new course on the GPS again, but it's *still* not working.

"Your watch won't work here." Valoisa's grin doesn't reach her eyes. She pulls out a small device that looks like a brick phone that's had unfinished open-heart surgery. She pushes a few buttons, and my watch pulses and tells me to take a left. "Oopsies," she says, before laughing. "I have access to your watch, your data, the card details it's linked to. Everything. Femi Fatona, families like yours often have secrets. I'm sure you don't want the world to know why your dad would pay five thousand pounds a month to an account held by Timothy Huxley. You *will* help me."

I break out into a cold sweat. Timothy was once married to Dad's sister. I haven't thought about him in a long time. My aunt split from him last year in part because he is a bit of a pig, but mostly because he embezzled funds from a prominent charity and defrauded a few others he was on the boards for. He avoided jail time the same way most people in his position do—he threw money at it until it went away. I don't know why Dad's paying Huxley anything, but it can't be for a good reason.

This cannot be happening.

"You're blackmailing me?" I mumble.

"Yes."

As much as I want to call her bluff, she's already made me look stupid. I don't need her to make an example of me, too. "What do I 'need' to do for you?"

"I need you to retrieve some batteries for me."

"Batteries?"

She folds her arms. "Yes."

"Yeah, but like what type? Are they AA batteries? Or …?" Her face is blank. "What do they look like, and what are they for?"

Her eyes spark. "A device." She digs a hand into her pocket and pulls out a pair of corroded, U-shaped batteries.

"I've never seen these before." I take one and study it, trying to see if there's any sort of classification hidden in or around the corrosion. *Nothing*. Except half of the logo for Jenkins & Children. "I wouldn't even know where to look."

"That's not my problem."

I offer the battery back to her. "I don't think I can help you."

"You don't have a choice. Keep it." She flashes a grin. "Feel free to walk away, but I will make sure people know your family is paying a man like Timothy Huxley handsomely. It's that simple. And don't even think about involving security or anything like that. We'll know."

I think through my options and find I have none. Waves of betrayal and disappointment ripple through my stomach, throwing it this way and that. *Get a grip, she's a stranger. You didn't know her.* Except a part of me thought I did. Understood her at least. I feel stupid.

"How many batteries? And how will I get them to you?" My eyebrows bunch together. "Hang on. Why can't you get them yourself?"

"So"—she leans in—"many"—close—"questions." Her hair smells like coconut. "I'll show you where to meet tomorrow night. I need eight batteries. And believe me, I would get them myself if I could."

"Why can't you?" I probe.

"Right." Valoisa takes a deep, deep breath. "This way, Lost Boy."

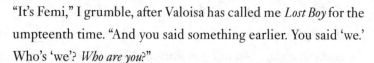

"It's Femi," I grumble, after Valoisa has called me *Lost Boy* for the umpteenth time. "And you said something earlier. You said 'we.' Who's 'we'? *Who are you?*"

Valoisa doesn't answer. Instead, she guides me through this labyrinthine forest, pointing out key markers that'll help me find my way back to the meeting spot: a half-burnt berry bush, the rusted remains of a bike—which strikes me as odd since the island isn't that old—and a field of mushrooms that look like a set of bleeding gums.

"Hey, come on—"

"Enelle, my cousin," Valoisa says, cutting through my words. "She's not much older than me. We're *from* here. Darlenian natives."

"Darlenian?" I tilt my head. "No, Richard *discovered* the island.

He made up the name Darlenia after his mum, Darlene. The only one who..." My words trail off. *Was he lying about her name?*

"Darlenia is the true name of our island. He stole it from us," Valoisa states. "Anyway, here we are." We're still surrounded by climbing trees and strange flora, but up ahead the forest thins, and guests walk along the paths, oblivious to our lurking eyes. "Up ahead you'll rejoin the redbrick path." She suddenly looks beyond tired. Shaking her head, she flashes an empty smile. "Tomorrow. Midnight. Don't forget our batteries, Femi."

I don't bother answering, knowing I don't have a choice but to play along, at least for now.

We're from *here. Darlenian natives.*

Valoisa's words stick like onion on my breath as I walk along the redbrick path. If Richard was lying, wouldn't someone have outed him by now? Then it hits me. Yeah, there was that rumor floating about... Darlenia being an immersive experience filled with actors and actresses. *Could this be part of the island experience?* It would make it easier if it was. But still...

She could be telling the truth, I allow myself to think, glancing down at the batteries in my hand again. Judging by her threat of blackmail, this probably isn't part of the island experience.

I replay the moment in my head. *Except she had no proof. I bet the ambush was staged, too.* My stress levels reduce a bit. *It's all smoke and mirrors.* I smile. *Fine, I'll play along.*

The first place to start is to find out what type of batteries these are. I spy the partial logo again. Of course; if there's one person who would know, it would be Dapo.

When I finally track him down, he's at an information kiosk looking straight-up shook. "Peanut head," I call. He glances my way, then does a double take.

"Femi." He walks over to me. "Y-you're...okay?"

"Yeah. Why wouldn't I be?"

"Your text? I tried calling. They said on the PA system there had been a minor security breach and anyone who received the pulse to their watch needed to get to safety. When you sent me that message, I thought—I thought—I'm in the middle of making them hunt you down."

"Oh, nah, I didn't get that pulse. I'm all good..."

My words trail off as I wonder if the "minor security breach" was somehow related to my meeting Valoisa. But since no one from security is rushing me, I guess not.

"Ugh, I'm going to have to tell them it was a false alarm." Dapo frowns. "But why did you text me *SOS*?"

"Oh, that...I thought it was an SOS situation, buuut it turned out not to be. I forgot to text and explain. My bad. But anyways, check it." I show him the batteries. "Look what I found."

"What are you doing with VaPo batteries?"

"VaPo?"

"Vanildehyde-ion polymer. Richard Jenkins developed them as part of his quantum hardware. They're industrial-grade and the kind you need to dispose of carefully. You just found them lying around?"

"Sort of. Industrial-grade? So, it's not like they're going to be in the back of a remote or something?"

Dapo laughs. "Exactly."

"So, where *would* you find them?"

"Why?" Dapo studies my face, and I do my best not to give anything away. "I'm supposed to believe all of a sudden you're interested in batteries?"

"Come on, bro, can't I be curious about stuff?"

"Sure. Well, uh, as I said, they're industrial-grade. So, you'd find them in stuff that requires more power. I think I remember reading about them being used to power vehicles and stuff. Judging by how quiet those resort vehicles are, I wouldn't be surprised if they were under their hoods." Dapo pauses. "You know—"

"Thanks," I say, walking away. I cannot stomach an impromptu lecture on facts and information I don't care about. "Catch up with you and Dad for bowling later this evening, yeah?"

Hands in my pockets, I go looking for a worker who can corroborate what Dapo said about the batteries. *But what then?* I'd know where to find the batteries with no way to actually get them out. I squeeze my eyes shut. What's the point in this challenge? Why have me running around looking for random batteries for a random girl?

Lost in my thoughts, I bump into something and look down. No, someone. The girl from the ferry arcade. *Mui.* She blinks once. Twice. Breaks into a smile.

"It's *you!*"

"Sorry, I didn't see you there." I help her up, and then she gives me a hard stare. "What? Did I hurt you?"

"You're not going to help Ken up?" She looks down at the space to her left.

"Who?"

"My best friend. You knocked him over, too." A couple heart-beats of silence pass, then Mui crosses her arms. "Well?"

I scratch my cheek. There's no one else here, but her glare is resolute. "Of course. Sorry, Ken." I step toward the space on her left and hold out my hand to help her imaginary friend up.

"Lower."

"Sorry?"

"Ken's hand can't reach yours. It's too high."

"Right." I lean down lower and pretend to sling a little boy onto his feet. "There we go."

"He says thanks. Even though you were rude initially. He also says you might want to dry your hands since his are wet. Where were you off to in such a hurry? You looked like someone on an adventure."

"Ha, nah, I'm looking for a worker who knows about cars and—" This is silly. "Why am I even telling you this? I'm not really—"

"You'll want to speak to Alberto, then." Mui turns to the empty space next to her and nods, agreeing with Ken, apparently. "Yeah, he knows *everything* about cars. Won't stop talking about them. He's the resort engineer. Ooh, ooh, ooh, tomorrow, let me and Ken take you to him. We can meet at the visitor center when it opens."

"Uh, I dunno. I—hey!"

Mui runs off.

I have no doubt she'll be at the visitor center tomorrow waiting for me.

CHAPTER 7

INVOLVED

I'M LYING IN BED, UNABLE TO SLEEP.

After my encounter with Mui, I decided I wasn't going to carry on with this weird quest I'd been given. Too much effort for no real reward. Instead I've been chilling and enjoying my day. Listen, they need to bring a bowling–slash–crazy golf fusion to the UK because it's too much fun.

But, as if by divine intervention, I received some texts a couple of hours ago from an unsaved number:

> Lost Boy, if you need confirmation that this is real:

> *Your trust fund.pdf*
> *Current account statement.pdf*
> And here's something Richard wouldn't want you to see:

https://thetruthof3n14d4rl.com/ttad?sslfdwg
=atcnve/

The two PDFs are real. I checked. The trust fund document is supposed to be behind layers of authentication while the current account statement shows a payment from my account to Timothy Huxley's. One great British pound. Except I didn't make the transaction. The memo line is a wink face emoji with the initial *V*.

Then there's the link. It's a blog post from Enelle Ruiz. I open the link.

> Our home in the heart of the Terline Forest yawns without fail when the sun rises. At least it sounds like a yawn when the kings and queens of their overlapping food chains rush by.
>
> They're all headed for the forest's edge. We've never understood this new habitual action, but we've had plenty of fun guessing what it may be. Perhaps they have long-lost family waiting for them? Or maybe there's a mystical gem that attracts them like a magnet? Mama thinks plainly they're brain dead.
>
> Whatever the answer, they turn back just as quickly, wailing when they do. For some reason they never go beyond. I think they experience the same painful ringing in their ears that we do whenever we get close to the forest's edge.
>
> It wasn't always like this. I'm not sure exactly when things changed, but it feels like in a blink the island

rejected us, and our wildlife became strange. I mean really strange. The animals shed their mundane colors for iridescent ones. Sea life we saw while we snorkeled was emerging onto the edges of the woodland that broke onto the shore. Our island was changing.

It was about to change even more with a modest knock on our door. No one *ever* knocked.

Before Mama or Papa could react I was already answering the door to a gangly man wearing a pink paisley mask that covered his mouth and nose. His blond hair was cut in a stylish bowl cut and he wore an airy white shirt. And then I noticed, by his black boots, as if he'd trained it, the kitten of a tasseled feline nibbling. It had a strange orange tag around its neck.

Even as a kitten, I could see its future. In a matter of months it would triple in size. Shed its brown fur in favor of an iridescent white. Soon, it would grow horns with rigid, red tassels. Soon, its teeth would be so jagged and sharp that they'd grow outward, leaving it with a permanent snarl. And yet this man seemed unbothered. Maybe he didn't know?

Even though I couldn't see his mouth I could tell by the way his piercing brown eyes crinkled that he was smiling.

The stranger: May I come in?

I had no idea what to say. All I could do was nod. I always heard Mama and Papa reminisce and lament about how many people used to live here. Maybe the arrival of this stranger meant Darlenia was changing for the better. Maybe I will come to see the sun on his shoulders.

Yes. There is still wonder left in the world.

thelake.jpg

infrontofthepalace.jpg

onthebeach.jpg

crimsonstingrays.jpg

The whole thing is damning: The stranger is Richard, that's obvious, which means he was lying about the island being uninhabited when he found it. Then there's the pictures, showcasing parts of the island even more breathtaking than what I've seen so far, and time-stamped several years before Richard supposedly discovered the island.

"He's a fraud," I mumble. I can't think of why he felt the need to lie or why no one has called him out on it. A bitter taste fills my mouth and I feel wobbly, like the ground is one big trampoline. "He's a fraud." It's difficult to catch my breath. "He's a fraud."

How has he gotten away with it? *Probably paid them off*, I muse. But why go through all that effort? *Because he would not have been seen as any different from his billionaire peers who bought something pre-existing, repackaged it, and took all the credit.*

My heart pulses in my ears as I think about the secret I now know and the reality of the situation. I rue the blackmail hanging over my head. If Valoisa had trusted me with this evidence up-front, it wouldn't have been necessary.

I roll over and glance at the bedside clock. It flickers to read 12:18 A.M.

I'm about to turn back when I catch sight of the clear night sky and the blinking stars through a gap in my curtains. I prop myself up on my elbows and I can't decide if I should head out to stargaze. My tongue roves over my teeth as I come to a decision. I'm not going to clear my head if I'm tossing and turning in bed all night.

"Go on, then," I mutter, climbing out of bed and getting dressed for the breezy outdoors.

After putting on my Flu Game Jordans, I'm ready to sneak out my window. Can't risk being caught by Dad or Dapo. When I land on a twig, the snapping sound is a foghorn in my head. My heart clenches. I say a quick prayer to keep both Dapo and Dad asleep in their rooms until the morning.

Satisfied neither of them are going to come bursting into my room to demand answers, I wander the resort grounds, passing more villas and a Harrod's as I look for a good stargazing spot. I let out a wide yawn—I'm bloody tired—but Valoisa's threat is a sturdy finger prodding my side. Hoping to distract myself, I remind myself I'm on a beautiful island. All around me, plant life glows—some brighter than others—and bugs chirp softly.

Movement in a tree above catches my attention. Illuminated by the glowing leaves is an animal that looks like a mini monkey with oversize eyes and large, rabbit-like ears. It spirals down the trunk of the tree and leaps into the heart of a bush. Seconds later it emerges with a bug hanging out its mouth—a mouth that looks like it's had glowing lipstick drawn on terribly.

SMACK. Something hits me in the side of my head. A Nerf American football is at my feet, and when I look in the direction it came from, Deja is grinning.

I shake my head. "That was on purpose, wasn't it?"

I launch the football back at her, but she steps out of the way. "Where are you off to so late?" she asks, skipping to me.

"Aren't you going to get your Nerf thingy?"

Deja shrugs. "It's not mine."

"Shouldn't you be in bed?"

"Yes."

"Then why aren't you?"

"Because," Deja starts, "Dad's at a casino night Mr. Jenkins is hosting. Dad won't be back until *late* late."

"So you thought you'd wander around the resort, alone, at night?" I quirk an eyebrow. "Why?"

"I don't know. Because lately I need time to think." A glint of sadness shimmers in her eyes and she looks down. "You ask a lot of questions, Femi."

I rub the back of my head with a hand, warmth tickling my cheeks. I'd give up three of my top beats for free to get a clue on what's going through her head. "Fair enough. I'm going to find a good spot to look at the stars. Want to come?" I would ask her what's up, but I don't think she's ready to talk about it, and I know she'd deflect. Maybe stargazing will put her at ease enough to share.

She brightens a little. "Ooh, of course! This reminds me of the last time we saw each other in Cornwall. Lead the way."

I lead, walking aimlessly until we find an open field that might be another golf course. We gaze up at the night sky, play connect the dots with the constellations, and talk about our futures. She beams at my plans to take a gap year. I nod while she unravels her own path in the world of law. We reminisce on the past. Like the time we went ice-skating together and could barely stay upright. The laughter flows for a while before we rehash a few more of our favorite moments together, until we settle into comfortable silence.

My thoughts return to Valoisa and my . . . situation. I bite the inside of my cheek and cycle through my options. I need to tell someone— Would Deja understand? There's a tightness in my stomach. When I explained the situation with my family, she wasn't exactly on my side.

You need to grow up. The voice isn't mine, but Dapo's, if his had more reverb and sharper tones. I nudge Deja, ignoring the way my skin sparks at the contact.

"Yeah?"

I take a deep breath. "Can I tell you something?"

"If it's about what you wanted to say last time, it can wait. Sorry about pushing you at dinner, I was in a weird place. Before this trip, I found out my best friend and my boyfriend . . ." Deja sighs. So *that's* why she looked the way she did. Part of me wants to poke at what she found out, and part of me fills with disappointment at her mention of a boyfriend. "The stars are so beautiful."

"Uh-huh," I say, looking right at her, taking in how the moonlight adds a deep blue tint to her skin, making it look like polished stone. "They are. But it's not about that."

She turns my way; her eyes search mine. "What is it?"

"I'm being blackmailed. I think."

Deja bursts into laughter. "You're what?"

I fill her in—how I got lost going after Richard, how I ran into Valoisa, how she sent me on this quest, how I'm not sure if this isn't all some big joke from the resort. Deja stays quiet until I finish.

Her brown eyes are attentive and empathetic. In that moment I see our future: me, an established music producer; her, a renowned lawyer; us, a power couple. My breath catches and I inch toward her. She doesn't move and our eyes stay locked. If I tell her now, could I—? Could we—?

Deja clears her throat and glances away. The moment ends.

"Wow…" she says. Then, a four-letter expletive. "So, you're being blackmailed, and Richard Jenkins is maybe a fraud. This was not on my resort holiday bingo card."

"I know. But you can't tell anyone about Richard, Deja, I'm serious."

Deja frowns. "Why not? Wouldn't the truth help your blackmailers out?"

"I have a feeling it wouldn't. Otherwise they would have said something by now…Unless they can't. Maybe they signed NDAs, like we did? Whatever the reason, it's messy, and if we complicate things, well, they know about my dad and Timothy Huxley."

"Damn, they know about that snake, Timothy?" She huffs. "So, what are we going to do?"

"We? No, there's no *we*. It's bad enough they have me by my neck. I can't involve you in this."

Deja grins. "Too late, you already did."

Later that morning—after I've gotten a decent amount of sleep—Deja and I arrive at the visitor center. It looks like another old building, this one much more flamboyant than Café Central. Complex patterns are sculpted and carved around and on the door, windows, and twin pillars. Because of my new knowledge of Richard Jenkins's fraud, my mind lingers, and I think of a hidden past and what the building might have been: a temple, an embassy, or maybe a museum. Whatever it was, it's now another thing lost.

Mui's already waiting for us in front. The moment she clocks us, she rushes our way.

"Femi!" she squeals.

"Hey, Mui," I say. "You all right?"

"Who is this?" Mui jabs a finger in Deja's direction. "I didn't know you had a sister."

"Ew, I'm not his sister," Deja answers for me. "And I heard you're going to help Femi out?"

"Uh-huh." Mui nods vigorously. "I am. I'm going to take him to the staff quarters to meet Alberto. I guess you can come with us."

Deja pulls at my top, and I lower my ear to her mouth. "She's adorbs," she whispers. "I like her."

"She's something," I whisper back.

"I'd love to come along," Deja says to Mui.

Mui nods, grabs my hand, and pulls as hard as she can. I don't move, a part of me hesitant to go down this road.

"Let's," she grunts, "go!"

Mui acts as our personal tour guide, pointing out all the quirks of the resort. Like how the amusing statues spotted all over, smothered in fresh bird poop, have the faces of the first staff members to work at the resort and their children. Or how there's a whole underground network known as Backstage. It's how the employees get to and fro, make deliveries of all sorts.

That gets me thinking. "Mui...how do you know so much about the resort?"

"Um, I'm not supposed to say, but...you seem nice." She looks to her left. Always her left. "You think I should tell them, Ken?" Turning her head as if words are being whispered into her ear, she nods and then smiles. "Okay, Ken says it's okay. So, uh, I know so much because Dad lives here while he works, so I get to visit when I can. But he's always so busy."

"I see." *So that's why she's alone so much.*

"Yep. We know this whole place inside out. Like every word of 'Stay Gold.'" Mui skips ahead. "Staff quarters are round the corner." I lose sight of her, but her voice says, "See? Here it is."

I catch up to her, and she's pointing at a structure of garish proportions. The white and pink, dome-topped building in front of us reflects the sparkling blue waters of the pond in front of it.

"Come *on*," Mui insists, grabbing my right hand and Deja's left hand, and pulling. "Let's go find Alberto. I know a special way in."

Mui takes us around the side, where full trash bags sit, shrouded in the shadow of a large tree bearing the same fruit Valoisa threw to distract the glass dragons. The smell is unbearable. One falls to the ground with a splat as Mui opens the side door.

We step inside, thankfully leaving the rancid smell of the fruit and trash behind. Winking chandeliers hang from the mirrored ceiling. Abstract art, framed by glowing flowers, decorates the walls. Mui walks, sometimes skips, ahead of us like she owns the place. The staff greet her with broad smiles and kind eyes.

Deja and I get the same treatment by association, which feels nice. It's a new sensation. I've followed behind Dapo nearly all my life, and it's always been cold. I'm the impolite and immature younger brother.

Memories come flooding back, dragging me under for a moment. If only he hadn't said what he said when all I was trying to do was help Mum. If only I hadn't pushed him.

If only he hadn't stumbled over a broken bit of pavement and into the road.

"This is Alberto's room," Mui announces. We're standing in front of a white door with pink ridges and freckled with blue and purple flower stickers. "I stuck those there," Mui says when she catches me staring. She knocks and smiles with pride. "I won a bet."

Moments later, the door opens and a man emerges. He's a tall, light-skinned man with short hair, shaved at the sides, and a mustache-goatee combo peppered with silver. Dark sunglasses keep his eyes hidden.

At the sight of Mui he smiles. "Mui Mui, what a lovely surprise. How are you? What can I do for you?"

"Bertie! We're good, thanks. And nothing you can do for me, but my friends over here—they want to talk to you about cars. They *aren't* brother and sister."

Alberto takes us in, his head flicking between me and Deja. Light bounces off his sunglasses lenses as he whips them off. "I'd be auto-ly delighted to talk about cars," he says in an accent I can't quite place. He stands there and stares me down for what feels like ages.

I stare back, but the mischief in Alberto's eyes forces its way through my dam of composure and I laugh.

"That was a terrible pun. I hope you know that," Deja states, but she's smiling.

"Made him laugh, though, didn't it? Right, enough chitchat, what is it you want to know about cars?"

"Well, I was hoping you could show me under the hood of one of the resort vehicles." I clear my throat. "Please."

Alberto shakes his head. "No can do, I'm afraid. They're parked in the depot if not in use, and that's off-limits. But what I can do, my boy, is talk you through the rough schematics and answer any questions you may have. Come on in."

CHAPTER 8

BACKSTAGE

M
UI, D
EJA, AND I LEAVE A
LBERTO'S ROOM, AND AS WE
walk I mull over everything he said, thinking through the options.
We were lucky, in that he volunteered a lot of information freely.
I can't decide if it's because he's trusting or loose-lipped. The batteries are in the resort vehicles and aren't easy to get to. Not unless
you know what you're doing, and I def don't. Alberto cheerfully
said trying to remove them would be like asking God to strike you
down with lightning, and the Big Man (his words) obliging you.

So that plan is out. But he did let slip they keep spares in the
Backstage general stores, and, thanks to Deja being subtle in butter-
ing up Alberto, I know where that is. The closest entrance into the
underground Backstage is via a walkway just behind Café Central.

Mui suddenly jumps in front of me, and I barrel into her,
almost knocking her over. I grab her by the shoulders.

"Mui," I say. "What are you doing? I could have hurt you."

"And Ken," she adds.

"Huh?"

"You act like he's not even here."

Because he isn't, I think, but don't say. I get it. I had an imaginary friend once. When you're that young, they're as real as the sand trapped in your socks after a visit to the beach.

"He doesn't mean to act like that. He needs reminding. That's all," Deja says.

"Apology accepted."

I bunch my eyebrows together. "But I didn't—"

"Where are we going now?" Mui asks.

Deja nods, looping her arm through mine. There's that spark again. "That's what I'd like to know."

"*We* aren't going anywhere." I unlink myself from Deja. There is no way I'm letting her or Mui tag along and be accessories to my situation. "Now, if you'll—"

"You're going to the general stores, aren't you?" Mui asks.

I open my mouth to lie but quickly decide against it, embarrassed that was my first response.

Mui laughs and high-fives Deja. "I knew it!"

I shake my head and laugh. "You're a sharp one, aren't you?"

"Not me." She shakes her head and glances left. "Ken. He sees everything. He always did—does. He always does. Isn't that right?" The question remains unanswered, hanging in the air. I'm not sure if it's for me or for Ken. "Uh-huh. So, Ken thinks you want to take some batteries from the general stores. Why?"

"I can tell you why, and then you can go and tell everyone else," Deja says with a devious smile.

Oh, she's good.

Before Mui can latch onto Deja's mischief, I say, "If I let you both tag along, will you stop being massive thorns in my side?"

"Deal," Deja says. Mui nods like a bobblehead and smiles.

The moment we start heading toward the walkway that leads behind Café Central, Mui breaks out into song. "*Heigh-ho, heigh-ho, it's down Backstage we go.*"

Lord, give me strength.

Along the way, a small glass dragon—this one the size of a house cat—scuttles across the path. My heart prepares to rev into action but settles quickly. Unlike the ones in the forest, this one has a visible orange tag around its neck and stops to lick my shoes. I smile, and make up a rhyme. *If you see orange, they're tame and fun. Anything but? You better run, run, run.*

It takes us about ten minutes to reach the walkway leading behind the café. Though it's not much of a walkway; it's narrow, and we have to slide through it with our backs pressed against the wall of the café to avoid thorny bushes, until we emerge into a small clearing. There's a door—wooden with white paint peeling off it—dead ahead.

Mui rushes forward and twists the golden doorknob. It's locked. My jaw clenches. *What now?* I close my eyes and steady my breathing. When they open, Mui is gone. I wonder if she got bored and left in search of another adventure. I try the doorknob again, more forcefully, but it doesn't budge. *Nope, def locked.*

Deja steps up to the door and looks around the space. "Maybe there's a hidden button or something?"

We feel at the walls, pressing in different spots high and low.

"What are you doing?"

Mui's voice makes me jump, and I turn around. She's wearing a quizzical look and holding a knife like an ice-cream cone.

"I thought you'd gone," I say.

"Yeah, to get this." She presents me with the knife. "We can unscrew the doorknob and unlock the door. You're both looking at me funny? Did I say something wrong?"

I share a smile with Deja and shake my head slowly. Mui is whip-smart. "Nah. Not at all."

The knife is awkward to use, and it takes me about fifteen minutes to get the doorknob unscrewed and a couple more minutes to find out how to unlock the door and open it. The first step is onto an escalator that senses our arrival and whirs to life. It carries us down toward Backstage.

The walls are lined with mirrors that warp our reflections. At the bottom is a path that goes left and right. A small sign indicates the general stores are to the right.

"You know," Mui starts, "Daddy's friends say you have to do everything here quietly."

"Do they now?"

A couple of workers amble by, and we duck into a shallow alcove that provides enough shadow for us to remain undetected.

"Have you heard?" one of the staff members whispers. They've got this deep bass in their voice. "Remember Elora? They told us she left for a competitor and put her on immediate gardening leave. Not true. Apparently they asked her to leave when she brought something up management didn't like. Something about her rights as a citizen."

"Seriously? What did she say?" says the other. A tenor if I had to guess. "And is it me, or are Mr. Jenkins and his team more tightly wound these days?"

"I don't know what she said, and who cares? If she was let

go because of an opinion, I'm worried. I knew they saw us as disposable, but man..."

Tenor sighs. "Yeah, but you know, to play devil's advocate, they don't let us stay here for an opinion. They..."

Once their conversation fades into the distance, we come out from our hiding spot. Deja complains about pins and needles, while Mui tugs on my top.

"Uh-huh, they *do* say," she says, going back to our previous conversation. "They say if you're not quiet, something will..." She brings her voice to a low whisper, and I lean in. "*Boo!*" In the same breath, she grabs my shoulders and I jump.

Scowling, I sigh. "Let's just get the batteries and go."

I'm annoyed. This was supposed to be a holiday—sun, new experiences, and as little time with Dad and Dapo as possible. But it's taken less than a day to scrub out the excitement I'd built up for the resort and replace it with unease.

We make a right, then a left, following the signs. Another right. Right again until, at the end of a hallway that slopes up, we arrive at the metal door for the general stores. Other than the smell of festering garbage on a hot summer's day, the most striking thing about Backstage is how muted it is. The opposite of the resort above us. There's no color, and it's quiet—the buzzing in my ears is faint down here. The walls of the hallways are mottled with dark lichen.

If Valoisa is telling the truth, what were these sprawling hallways before they became transport tunnels and storage facilities?

We slip inside the general stores, and it's wet and dark and vast. Our footsteps slap against the stone floor, drowning out loud dripping. Deja and Mui follow behind as I search the various shelves like I'm in IKEA. The batteries are tucked away in the far-left corner of the room. I take as many as I need and sigh, relieved.

From behind me there's a grunt. I turn, and Deja's looking up with wide eyes, pointing with a trembling finger. Her gaze is fixed on a large, brown furry moth with a golden, mosquito-esque needle on the ceiling. Even with its wings tucked in, it's about as wide as a microwave and the length of an acoustic guitar. My eyes rove over the body.

If you see orange, they're tame and fun. Anything but? You better run, run, run.

Maybe its tag is hidden? Or maybe it isn't. Every nerve I have frays like one of my chewed hoodie strings, and I step backward carefully. *If in doubt, don't stick around to find out.* Deja backs away, too. But Mui, she's smitten, staring up at the ceiling with wide eyes and an open mouth. She brings out her phone and locks its camera onto the moth.

I stoop down. "Mui, don't. Let's go—"

The flash on her phone goes off.

For a long moment nothing happens—then the animal's golden needle twitches. There's a hiss, like air being sucked through teeth. The moth spreads its wings wide, and, in a flutter, peels away from the ceiling.

Mui shrieks. Deja mumbles gibberish.

I don't think. Stuffing the batteries into my pockets, I spin, hitch Mui onto my back, grab Deja's hand to jolt her into action, and bolt for the exit. We manage to reach the door, and I'm able to slam it shut. With both my hands on it, I take a moment to catch my breath. *Inhale. Exhale. In—*

The moth's golden needle punches through the metal door. Mere inches away from spearing my stomach.

Pardon?

"Nope." I swallow and, with my head, gesture at Deja and Mui to run. We shoot down the hallway toward an exit. There's another punching sound. And then a thumping slam.

That'll be the door.

With adrenaline pumping, I lose track of where we need to be heading, and we burst into a small kitchen space. A few security guys sit at a table, chatting and eating doughnuts and drinking coffee. They stare in our direction with probing glares.

"Hey," Mui says, waving.

"*You* shouldn't be here," one of the men says with a frown. Ah, that's the bass voice from earlier. He also seems to be the leader.

Mui giggles. "I know, but—"

"We got lost," I say, talking over Mui so she doesn't make things worse. I edge backward toward the light switch. "We're guests."

"Guests," Bass parrots. "Look here, you're—"

"I'm afraid we really must be going." I flick the switch and plunge the room into darkness before legging it out of the room. The calls of security bounce off the walls. Their footsteps echo, and their flashlights dance, never quite landing on us.

"Mui, you and Ken okay?" She glances up and nods. "Deja?" Her cheeks are flushed, and she gives me a slow smile and a nod. "Good, good. We're almost there."

Once we're back through the door we took to head down into Backstage, I lie on the ground next to Deja, gasping for air and allowing blood to flow back into my sore arms. A shadow falls across me, and I look up at Mui. She's smiling.

"That was the most fun Ken and I have had here. Ever! *EVER*. That moth was huuuuge!" She spreads her arms to illustrate how wide. "And then Carlton was like, 'You shouldn't be here.' He looked so mad when you talked back to him."

"Hold up." Deja sits up. "Carlton? You knew those security men?"

"Uh-huh. He knows Daddy quite well." My mouth drops open ever so slightly. "Yeah, he's actually quite nice."

"Nice," I say, holding back the urge to kiss my teeth. "Mui... you could have told us. You know, before we went running." I rub at my temples.

"I tried!" Mui insists.

"To be fair," Deja says. "You didn't give her much of a chance to say anything before you turned off the lights."

"Touché," I say.

"Anyway, I've got to go. Daddy's messaging me on my phone, and I don't think he's happy." Mui waves her goodbyes and sets off running, leaving me and Deja alone.

"What the hell," Deja says. She bursts into infectious laughter, setting me off as we replay what happened. I get to my feet to mime Deja's look when she saw the moth.

Deja grabs my forearm to steady herself as she gets onto her feet. Once we stop laughing, we lock eyes. I'm transported to the last time we were together, knowing what I would do differently now. She would know how much I liked her—how much I loved her. *Because she deserves to know the truth.* Everything begins to feel dull and empty and—

Deja gives me a shake, pulling me into reality. "Earth to Femi. Dad just texted me. Our families are eating together. Let's go join them."

CHAPTER 9

ENELLE

Deja and I join our families for brunch, and it isn't terrible. I order Lapsang souchong–cured haddock and twice-cooked eggs, which I wolf down.

"How was the first day of the Somerberg Conference yesterday?" Dapo asks, cutting at his bacon.

Dad perks up and puts his cutlery down, before wiping his mouth and smiling. "Great. I met this nice lady from Sri Lanka who was telling me all about how proud she is of her children. They all run publicly traded companies. Maybe that'll be you one day, Dapo."

Why not me? I think. Not that I have any desire, but still it stings.

Dad continues. "Richard spoke about how the current political climate is divisive and how he is seeking to introduce positive change by funding numerous campaigns for the leaders of tomorrow across the world."

"Eat the rich," I declare, and everyone gives me a look like

I've offended them. "Relax, it's a joke. But seriously, politics is so messed up at the moment. These parties need to shape up. They have all these ideas, but they need to remember they serve the collective citizens of their respective nations, not the power government brings."

"Yeah," Dapo says. He draws out the word like okra soup. "That's right."

"Well said," Mr. Merrick adds. I haven't seen Deja's dad since we arrived, and apart from the noticeable hair loss, he hasn't changed a bit. "And another thing about those morally bankrupt fools running the country—they wouldn't know a good policy if it came up to them and paid them a hefty sum under the table."

He ends up going on an almighty rant. Halfway through, my phone buzzes. It's another couple of texts from Valoisa.

I won't take your silence personally, Lost Boy.

Don't forget my batteries.

Dread gathers in the depth of my stomach, weighing it down. I know she has every intention to expose my family if I don't comply.

I spy Dad giving me his what-have-I-said-about-no-phones-at-the-table glare and put my phone away. If only he knew.

"Why don't *you* run for Parliament, then?" Deja asks.

"Because," answers Mr. Merrick, "there are far too many suspect pictures of me on people's phones. Can't risk it. I don't want your mother to leave me."

"Ew." Deja scrunches her face while her dad bursts into

deep-bellied laughter. "Anyway, isn't it nice? To be together like this again?"

"Absolutely," Dad affirms. He talks about what he's enjoying on the island so far, from the interesting wildlife to the way everything seems to run so smoothly. But, for me, the sense of awe Dad describes has soured. Between Richard's secret and my blackmail situation, I'm disillusioned with the whole experience.

"Femi, what about you?" Dad smiles. "Anything you've enjoyed that you can share? Maybe something you, Dapo, and I can do together once I'm done with the conference today."

"Not really," I say.

"Are you okay?"

"Yeah."

Dad's smile is tight. "Why are you suddenly being short with me? If you're not well, there's the medical center. Maybe we should book you—"

"Dad, I'm fine. Honestly, I'm tired. Sorry."

"How come you are tired all of a sudden?" I keep my lips pressed tight together. "Well? Have you been . . . drinking?"

I hold his steady gaze and clench my jaw, knowing if I speak, I'll be unable to control my tone. Silence reigns before Deja's dad burps and bursts into uneasy laughter.

"David, let him be, eh?" Mr. Merrick pats Dad on his shoulder. "Who wants dessert?"

Straight after brunch Dad forces me on a video call with Mum to "explain my attitude." I don't think I've ever uttered more one-word responses in my life. Over it and over him. He *knows* I don't like being put on the spot. To her credit, Mum has more sympathy for me in situations like this.

I spend the rest of the day holed up in my room watching movies back-to-back, counting down until I need to deliver the batteries to Valoisa. Deja won't be coming with me—she and her dad are watching a movie at the resort's cinema—but she told me to come knock on her window once I'm done. Villa 48, window to the left of the front door.

As the time gets closer, I wait for quiet to settle in our villa. For lights to turn off. For doors to close. And then I pry open my window and clamber out. Humid rain falls as I make my way into the forest, and petrichor fills the air.

Valoisa doesn't appear for at least another twenty minutes.

"You're late," I state.

She shrugs. "Do you have what I need?"

I pull out my phone and show her a selfie of me with the batteries. "I do."

"You were supposed to *bring* them." Her tone is sharp. "This isn't a time for joking. You realize I can ruin you?"

"You see, I did some thinking. Yeah, you might ruin my family, drain our bank accounts, but my friend said something that made me think. While I need you not to do that, you *needed* me to get your stuff. For whatever it is you need them for—why do you need them, by the way?"

Valoisa takes a deep breath. Her smile is brief and shallow. "Not so docile, I see."

"No." I smile back. "If you want the batteries, I need two things." Valoisa purses her lips but doesn't say a word. "First,

I need to know that by giving you the batteries, I'm not doing anything that's going to land me in trouble. Second, I need to know once you get them, you'll leave me and my family alone."

"I promise you both those things will happen. This is all for Enelle," she starts, her voice trembling. "She's in a bad way at the moment, and she's terrified she's getting worse—her pain's chronic. The batteries are going to power a device to help ease things for her."

I nod, then frown. "These batteries are industrial-grade, though. Must be some hell of a device..."

"It has to be, to help Enelle the way it needs to."

My gut twists. I know what it's like to put your hope in something to make everything right. When Mum told us about her lupus last summer, I spent hours online getting spooked by all the ways it could complicate things. And even more time looking for solutions. I got her to agree to try something a bit more experimental, that could make the effects negligible— something Dapo didn't agree with and which led to our falling-out. Then the incident between us. And it's been worse since.

"I get it. But if I'm going to give you these batteries, then I need to trust you. Tell me about yourself and Darlenia."

She opens her mouth but closes it a moment later. After a few heartbeats, she turns to me with eyes full of determination. "You saw the blog post. This... isn't the real Darlenia. It was so different before Richard appeared nearly twelve years ago. It was thriving. Then when he came, and he brought his money with him, people were forced into a decision by the sheer magnetism of his resources: work for him as live-in staff when his resort opened; leave the island with a sweet payout; or stay, but on the outskirts.

"Most left, while a handful became staff. I don't tend to see them around much."

I nod, sympathy crystallizing in my thoughts. It must have been lonely. The whole thing sounds like gentrification on an unprecedented scale. Another word comes to mind, too—*colonization*. Both in the name of empire and in the name of Richard's self-interest. Valoisa talks more about Darlenia, and it's clear how much this island means to her—it's where she grew up, where she learned to engineer and fish, where her home is.

"Try not to move too quickly," she says a few minutes later, when we're deeper into the forest. Insects chirp every now and then. "Most of the beasts of the forest are asleep, but the sleepless ones are easily startled and, though you are with me, they know you don't belong here. Especially the land eels."

"Land eels?"

Valoisa nods. "The Ghosts of Darlenia. They can't see, but they perceive. They are cunning creatures that come slithering out when there's rain—which isn't often. A kill here and there. It is enough for them for weeks. But that's not even the most interesting thing about them. Their skin only ripples when they're hunting. And when they hunt, they want their prey to know it. In fact, they bank on it. That is when they act."

"Seriously?" My heart thumps in my chest.

"Come."

The deeper we go, the taller the flowers get, and the smell shifts, too. All I smell is excrement and earth. Entering Darlenia already felt like a whole new world, and now it feels as if I'm entering another. We emerge upon something spectacular. A tall and square white brick terrace, at least five large fridges high, is laid out in steps like a theater. On each step moss and flowers glow. There are narrow arches that burrow into the center of the structure while worn stairs lead upward.

This is the *real* wonder of the island.

"What is this?" I ask.

"The Gardens of Laudadon. Apparently back when we had a monarchy, the queen built this place for her beloved, who was never identified. I would spend hours here as a kid. Exploring the ins and outs." Several beats of silence. "I want most of the Darlenian people to return," she declares. "I want to open up our part of the island and show off Darlenia and our heritage. I want people to understand what it is to be Darlenian. But Richard won't."

"Why not?" I suspect I already know the answer. I'm surprised he didn't come for this structure.

"When Richard arrived, he signed a deal with our government. They didn't even put up a fight. Overnight they gave up sovereignty and control of the island in exchange for huge payouts from him for each citizen and ironclad NDAs to never speak out. Part of the deal was automatic Portuguese citizenship for those who chose to leave—since Portugal was the closest country willing to strike a deal—to hide any trace of Darlenia."

Deep anger bubbles within me. "It sucks no one can speak out about what happened. I'm glad you shared it with me. If you wait here, I can come back with the batteries." I turn to leave, but she stops me, grabbing my wrist.

"Do you want to meet her? Enelle." When I nod, she flashes me a smile that reaches her eyes. "Let's go."

She leads me through more dense, lush forest toward her home, in Valoisa's words, located in the "nostril" of the forest. Slowly, slowly, the ground becomes more rugged. I regret wearing my Jordans, wincing when I hear a squelch and spot a splash of mud on the leather and laces.

The plants are a lot more unruly, unlike the sculpted and prim bushes on the resort grounds. The grass ringing the trees— thin and tall—is a mix of yellow and green. The flowers that sprout in random clusters are mesmerizing and jarring. Their petals are the color of a deep bruise, while having the look and feel of saggy skin, and I wince. They've blossomed on stems leaking a whitish sap that makes my stomach turn with nausea. I feel my mouth fill with saliva. A surefire sign I'm about to puke if I keep staring at the sick-looking flowers.

And yet this is the true island.

Valoisa pauses and signals for me to stop and be quiet. Up ahead, a young boy with umber skin and loose curls, probably no older than Mui, sprints across our view in a red vest. He's chased by a man with the same shade of skin and broad shoulders.

"Yos myo, Socri! Disaxiliras!" exclaims the broad-shouldered man. They disappear into the greenery.

"One of those who stayed behind?" I ask.

Valoisa nods. We walk on, and appearing on either side of us are tall rocky walls that brush the thick canopy of trees overhead. There is no other way but ahead. Passing through the natural pathway, we emerge into a clearing. I swallow.

In front of us is a small cottage, crooked like my right eyebrow. But along the walls and on the trunks of the trees are … "Jellyfish?" I wonder aloud at the glowing masses.

"Wunderjellies," Valoisa corrects.

One drifts off the tree trunk and pulses through the air across our path toward the other side. As if the air is water.

"Harmless. They'll return to the reefs by sunrise," she says. "Right now, they're grazing on the moss. There's not much food in the reefs for them anymore. They never used to come on land. I'm not sure what changed. Enelle's inside."

We cut across the clearing to the house, and I follow Valoisa inside, where I find myself facing a woman who must be Enelle. Sitting in a rocking chair, she seems beyond tired and older than the few years that are supposed to separate her from Valoisa. She's not even looking at us but toward the window. Her skin is the same shade as Valoisa's—umber with a cool undertone. Her hair is in elegant canerows. A small radio plays a crackling, jazzy tune.

I look around the room, and it looks as messy as my bedroom back home.

"Eni," Valoisa says. Enelle's head turns our way, a soft smile reaching her bloodshot eyes and bone-white eyelashes. I fight to keep my face neutral, despite how striking she looks. "I brought him."

"'The winds of change grow. Anticipation tastes sweet. Spring is among us.' Do you know who wrote that?" Her voice is much gruffer than Valoisa's.

"Austin Seinfeld." Valoisa steps in and around the mess. "It's time for your meds."

"No thanks."

Valoisa pours some purple liquid onto a spoon. "I wasn't asking, Eni. Not when you had a flare-up this morning." She forces the spoon into Enelle's mouth. "Fabulous."

"Witch," Enelle mutters. I burst out into laughter and she turns on me. "You. What do you want?"

I point a finger at myself. "Me?"

"Yes, you. You're the one I'm looking at, aren't you?" Enelle glances at Valoisa and shares a wry smile with her. "You're right, you have brought me a Lost Boy."

"I'm not lost. I read the blog post you wrote. And Valoisa told me what Richard did. I wanted to say I'm sorry for what's happened."

"Me too." Enelle yawns. "Val told me about the batteries. Thank you so much—this will really help. Come closer." I obey. She points toward the kitchen. "In there is the device. All I need you to do now is put the batteries in and plug it in. Val will give you more instruction. Please do this for us. We can't enter the resort."

My curiosity puppets my mouth. "Why not?" I know they have NDAs, but surely that shouldn't stop them moving around the island.

"Lost and nosy, I see." Enelle's lips form a smile as sharp as broken glass. "Because the ones who stayed here have an agreement with Mr. Jenkins. Everything north of the pearl path belongs to him. And if we are caught crossing that line, then he can seize what's left of our land."

"How many of you stayed?" I ask, remembering the boy and the man.

"Too few of us, my sweet." With both hands, Enelle grabs mine. Hers are warm and soft, and they tremble. Her eyes water, and I see the misery written all over her face. Empathy sears through my gut with the heat of an iron. "Val says you help us out of the kindness of your heart. You're doing the right thing. The island is most grateful."

I swallow and nod. Valoisa hovers behind, waiting, and I glare at her. She's been feeding Enelle lies. Still, face-to-face with Enelle now and seeing her in pain, there is a part of me that does want to be helpful.

Enelle points up at the ceiling toward what looks like a smoke detector. "Valoisa, the battery is low, replace it. I'm starting to feel that cursed frequency."

Valoisa nods at Enelle and then says to me, "This way."

CHAPTER 10

THE DEVICE

VALOISA GUIDES ME INTO THE KITCHEN, STOPPING IN front of a pulsing light on the counter. It's coming from a boxy device riddled with snaking wires and empty slots. For where the batteries go.

"Impressive, right?" Valoisa asks, gesturing at the device with her chin. With deft movements she grabs some stray parts on the counter, cuts some wire. She consults a piece of paper while fiddling with the device. "It's ready. All it needs now are the batteries."

I frown. "How's it supposed to work?"

"It's a bigger version of what Enelle was complaining had a low battery. It will send out frequencies to help alleviate the chronic pain she's in."

"How does—"

"Don't ask me how it works. All I know is the device on the ceiling gives her a small range of movement. If she goes too far, the pain is likely to flare up. This device should allow her to move more freely. I'm the one putting it together, but Enelle's the brains." She laughs. "She's always been like that, speaking in riddles. Writing in her notebooks. Thinking up solutions. Giving orders. It can be so frustrating not fully knowing what's going on in her head. But I go along with it, because the end result is impressive. I caught the engineering bug from her."

"I know what you mean."

"Huh?"

"I mean, I've got a brother. He's never letting me in. Always telling me what to do. If only he—" I stop myself. *She doesn't want to hear you whine.* "It's whatever. Let me know when to meet so I can bring you the batteries."

"No, not quite, Lost Boy."

"What is it?"

"I need you to put the device in a specific place at a specific time. I can show you on the map."

My head shakes as the words tumble out. "I—I dunno. And I barely—look—I'm not sure—"

"Please. We won't ask for anything else. And after this, we will delete your data." Her gaze pierces through me like a needle, numbing my resolve. "I get it, we're strangers. But Enelle needs this. You *saw* her. It'll be easy."

"But why can't you plug it in here? Isn't closer better?"

"That's what I thought, but Enelle said at such close range, it would do more harm than good. But we can't go as far as we need to because Mr. Jenkins, or that yava Ellen, will know if we try. We can't take that risk."

My gut crumples. *Idon'tknowIdon'tknowIdon't—*

I lock eyes with Valoisa and find no lies in them. Combined

with the looming threat of blackmail, I relent. "Okay, I'll do it. Where do I need to go?"

"Let me get the map," Valoisa says, smiling wide and departing for a moment. When she returns, she guides me through where I need to put the device and plug it inside a building, pointing it out on the physical map. The building is on the east side of the island, north of the pearl path. She warns me not to put the location into my watch's GPS. In case they're watching.

"In the back room," she says. "Find the socket facing the window and plug it in."

My eyebrows squish together. "Hang on, if it has batteries, why do I need to plug it in?"

"So the batteries aren't depleted. And if there's an outage, the device can keep running."

"Fair point. And what do I say if I get caught?"

"Yos myo, don't worry so much. You'll be fine." Valoisa smiles at me. "I can't thank you enough, Femi."

"You're welcome."

I clear my throat, my heart thudding in my rib cage like there's not enough room. She gets on her tiptoes and gives me a soft peck on my cheek, sending a jolt of energy through me.

The moment is tinged with guilt when I think of Deja. I haven't done anything wrong, but the sinking feeling in my stomach suggests otherwise.

"I should get back to Enelle, see how she's doing. Once again, thank you. Beyo ye sol an tyos umbros."

I tilt my head. "What does that mean? Something good, I hope."

"Of course, Lost Boy. It means 'I can see the sun on your

shoulders.' It—how do you say—is a better way to say thank you. It means to have a deep appreciation for a person. But know this, too: If you screw us, we will not forget or let it go."

"Noted."

Enelle's coughing bursts the silence between us.

"Duty calls," Valoisa says, leaving me in the kitchen alone.

With a heavy sigh, I turn away, heading out the front door.

Deja comes to her window on my second tap.

"How was your late-night tryst with your blackmailer?" she asks, leaning out her window. "Do tell."

I give her the rundown of meeting up with Valoisa, going to see Enelle, and realizing they're telling the truth about Richard and the island. "You know, she's unorthodox, sure, but in another life I reckon we could have been good friends," I conclude.

"Talk about Stockholm syndrome, eh?"

"No, it's not like that." I laugh. "Come on, there's—"

Deja reads from her phone, "Stockholm syndrome is defined as feelings of trust or affection felt in many cases of kidnapping or hostage-taking by a victim toward a captor." She looks up, her tone firm. "Tell me this doesn't sound like that?"

"Okay, I see your point. But, Deja, if you'd been there, you'd have seen—heard—her sincerity. You know what she's been through with Richard."

"And I sympathize, but that's not an excuse to blackmail someone."

A long moment of silence stretches between us, damp and uncomfortable. "You're right," I say softly. I hate when she's not happy with me, and I search my mind for anything that'll put a smile back on her face. "I've just remembered something. You know that time we—"

Deja yawns. "I'm beat. Let's catch up tomorrow? If that's okay?"

"Uh, yeah no, that's cool. When should—" Her window closes, and she draws her curtains. I click my teeth and wander back toward my own villa, hands in pockets, replaying my interaction with Deja.

Unease twists my stomach inside out as I swing between going back to ask if she's cool or leaving it because I'm overthinking. I decide that, to make it up to her, I'll make her a beat. Something to let her know how special she is to me.

"Femi?" calls a familiar voice. I turn. *Mui.* She skips toward me. "Shouldn't you be in bed?"

"Well, yeah, that's where I'm headed. What about *you?*"

She shrugs. "*We* are looking for treasure. I hear people bury stuff here."

"And your parents are okay with this?"

"Well, parent," Mui starts. "Mum isn't here. Only Dad is, and he's servicing the vehicles with Alberto, getting them ready for tomorrow. He thinks I'm asleep and doesn't even get back indoors until the morning."

"Okay, then, tell me about this treasure." I bend down. "Have you found anything good?"

"Yes, of course. We're great treasure hunters." She brandishes a worn-looking silver spoon. "See?"

"Ooh," I say. "That's a great find. Well, don't let me hold you up hunting for treasure. See you around."

Mui scampers off, only to skid to a halt and turn back around. "Wanna come with us?" She stares at me.

As much as I would love to crash on my bed, maybe I should care about someone as young as Mui wandering into areas she shouldn't. These animals aren't as docile as Richard claims.

"Go on, then," I reply. "Lead the way."

It's soon clear there is no rhyme or reason to Mui's method of finding treasure. It's adorable to see her displacing rocks, peering into bushes, moving garbage cans out of the way.

In the middle of looking in yet another bush, she says, "Who was that girl you saw in the forest?"

"Huh?"

"Tonight, I followed you for a bit. Were you being mischeeky-ous?"

Mis—what? Ah. "You mean *mischievous?*"

Mui nods, using her hands to scrape away some dirt. "Uh-huh. That's what I said, *mischeeky-ous.*"

"I suppose I was."

"Don't worry. Lips sealed." She spins around and brandishes a shiny-looking rock with a mesmerizing swirl pattern. "Treasure! Okay, bye!"

Before I know it, Mui rushes off, swallowed up by the silkiness of the dark.

After considering whether I should go after her, I decide she'll be all right—she knows to keep to the paths. Instead, I trudge back to the villa and collapse onto my bed, staring up at the ceiling. My thoughts are filled with Deja and Valoisa and Deja and Valoisa and Deja.

> Dejaaa, sorry if I upset you. Didn't mean to. Good night and hope you sleep well

Right. That'll do. I'll—
My phone buzzes.

> Didn't upset me. It's fine. Night x

Her message is so blunt. I rack my brains searching for anything that could have offended her but come up short. I'll have to trust that if she were upset with me, she'd say so.

CHAPTER 11

PLUG-IN DAY

After a terrible night's sleep, I press snooze on my alarm three times before getting up and showering. I glance at my rucksack that has the device in it, chewing on my fingernails. I'm supposed to plug in the device this afternoon.

Or I could find somewhere to chuck it. But every time that thought crosses my mind, it's rubbed out by the sounds of Enelle's cough and the pleading on Valoisa's face. I might not be able to say anything about what Richard's done, due to my NDA, but I can still help Valoisa and her family. Even if blackmail hangs over my head like a sagging ceiling.

I put on my rucksack and head into the living room. Dad's already gone to the conference center, and there's no sight of Dapo. In the kitchen, I go for a glass of water, seeing the sticky note Dapo's left on the counter:

Gone for a run.

FYI: I'm going to go to the Making of
the Resort Museum.
Meet there @ 11:30 in case you wanna
hang
D

It's 11:15 A.M. right now. On the one hand, I don't want to go. On the other hand, this is an olive branch I know I should take if I hope for our cold war to thaw. Plus, knowing what I know about Richard now, color me curious.

Screw it. Let's hear what Richard has to say at the museum.

I put in my earbuds and browse through several playlists on my phone before choosing one that always calms my nerves. The volume is low enough that it doesn't make my hearing worse but loud enough to distract me from the constant buzz in my ears.

As I follow my watch's proposed route to the museum, several golden-beaked birds saunter along the pearl path in a single-file line. From the largest to the smallest, each has an orange tag. I creep closer. A couple of beaks turn my way, but none are startled by my presence when I crouch down. I follow them for a bit, picking up an iridescent feather that falls free. Before they veer into a bit of greenery, I point and scan with my watch. The app on my phone pings:

> **_Golden raptor_**—Believed to belong to the
> Vehemgypinae family. A subfamily of the
> Sagittariidae family. Their distinct golden beaks are
> functional. When they catch the sunlight, it blinds
> their prey. The feathers, however, have no clear

reason for their iridescence. Some golden raptors
have been spotted with patches of brown feathers,
which suggests they may not have always had
iridescent feathers.

I don't see any more animals and the walk is quiet.

It gives me plenty of time to think. About a lot of things, but my focus is on last summer. My thoughts always circle back to then. I nibble on my bottom lip and sigh over and over. Then, like a switch, my regret twists into anger.

Why would you tell Mum to try something that's not fully proven yet? Are you a medical professional? If you cared about her, you wouldn't have suggested something so risky.

The words belong to the Dapo from last summer. I don't remember much else in terms of what was said, and my brain has given up trying to piece it together beyond a certain point. I saw red and I pushed him. Hard. He stumbled on a broken bit of pavement and into the road. There's no sound. I see him get struck in the hip by a car and he's writhing about in pain.

And I'm sorry.

I go over to him, but he waves me away. His eyes are wet, and he's saying something. There's no sound. But I don't need sound. Not when he looks at me like he hates me. It makes sense. He had one of those last chance football trials coming up. And because of me he never did go to them.

His last chance gone, like that.

The flashes fade to black and I pull out my earbuds. The steady hum of the island comes rushing back, and in a weird way it's a relief.

Dapo's standing in front of the museum, waiting. He nods curtly when he sees me and when I'm within earshot, says, "I didn't think you'd turn up. I was about to head inside. What's in the bag?"

"I didn't think I'd come either but I thought, why not." I glance down at my bulging bag. "And just some music stuff. How was your run?"

Dapo shrugs. "Decent. Boring as hell. I got us the…" His words trail off as his attention is drawn to something else. I follow his gaze. Some*one* else.

"Ellen," he mumbles, striding over to her. I follow. "Ellen," he says again, louder this time.

She stops, and in one smooth, fluid motion, turns to face us. "Do I know you?" She doesn't smile.

"Uh…" Words jam in Dapo's throat. She goes to leave, and when I nudge him with my elbow, he finds his voice. "Wait. I—you don't know me, but I know you. Yeah, Mr. Jenkins's right-hand woman. He wouldn't be half the man he is now without you."

"Flattery is cheap. Do you want something?" Her tone is bored, but it looks like his flattery bought him a few moments of her time. "What is it?"

Dapo doesn't say anything. I think he's starstruck, so I nod and jump in, dialing up my levels of mischief. "Yeah, actually. I was wondering, do you know who Enelle Ruiz is?"

The little color Ellen has drains from her face. "Where did you hear that name?"

"I…uh, saw it carved on a tree somewhere," I lie. "Sorry, I— Did I say the wrong thing?"

"No."

"Oh."

Ellen's gained most of the color back in her face. "Oh, indeed. Anything else?"

Her phone trills at the same time and she picks up.

"Rich, hey. Another one? Uh-huh. Yep, it seems like they're happening more than usual." She listens for a moment. "Totally understandable. Do you want me to get Alberto to—no? Okay. Yep, I'll make the arrangements. Anything—" She looks at her phone and sighs. Then she looks at us.

The expression she gives us isn't a glare, but it's a close cousin. She sizes me up before her face softens. "If you have any other questions, you can use the watches we've provided, or there's a helpful information center you can go to. Now, if you'll excuse me, I need to go."

And then it's me and Dapo again. The conversation Ellen was having on the phone sticks with me. *What's happening more frequently?* I work through possibilities in my head—cyberattacks, complaints, bad reviews.

A hand lands on my shoulder.

"You didn't tell me you'd made a friend," Dapo says. He points toward a young, beaming girl rushing toward us. She's waving as she runs. "Who's that?"

"Mui," I say, unable to hold back my smile. "And Ken."

"Ken?"

"You'll see."

When Mui arrives, she looks from Dapo to me and back again. "Wow, you guys look alike. You must be brothers, then." Mui examines Dapo. "He looks nicer than you, Femi. But he's sadder."

"Sadder?" Dapo asks.

A nod. "Yes. You sort of look like Daddy when Ken got lost. So I dunno what, exactly. I just know you're sad."

"Interesting."

I wonder if Dapo's caught up in what happened last summer, too. If he still hates me. I don't want to dwell on that. But then another thought flashes. "Wait, who is Ken to you ... other than your best friend?"

Mui lifts her chin and declares, "He's my brother."

Dapo looks stricken at her response. Unease claws at my insides, but words fail me. I have no idea if it's my place to say anything at all. Instead, I exhale and plaster on a grin. "So, Dapo, I'm thinking we skip the museum and go to Café Central." I lean in and whisper to him, "Don't ask me why, but I don't feel comfortable leaving her alone, and I bet she'd rather eat than go to a museum." He nods. "Mui, you in?"

"Yes, yes, yes," she answers.

It's not long until we're all sitting inside a buzzing Café Central. A plate of fresh fruit rests between us. I look around. I've been so preoccupied with my own situation, I hadn't noticed how, over the last day, the number of guests on the island has swelled.

Huh. They must have ferried more people in even though Dad's conference started already. That could explain the new faces among the guests and Café Central staff.

The bag containing the device is by my feet. Every time I remember I have it on me, my heart thuds in the back of my throat. *Stop thinking about what could happen if you're caught.*

"You all right?" Dapo asks. "You seem quieter than usual."

"I've been better, but yeah, I'm good. Tired." We leave it at that.

Later, after some of the best smoothies I've ever had, we leave Café Central, stepping into a humid hug and onto the pearl path. Dapo suggests we get some ice cream from the combination Harrods and Waitrose. It's not far at all, and the suggestion slaps a wide grin on Mui's face, showing as many teeth as possible.

But when he suggests we sit in the gardens near Ethereal Lake, Mui's smile vanishes.

"I'm not sure," she says, trembling. "Ken and I don't like large puddles of water."

Dapo crouches in front of Mui. "You're not the only one," he says. "I'm the same. But we won't be close enough to fall in, and even if you did, Femi's a good swimmer, so he'll go in and get you." He glances up at me.

"Of course," I say. "Mui, you're safe with us."

It takes a moment, but Mui eventually nods, and after conferring with Ken, brightens up.

The three of us soon sit on a bench eating ice cream, looking out at other guests and admiring the lake that lives up to its name. The surface glistens like it's coated in pink oil. Guests wade and splash and swim, squealing in excitement. Fish with golden scales leap in graceful arcs.

Some peoples fawn over the golden raptors. The animals lope across the grass, wings tucked in, and stagger and bump into things like they're drunk. I think they might have bad eyesight.

"Question," I start, "what would you do if this whole island was founded on a lie?"

Dapo pulls the ice-cream cone from his mouth. "A lie? What sort of lie?"

"Let's say—"

I flinch as a boy in front of us exclaims, "*Ouch!*" His face is scrunched in confusion at the golden raptor in front of him. "*Ouch!* It bit me. That really hurt."

Blood drips from his left hand, and he takes half a step back. There's a small bit of red on the tip of the bird's beak. The boy raises his other hand, balling it up into a fist, ready to bring it down, but he freezes when the golden raptor spreads its wings.

The boy stumbles backward and falls while the bird lifts off. Squawks fill the air as, all around, golden raptors take flight. A sense of dread ripples through me as they circle above as if we're prey.

Murmurs rise at the strangeness, but no one moves. They stare and smile and gasp. On the branches there are more golden raptors, still and watching us with a chilling focus. *Where did they all come from?*

Dapo stands from the bench, not caring as melted ice cream slides down his hand. "Both of you. I . . . I think we should go."

"Why?" Mui asks as she licks her ice cream. "Oh. Look at all those birdies. There's so many."

"I think that's Dapo's point," I say.

There is a sudden screech—like microphone feedback, localized inside my head—and I prickle all over. I drop to my knees, forgetting all about my ice cream as I slam my palms over my ears.

Seconds later, the sound disappears, settling into the familiar hum of my tinnitus. "Did you lot hear—"

I freeze, open-mouthed, as the flock of birds float to the ground like large sheets of paper, as though any predatory urge they had has gone. Some birds land and stand still, stuck in a trance.

Ellen appears. Alberto is by her side. "Excuse me, excuse me. Can I have your attention, please?" Once everyone is focused on her, she smiles. "Transparency is key. Please tell them what you told me, Alberto."

Alberto nods. "Certainly, ma'am. I was telling Cuplow that we had a blown fuse in quadrant C132. You see, it's very peculiar what happened. It's as though there was a burst of electro—"

"And what does that mean for our esteemed guests?" Ellen asks.

"Yes, of course, ma'am. So what that meant is that the control system in this part of the resort was down and the animals— these gorgeous birds here—were . . . temporarily confused."

"Confused!" a woman with pale-pink skin, strawberry-blond hair, and prominent freckles exclaims. Her voice is shrill, and posh as British royalty. She's standing by the boy who was bitten. "My precious son could have lost his arm."

"Really?" The boy looks up at her in complete horror. He grabs at her hand, and she swats him away before folding her arms.

"Not now, darling, Mummy's telling off these incompetent fools."

Ellen goes red. "My humblest apologies, but I can assure you, Ms. Bedeau, this won't happen again. As the resort manager, I am one hundred percent committed to the comfort of our guests. Now then, to apologize for our little faux pas, we have given you access to Mr. Jenkins's personal restaurant for tonight so that you and your family might enjoy a complimentary dinner on us."

"Mr. Jenkins's personal restaurant?"

"Of course. In his private residence."

"Complimentary, you say?"

"In every way."

"Well then," Ms. Bedeau starts, unfolding her arms, "we'd be delighted to accept your olive branch." She turns and leaves, dragging her son along behind her. "Come along, Cyril."

My gaze homes in on Ellen, her face creased with worry, shoulders tight. She whips out her phone and types away. I'm reminded of Dapo. If he didn't freeze in front of her, they'd have gotten along well, I reckon. Both with rods up their—

There's a sharp pain in my toes, and I look down at a grinning Mui, who removes her foot from on top of mine. "Why?" I ask through tight teeth.

"'Cause," Mui answers with a shrug. She shows me both her hands. Empty. "Done! Thanks for the ice-cream treat." She steps toward me and hugs me tight, taking me by surprise. "I need to go, but let's hang out soon."

I hug her back and say, "See you soon."

She scurries off. I turn to Dapo, and he's also scurried off, trailing after Ellen leaving me gazing at the Ethereal Lake. There's a bit of time to kill before I need to plug in the device. I'll get to the place early and chill. Burn of all the nervous energy I have before I do the deed.

Do the deed. I chuckle. Wrong choice of words. I'm … 60 percent comfortable with what I'm about to do. The uncomfortable 40 percent is worry about getting caught. *But you're helping.* With a breath, I close my eyes. Flashes of Enelle coughing and Valoisa caring for her appear in my mind; I see Richard on the ferry again, this time he is less like the sun, and more like a black hole. The images unwind into sounds and riotous color. Pain builds behind my eyelids.

I open my eyes. I take in the resort around me as I walk. Everywhere I look, I see Richard's lies. New buildings constructed to mingle with the old. I suspect the statues of adults and children dotted around are not of founding staff members but original residents of the island. Details that seemed purposeful and atmospheric—faded doors to buildings, covered in vines; strange symbols etched onto brick—take on a new meaning.

After a short walk I'm standing in front of a box-like concrete structure with a white door. Like Valoisa described. The white door is unlocked, and I step into a space coated in a film of dust. I make my way to the back room like I was told to do, passing old desks and a chalkboard on the wall, and search for the socket that faces the window. It's in a room full of stacked chairs and books. Once I find it, I pull the device from my rucksack, insert the batteries, and plug it in. Then it's all about the wait.

T minus fifteen minutes until I turn the outlet and device on.

Thinking over the drama of the last few days, I half giggle from exhaustion.

When the time comes, I turn on the outlet and hold my finger over the device's power button. All I have to do is press, and then I can walk away. Except my stomach churns, and I have to take a couple of deep breaths, frozen by the fear that the moment I turn this on, security will come rushing in.

"You can do this," I mumble, remembering the way Valoisa looked at me. Enelle's blog post. Her coughs ringing in my ears. The images are swallowed whole by Richard's face, and I push the power button. Nothing happens for a few seconds, and then the device lights up, a beacon of pulsing. There's a whirring sound of the internal fans, but that's it. I stay in the room for a short while in case I need to undo what I've done. Nothing happens. There's no explosion. No alarm. Security doesn't come rushing through the door to apprehend me.

Satisfied I can breathe easy again, and glad it's all over, I drop a message to Deja.

> Want to do dinner?

> Sure x

CHAPTER 12

THUD

I STAND STILL ON THE REDBRICK ROAD, *DRAWN TO THE sudden appearance of a brilliant white light. The ground rumbles, and I am lifted from my feet and shoved backward. Slammed square in my chest by an invisible force.*

Hunched over, shards of light linger in my vision, and my skin tingles. I look up. There is a single plume of smoke. The air turns acrid and rotting. Every breath I take cuts my throat like I'm swallowing bobby pins. Every breath burns my lungs, and I taste blood.

I want to cough but can't. I have no mouth anymore, and no matter how much I will myself to, my vocal cords will not cooperate to give me relief. My eyes water, and my hands claw and scratch—tearing flesh to make a mouth for myself. I want to scream but don't. I feel no pain anymore. When my fingers pull away there is blood. Thick like syrup.

With a rumble from above, the sky cracks open with rain and hail and—

I sit up in bed, drenched in sweat and gasping for breath. A nightmare. They're as rare to me as the flowers on this island. I want to say the nightmare bloomed at random, but I know it's because of the device I planted. I can't shake this fear Richard and his people know what I did or will soon find out. That at any moment they'll burst into our villa. That it'll mean irreparable harm to Valoisa and Enelle.

My room is stuffy, so I open my window. The sky is full of fast-moving clouds against a night sky freckled with winking stars. The redbrick path is tinted in blue and shadows. The resort is still and everything is okay.

When I head to the kitchen to get a bottled water, light flickers around the edges of the living room door, which is ajar. I step inside, and Dapo is on the couch. He pauses what he's watching.

"Fems, you all right?"

I nod. "What you watching?"

"*The Usual Suspects*. The one with that disgraced actor?"

"Disgraced actors are such a wide pool, bro—you know that, right?" The name of the movie rings a bell. It was on the 100 Films to Watch Before You Die list, and before I pushed him into the road that summer afternoon, Dapo and I had made it over halfway through watching all of them. We said we'd finish the list together. "Any good?"

"I've only just started. Do you want watch? I . . . know it was on that list we were going through."

"Sure."

We sit side by side on the sofa. We banter. We laugh, like old times. We make fun of the parts that have aged like sour milk, and the invisible space between us shrinks. But as the darkness thins into morning light, I know it'll widen again once the movie ends.

One moment of bonding won't rub out what I did to him. Even though he's never said the words, I know he still blames me for what happened last year.

Much later that morning, Dad, Dapo, and I decide to eat breakfast in the outside seating area of the Bluebird Café—an impressive building made of pale-green glass, where the staff members greet us with big smiles. Well, Dad and Dapo decide that's what we're doing. I'm forced to tag along.

No one is sitting inside, and there aren't many people using the outside seating area either, maybe because of the heat. At the moment, it's just us, some families and couples, and a lone woman with bleached-blond eyebrows reading a book with headphones on a few tables over. Our table looks out onto a large field of low-cut grass that borders the edge of Valoisa and Enelle's forest. I wonder if this café marks the boundary of Richard's land on this side.

With my earplugs in, to keep my tinnitus manageable, I'm able to focus on the layers of green shrubs, dark-blue bark, and orange leaves. Knowing deep within the forest, Valoisa and Enelle go on with their lives as forgotten relics. Anger builds at their forced invisibility.

"What are you eating, Fems?" Dad asks.

I shrug. "Dunno yet."

The sun's glaring down at us, and I'm forced to squint while I read the menu. All of it is stuff I've never tried before. The question is less about what I want and more about guessing how risky things sound and how adventurous I want to be.

Braised Moulak worms over corn fritters is my decision. The menu has assured me the "worms" are a worm-like vegetable cultivated on the island. I sink back into my chair and twiddle my fingers.

"So, my sons, talk to me." Dad plants a hand on our shoulders and squeezes. "We're here to bond. And now that the conference has ended, we can focus on doing that."

"About what?" I shrug off his hand. "I've told you, you can't start a convo like that. It's inorganic."

"Inorganic? *Nooo*. I am making conversation." He speaks as if he's a robot and attempts to move like one, which makes me burst into laughter. How he convinced Mum—a cool, calm, collected woman—to marry him is beyond me.

"Well," Dapo says. He adjusts the collar of his oversize shirt. "I heard back from three of the internships I applied for."

Dad shifts his chair so he can give the Golden Son his undivided attention. "And? Go on?"

Silence bubbles at the tables. I kiss my teeth. "Just tell us and be done with it, man."

Dapo throws me a withering look before saying, "I got all of them."

"My boy!" Dad exclaims, bursting from his seat and patting Dapo on the back. "Praise God, praise God. So which one will you choose, or you haven't decided yet?"

"I've decided. I'm going to intern at the Ministry of Interdi—"

A sharp, silent pain spears through my eardrums, and I spasm in my chair. Several pairs of eyes snap to my direction. *What the hell was that?!* "Did you two hear that?"

"Hear what?"

"A…" I pause and pull out my earplugs. "Strange." There's no ringing. It's crystal clear. As if whatever just happened got rid of my tinnitus for good. "Sorry, I thought—" The ground rumbles beneath my feet. "Tell me you at least *felt* that?"

"Felt what?" Dad says. Dapo looks out at the forest, not bothering to answer.

THUD.

I glance over. Dad's coffee wobbles. As it starts to still, another *THUD* sends it sloshing.

"Kí ló n ṣẹlẹ?" Dad says.

THUD.

"Look," Dapo says, pointing up. I look, and there against the blue sky is a swarm of golden raptors clumped together, pulling at something. Squawking. Fighting. Ripping. Among the frenzy are screams. In an instant the flock disperses, and what they were clawing at descends into a free fall. Limbs flap in the gentle breeze. A scream carries through the air.

"Is that…" I can't quite believe it.

"Yeah," Dapo murmurs as a body falls into the field with a bone-splintering crunch.

II
GUILT

"My pride may course through,
but I still bleed red
In a deep shade it runs like syrup does
As the mortal wound forms a crown
of dread."

—Xavier, "The Beast in Us" *Deluxe* **album**

"Personally, innovation is a life and death
pursuit. I take him[1] as seriously
as I take my own life."

—Richard Jenkins, *Vanity Fair* **interview**

---

1. Richard Jenkins has been known to personify defined concepts. When prompted further on this, he claims it is a necessary act of respect for his craft of pure creation.

CHAPTER 13

JUMP SCARE

Dad slams his hands on his head. "Ye!"

My insides curdle. I turn to Dapo, who looks calm. No, he's in shock. The now-blaring alarms aren't enough for him to look away from the body that fell from the sky.

The ground continues to rumble.

"What the hell!" I don't know if I shouted that or not. I think I did. I can't hear anything over the sound of my heart beating in the back of my throat. Everyone jumps from their seats, exclaiming in different languages. Likely wondering if what they saw—are seeing—is real or part of some sort of twisted performance.

But there's no way! How can a body falling from the sky be a performance? How can a person's bones, poking through their ruptured flesh while blood pools, be entertainment?

There's no way.

Then I hear the scattering of chairs and toppling of tables. A few tables over, an animal appears. I remember Enelle called it a tasseled feline in her blog post; it's larger than I expected, far exceeding her description. And while it has what looks to be a permanent snarl and emits a deep, rumbling growl that threatens violence, it also moves with unnerving flexibility as if it's double-jointed. When it yawns, its jaws open far wider than they should.

Dad pushes past me and grabs a chair. Lifting it high above his head, he throws it at the rippling beast. When it hits, the beast lets out a low growl and stands still. A cluster of small flies shimmies across the beast's face. It's sizing us up. My feet are welded to the ground, and my heart swells. Throbs. It's ready to burst through my chest, my eardrums, and my feet.

Dapo's still staring at the person who fell from the sky. Dad's—

He's staring down the tasseled feline. "Femi," Dad says forcefully. "You and your brother go and get to safety."

"I'm not going to do that. You won't be able to—"

"Son, it's okay. Please. It's—"

None of us see the outstretched paw coming. It flashes like a whip and cracks against Dad's ribs. He staggers back a quarter of a step before dropping to the ground. A stream of strained Yorùbá fills the air as he rolls onto his side.

Two waiters and the cooking staff emerge, banging pots and pans and shouting nonsense at the animal. There's a moment of uncertain stillness before the massive cat's ears droop and it gallops away, heading toward the forest.

"Dad?" I glance at him on the floor. "You all right?"

"Of course, son." He forces a smile and wheezes. "Caught me by surprise, that's all."

Dapo's still staring into space, so I get up and stand in his face. "Bro. Hello. Hello!" I shake him as hard as I can, and that does the trick. He blinks and looks at me, as if seeing me for the first time since the person fell from the sky. "I don't know what that was, but maybe—"

There's a brief screech before a voice sounds out over the loudspeaker. It belongs to Ellen.

"Attention, esteemed guests! We regret to inform you that due to a system failure in our control room, an unfavorable situation is developing at the resort. Security measures are down. This makes the animals unsettled. Staff are taking the necessary steps to resolve this."

THUD.

"In order to ensure your total safety, it is paramount that you find shelter in an orderly fashion as soon as possible. Ensure wherever you find is secure, and keep windows and doors firmly locked until we . . ."

A chill of fear crawls under my skin and wrinkles my insides. It's hard to breathe.

"It is recommended you do not attempt to retrieve anything you may deem of value. We will keep you updated as to what your next steps should be. In the meantime, we ask you to keep calm and orderly, and find suitable shelter during this ongoing situation . . ."

"Please make your way inside," beckons a voice from behind us. It belongs to one of the waiters. His skin is dark. Could he be one of the Darlenians who chose to work at the resort? If he is, I wonder if he regrets his decision now. His locs sway gently as he peers out from behind the front door of the Bluebird Café, trembling.

I step to Dapo and nudge him with my elbow. He glares at me. "Come on," I say.

We head inside with Dad, and the waiter locks the door behind us. Not everyone's come inside. Some have decided to flee along the redbrick path in the direction of the guest villas. The closest villas are only about five minutes away. The furthest are a fifteen-minute walk.

The café is stuffy with the constant flow of air-conditioning snuffed out. My body is warming up and up. Other than the staff, there are a few couples, individuals, and a mother and son who I recognize as Ms. Bedeau and Cyril, who stay.

Dad pulls out his phone and presses it to his ear, holding it there for several seconds before pulling it away and kissing his teeth. "Ah, why isn't your mum picking up?"

"Here," I say, taking his phone. "Maybe—"

"It won't work," Ms. Bedeau says. "There's no signal, goodness knows I've tried. Watches are useless, too. We're royally screwed."

Cyril cocks his head. "Mummy, why are we screwed?"

She bursts into uneven laughter before wrinkling her nose and warping her freckles. "We should have gone to the south of France instead."

"Why didn't we?"

"Cyril. I can't, not right now. I can't. Let Mummy have a moment." She turns toward our waiter. "So?"

"So?" the waiter with locs replies with a blank stare. There's no brilliant smile. Customer service is not at the top of his list.

Ms. Bedeau huffs in a way I imagine she's huffed at Cyril thousands of times. "What happens now? Isn't there a procedure? I presume you have a panic room you ought to take my son and me to?" Again, a blank stare.

"Uh," I say, inserting myself into the conversation. "If I heard the announcement correctly, we're supposed to wait here."

Ms. Bedeau smiles, shallow and brief. Then she glares at the assembled staff—three cooks somehow standing in height order, and, other than the waiter with locs, another waiter, who is sweating profusely.

"I *heard* what the announcement said," she says. "I don't think you understand. My son and I are regulars here and pay for the exorbitant resort care." She flashes her watch in their faces. It's not like the ones we're wearing—it's a plush green to our navy. "I demand you take us to the panic room for guests like us."

"But...there is no panic room," the shortest cook says. "It is as this boy says—we must wait until we are given instructions."

"You're lying." Ms. Bedeau's gaze roves around the room. Then her shoulders sag. "Oh, you have got to—"

Cyril shrieks, before bursting into big sobs. "H-h-h-he's *GOT NO BODY*."

I turn and see him looking and pointing at—

A head.

It's all that's left of the body. On the other side of the windows, the hair on the head is matted with blood and tangled in a glass dragon's teeth. The head dangles, and a dead face stares out at us, one eye missing, the other bulging. Its mouth gapes in frozen horror. Its skull caved in like it's been kicked. Hard.

My stomach clenches as I keep thinking of the way the body fell, and it sends a shudder through me. There's a blur of movement in my periphery. Ms. Bedeau. She rushes to her son and wraps him in a big hug.

"It's okay, darling. It's okay."

"I"—sob—"want"—sob—"some"—sob—"chewing gum," Cyril manages.

Ms. Bedeau sighs, tucking stray strands of her strawberry-blond hair behind her ear. She turns to the staff, who all shake their heads. After going around the room asking the other guests, finally she looks at my family. "Got any?"

Dapo's still out of it, and he shakes his head like he's not sure if he's doing it correctly.

"Nah, sorry," I say.

Dad offers her two Werther's Originals. She rolls her eyes before muttering to herself.

"Let's go to our room," Ms. Bedeau says. "We'll get you some gum and find the panic room."

She takes Cyril's hand, and they amble toward the door. They're halfway there before our waiter clears his throat and says, "Excuse me."

"Yes?" Ms. Bedeau doesn't bother turning around.

"I would strongly urge you not to leave. It is not safe, plus there is no—"

"Thank you for your concern. But we will be fine. I'm sure someone will know where the panic room is."

When the door closes behind them, the sweaty waiter turns to us. "Would you like something to drink while you wait?"

"Wait for what?" I ask, confused. The waiter's smile is hollow, apologetic even.

"Your food. We were mostly done before the . . . interruption. Not to mention who knows how long we'll be here for. It'll be ready in a moment. Please, take a seat while you wait."

CHAPTER 14

STAFF QUARTERS

Dad, Dapo, and I sit around a circular table and share glances with one another. We're all still processing that a man fell from the sky and exploded in a fleshy mess. The animals aren't docile anymore. I chew off the end of the nail of my index finger, yanking it off so close to my skin that it stings, and a small bit of blood beads.

And we're sitting here waiting for food. Terror stabs at my insides while everything unravels.

Dad takes a deep breath and breaks the silence. "My sons, you good?"

I ignore Dad, sucking on my finger, tasting the metal tang of my blood. My gaze blurs, and I blink it back into focus, drawing in a deep breath. Turning around in my chair, I catch the attention of the waiter with locs. "Have they told you what's up with the system?"

"Not officially, but we're getting word it's because of an animal getting somewhere it shouldn't have, and it short-circuited everything." The waiter with locs takes a deep breath. "When we know more, we'll let you know. Would you like some more water?"

I frown. "How does that explain the attack?"

"I don't know. That's all I was told, okay. Maybe something triggered the animals. Water?"

"No thanks." I whip back around, smothering my trembling hands and exhaling. Did Richard and his team see the animals starting to act feral and have they been trying to rectify that? I think back to the fragments of conversations I overheard, the incident with Cyril, and the security breach that happened the day I met Valoisa.

Then I'm thinking about Valoisa and Enelle, and I'm hoping they're okay. They know the island and the animals well, but even they were wary. And what about Deja and her dad? I wish I knew they were okay, too.

"Sons? Talk to me," Dad says. Sweat beads on his forehead and he wipes it away as he turns to Dapo, who grips his cup with both hands and won't stop staring at it. Even though it's empty, he still mimics drinking something. He waits for the smallest drop to fall into his mouth.

"Dad," I say, "read the room. We don't want to talk."

"We should talk."

I tilt my head and narrow my eyes. "Are you serious?"

Dad winces before schooling his face into a hard frown. "Watch your tone."

At that moment the waiters arrive, laying plates of food in front of us. Dad and I break uneasy eye contact.

"Dapo, say grace," Dad orders.

He does, and a part of me finds comfort in being able to do normal stuff like this. But when Dapo is done and I stare down at my dish—Moulak worms—I lose all desire to eat. The glistening oil reminds me of dead, wet eyes. The shades of red of the tomato are a reminder of the man who fell from the sky.

I put down my cutlery and push the plate away from me. I focus on my breathing to combat my churning stomach.

"Is there something wrong with the meal, sir?" the sweaty waiter asks me.

I shake my head. "No, no it's me. I'm not feeling too well."

Meanwhile, Dad's slurping up everything on his plate. Oil splatters and sprays.

I turn away from the table and retch, emptying my stomach onto the wooden floor. "Oh, man."

"Sir!"

I wipe away loose chunks of food from my clothes and shoes with a napkin before getting up and staggering toward the bathroom. Barreling through the door, I lock it behind me, brace myself on the sink, and hurl again.

There's nothing left in my stomach but bile.

Get it together. I splash water on my face, but every time I blink, that dangling head is staring at me. Eye still, skull caved in. I rub my eyes, trying to scrub away the image, but it clings. I see the man falling, falling, falling.

Suddenly it's hard to breathe and my clothes are too tight. I pace around the bathroom.

THUMP THUMP THUMP.

A fist bangs against the door. "Femi, are you all right?" Dad calls. "You vomited and just ran off."

"I—I'm fine," I reply, composing myself. "I'll be out in a moment. I'm fine."

A few more splashes of water help cool me down.

"Femi!"

"Dad, I said I'd be out—"

On the other side of the door, Dad erupts into a coughing fit, and there's a thud. I unlock the door in a hurry. Dad's collapsed into a crumpled heap, his face scrunched in pain.

"D-Dad!" I say, rushing to his side. I'm met with a lopsided smile on his face that flickers into a wince every other second.

"I shouldn't have banged so hard, eh?" Dad squeezes out. His breaths are heavy and labored.

"Stay right here, I'm going to get help." I rush back into the main area of the café. "Do you have any medical supplies?" My question is aimed in the general direction of the staff. "My dad's hurt." When I look at Dapo, his stare looks a bit more focused now. "Dad's hurt."

We head back to Dad, where the waiter with locs steps forward to examine him. He applies some pain relief gel. When he rises up, he tuts. "The bruising is bad. And it's swelling fast. Someone needs to look at him."

"Who?" Dapo demands, kicking into gear. "I need you to tell me who."

The sweaty waiter answers, "Whitley. But if he's anywhere, he'll be in the staff quarters."

I nod. "I know where that is."

"You can't leave, it's dangerous," the sweaty waiter says. "I was informed there were several major system breaches. What what we saw wasn't the only attack."

"Our dad needs help," Dapo states. "Someone needs to look at him. You said it yourself."

"I did, but—"

"So, what's the problem?" Dapo questions.

As Dad, Dapo, and I make our way to the staff quarters we keep a sharp eye out for any more dangerous animals. The silence is thick and heavy and leaves me room to stew in my thoughts—to allow worry to scratch at my chest as I ponder Ellen's words.

System failure.

The favor I did for Enelle and Valoisa clouds my mind. Was this somehow my fault? But when I turned the device on, nothing happened. Valoisa and Enelle wouldn't do *this*.

Would they?

No, of course not. They just wanted to ease Enelle's pain.

Dad's ragged wheezing punctures the thought, reminding me there are more important things to focus on. When we get to the door to the staff quarters, I push the metal bar down. It budges only a fraction.

In the window to the right of the door, there's a flash of movement. There must be people inside, and they've barricaded themselves in. "Hey!" I yell while knocking. "It's just us. My dad's hurt!"

"I'm fine," Dad wheezes. "Really."

"You're not fine." Rolling my eyes, I continue. "He needs help. Please!"

After an uncomfortable silence, there's scraping and shuffling, and the door eases open. Alberto appears, signature sunglasses hanging on the collar of his T-shirt. Lips in grimace. "My boy." A heavy hand comes down on my shoulder and sends me wobbling like a tree in a strong wind. "Come in and let's get your dad checked out. He's not the only one."

Dapo, Dad, and I are led by the doctor, Whitley, to the small room where they keep the medical supplies. On the way he fills us in on what's what: There have been a handful of incidents of the island's animals turning feral, and now some staff members and guests are in the large living room hiding. Others keep watch on the entry and exit points of the building. There are hurt people tucked away in other rooms, too.

I lean against the counter, nibbling at the dry skin on my bottom lip while the doctor prods and pokes and examines my dad.

"Get me some ibuprofen, I'm fine," Dad says, slumped on one of the chairs. "Don't worry about me." His voice is strained.

My head shakes. "You're not—"

"Don't. You. Worry. About. Me," Dad sings, before bursting into a shallow cough. "See?" The chair scrapes against the floor as he gets to his feet and attempts the latest dance trend, pushing the doctor away.

He has all the grace and rhythm of a hippo on ice. I burst out laughing while the doctor sighs and fishes out ibuprofen.

"Okay, you win. But take it easy. You've got some deep bruising, and I can't be sure your ribs aren't broken."

"Dad, come on," I say. "Listen to what he's saying. Don't overdo it. You're old."

Dad scoffs. "Cheeky. Now the ibuprofen, please." He holds his hand out.

Before the packet of pills lands on his palm, I snatch it away. "No more dancing, okay?"

"Fine. You're just jealous." I hand the pills over, and Dad swallows them down without water. "Maybe one day you will—"

"Let me go, that's my *child*," roars a voice in the other room.

I stand at attention. Dad's already halfway out the door, wanting to see what all the commotion is about. Drama is nature's painkiller. Dapo's right behind him, along with the doctor. *What's going on?* Curiosity gets the better of me, and I follow. Conversation wobbles from the living room in bite-size pieces.

"If it were your..."

"...but it's not..."

Two people are facing off. Ellen and an Asian man who's not much shorter than her, wearing glasses and the standard, military-style staff uniform, winking gold buttons and all. Two men stand guard on either side of him, one tall with scraggly orange hair, the other short with bushy eyebrows. Both are built like rugby players.

Across the room I spy Deja and her dad. They look shook, but I'm filled with relief. Though when I catch Deja's eyes, I know she's seen some wild stuff, too. My attention returns to the confrontation between Ellen and the man.

He rubs the back of his neck and puts his hands up in surrender, saying, "Ellen, please, she's my *daughter*. You don't understand."

Ellen's foot taps against the carpeted floor, her eyes fixed on her tablet, before turning her gaze toward us. Past us. "If we open the doors, who knows what'll happen. I'm sure she'll—"

There's a scream. It sucks the air out the room all at once. Curiosity and fear mingle, sloshing through my limbs. Rushing to the nearest window, I peer through the curtains, and in that moment, my heart lurches up my throat and stalls.

Mui.

And she's running from a glass dragon.

INTERLUDE

MUI

MUI LAU SAT ON HER BED, PEERING OUT THE WINDOW. She had begun to notice summer was slipping away: The leaves were turning brown, making them perfect for stomping on, and the blackberries were swelling, making them perfect for picking.

These were two things she relished, two things that would bring a smile to her face.

Except Ken wasn't here, and that sucked all the fun out of the changing seasons. He'd been gone for about a month. And while he was out of sight, and thus out of mind for many, this wasn't true for Mui. She was sure—in her bones—he would return. He'd made a promise to her before he'd gone back into the lake near their house.

If Mui were honest with herself, she would have admitted her twelve-year-old brother, Ken, was never coming back. But that was a big thing to ask a seven-year-old. Instead, she left the truth alone in the hope she would never have to confront it.

It was easier for her this way. Anything to not grapple with the guilt she knew was there but didn't quite understand.

Everything in her mind boiled down to three *ifs*: If only she hadn't been so easily bribed to sneak out while their dad napped. If only she hadn't tried to swim farther than she was capable. If only she hadn't begged and begged and begged Ken to go back after her bracelet.

If only, if only, if only.

But this was all new to her, and she didn't know what to do. She fell back onto her bed and curled up into a ball, taking deep breaths while trying to steep in the quiet around her. She delved deep into her imagination, trying to be somewhere else: on top of the nearby hill, where the sky was within touching distance and their house was a small box a couple of ants could live in.

"Mui, aren't you packed yet?" asked her mother's voice, slicing through Mui's imagination. "Your dad's going to be here in no time." There was silence. In an act of spontaneous and random rebellion, Mui ignored her mother. "Mui," her mother said. Not unkindly, but there was a tone of warning.

"Almost," Mui offered. "I just need to . . . need to . . ."

Mui's bed groaned as her mother sat and stroked her back. "It's okay. Look, you don't have to go if you don't want to. But *we* think it would be good for you. To see some adventure. Dad's new job at the resort has some amazingly weird wildlife like the animals Ken used to make up and draw. Do you want to see?"

Mui sat up and eyed her mother, who couldn't help but laugh at her daughter's curiosity. "Where?"

"Here. Dad sent a couple of pictures."

Mui's mother proceeded to show her dad posing with the

most beautiful-looking birds, glass dragons[2]—according to her dad—and plants that glowed in the dark. For Mui, the pictures seemed impossible. Unreal. Magical. In some ways, they were. The pictures should not have existed because of the island's strict policy. Her father had bent and broken rules all so he could spark joy in his daughter again.

Instead, it sparked an idea.

"Okay, okay," Mui said, full of determination. "We will finish packing."

"We?" Mui's mother smiled. "I won't be going. Your father and I are … well, we don't do everything together anymore. Remember?"

"I knoooow. I was actually talking to Ken."

Mui's mother immediately looked shocked. "Ken?"

"Yeah. He's over there." Mui pointed toward the chair in the corner of her room where Ken sat, dripping wet. He waved at her and smiled with that impish grin of his. Far too wide with as many teeth as possible showing.

Mui's mother blinked at her. She recalled a conversation she and her ex-husband had had with a former friend. "Don't be surprised, children cope in a multitude of ways …"

Unsure what to do, Mui's mother did what she thought was best—she indulged her. Plastering on a smile, she said, "Of course. Well, I'll see you both downstairs."

"Okay, Mummy."

And like that, Mui had magicked her brother back.

---

2. Mui was astounded to find out that, despite their name, glass dragons weren't actually as fragile as glass. Their name derives from their skin, which is translucent enough to see inside. Glass dragons are anything but fragile.

CHAPTER 15

BRAZEN

No, no, no.

Every stride Mui takes, I take with her in my mind. Nervousness swarms my insides. She finds shelter underneath one of the resort vehicles and kicks away the small glass dragon.

"We have to help her," I blurt.

Ellen's thin lips part. "No can do, sorry. She's being pursued and we can't risk threatening our safety."

My fists clench. "The glass dragon won't give up. But she'll get tired. You can see where I'm going with this, right?"

"Have you seen what glass dragons can do?" Ellen counters, her words stern. "We cannot risk the—"

"Are you serious? You're basically—"

A hand comes down on my shoulder. I crane my neck. *Dapo.* "Fems," he says. Even though most of his shookness has thawed, I can still see the traces of fear. "Hate to be crude, but logically, we can't do anything without compromising the safety of others."

Anger jolts through me, a static shock. "She's a kid. And helping someone in need is logical. Not leaving them to die."

"I— Yeah, okay, you're right. But it's not safe." Dapo pleads with his eyes. "If you go out there, you'll die."

Deja comes up alongside me, too. "Fems, I know you care about her, but what Dapo probably means is before rushing in, let's take a moment to think up a sensible plan."

"We don't *have* the luxury of a moment. We need to just…" My words trail off. I could go on and on and on, but I know, looking at Deja and Dapo, that it would be like speaking to a brick wall.

I roll my eyes and put my hands up in defeat because that's what they want. To be right. So I let them. Besides, I have an idea. "Fine. I get it." Eyeing the men at the entrance, I walk over to Mui's dad, who sits off on his own. Deflated. "Sorry, do you know where the toilet is?"

"Toilet?" He looks at me like I've shoved soap down his throat.

"Yes. The toilet." I bring the volume of my voice lower. "I need to take *care* of something." *I hope he gets what I'm not saying.* "Preferably a toilet that isn't likely to be occupied."

Mui's dad frowns. *Come on.* I push my eyebrows up a smidge. Glance at the window. Realization.

"Ah, the toilet," he states, doing his best to keep the hope out of his voice. "That isn't occupied."

"Exactly. Where do I go?"

"You don't want to go to the main ones. They're bound to be…occupied. But if you head out of here and turn left, on the right there is a corridor that leads to a set of shallow stairs.

That's the door you need to...do what you need to do. I'd lead you there myself, but..." His eyes land on the men who watch him closely. I nod. *Thanks*, he mouths.

Five steps are all it takes for Dapo to call out to me, "Where are you going?"

"Toilet." He says something else, but I'm already out the door and on course. I can't stand here and do nothing. Right now, all that matters is helping Mui even if it means I have no plan. Sometimes you have to go for it and ask for forgiveness afterward.

Doesn't take long until I'm in front of the door Mui's dad mentioned. I open it and step inside. It's a small, musty space with cleaning equipment; my eyes are drawn to the sunlight that spears in through a dusty grate. *A way out.*

Moving the cleaning equipment aside, I carve a path to the grate. After a few tugs the grate comes loose, more sunlight rushes in. I crawl out, take several deep, quick breaths, and make my way around the building. A sudden surge of pain sears my temples. My legs wobble.

Even my body knows I'm doing something dangerous.

"It's okay, it's okay, it's okay," I whisper.

Mui is still camped under the car. Her leg's all scratched up, but she's keeping the glass dragon at bay. It hisses.

I look around, thinking.

In my periphery, several pieces of fruit from the tree by the side entrance lie on the ground. Edging over, I pick up a bruised fruit and hold my breath, preparing for the smell. When I squeeze hard, the fruit bursts. Oozes.

As I move toward the glass dragon, it clocks the smell of the fruit. *Good.*

"Don't worry, Mui. It's going to be okay!"

"Femi!" Mui blubbers.

I hurl the fruit as far into a cluster of greenery as possible. Just like in the forest, the glass dragon is drawn to the fruit, charging awkwardly after the smell.

I rush over to Mui, getting on my hands and knees, and peer under the car. "Hey."

Mui stares back at me wide-eyed and open-mouthed. "You saved us," she gasps. "Thank you."

Us? It takes me a moment to realize she means her and her brother, Ken. "No worries." I reach for her and ease her out when she grabs my hand. She dusts herself off, wincing as she takes a step. Threads of blood trickle down her shins. "Piggyback?"

She nods and I crouch down. Warmth flutters through my chest. So do vindication, relief, and pride all at once. Is this what it's like to be a big brother? Does Dapo have the same sense of . . . duty?

I'm lost in my thoughts until I step on an overripe fruit and pulp splatters all over my Flu Game Jordans. I kiss my teeth, while Mui flinches and gags at the smell now polluting the air.

Hisses seep into the air, and unease splinters through every fiber of my being. There are several scattered screams. Not close enough to send me into panic, but not far enough away either.

Mui tenses, and her grip around my neck tightens. "I'm scared."

"Me too, Mui. Me too."

When we emerge in the living room back in the staff quarters, Mui's dad rushes toward us and sweeps her into a hug. He's blubbering, tears of joy dripping all over his face. Mui laughs and squirms in his embrace.

"You're getting us all wet."

"Sorry, sorry, but I'm just so happy." Mui's dad turns to me and bear-hugs me. "Thank you so much. Truly."

"Happy to help," I say. All that matters is that Mui is safe.

The moment I turn away, my gladness evaporates. Dapo and Dad are both glaring at me. "Why the long face?" My attempt at humor falls short as he stares.

"I'm glad you're both okay. But what if that stunt of yours hadn't worked?"

"But it did. We made it back."

Each second of silence thickens the tension. Dapo opens his mouth but relents, instead shaking his head and walking off.

"Whatever," I mumble. *Of course, he thinks I did the wrong thing.* There's a tap on my shoulder and the familiar smell of vanilla. "Deja, look, I know—"

"Idiot," she breathes, turning me and pulling me into a hug. "Sometimes I wonder if your stubbornness is a blessing or a curse."

"A curse, if you're not careful," answers a voice. It's Ellen. And she's wearing a subtle scowl. "A word, please." She doesn't wait for me as I follow her out into the hallway. Satisfied we're alone, she says, "Thank you" so quietly I nearly miss it. She presses on. "I didn't want to consign a young girl to death, but they look to me for leadership, yes?"

Excuses, excuses. "Yeah, cool, I get it."

"Look, I get why you did what you did. But it can't happen again. There's protocol for things like this. Understood?" *Ah, so she's telling me off.* Fingers snap in my face and I frown. "Focus. Now then, are we on the same page?"

"Yeah, we're on the—"

Both of us turn toward the sound. It comes from the door that sits at the bottom of the shallow stairs. The room I escaped from. It's also the way I came back in.

Did I put the grate back on?

THUMP.

A sick feeling tangles my insides. My first instinct is to cobble together a few words that I'm unsure count as a prayer. Then Ellen starts sniffing. I do, too, because there's this smell . . .

"Hang on, can you smell that?" Ellen asks. "*What* is that smell? It smells like . . ."

"Sweaty feet," I finish. Looking down, I spy a piece of fruit stuck to the sole of my shoe, and sigh. There's another thud. Distant, echoing screams. *No, no, no.* The hissing of glass dragons booms in my eardrums. It's hard to breathe. To move. To do anything.

Then there's silence.

But that doesn't mean they've given up.

"Leave," I breathe.

"Huh?" Ellen asks.

"We"—I swallow—"need to leave. Is there another way out?"

Ellen cracks her knuckles. "We need to hold tight and wait per resort protocol. There are plans for circumstances even as confounding as this. A team will be working to get our control systems back online so we can resolve this issue with the animals." She turns and heads back into the living room. "Rest assured, everyone. It's all under control."

I follow, body trembling and fists clenching and unclenching. "You don't understand. We're not safe here. Those hisses. This is an ambush."

"I don't hear any hisses." She turns away from me, but before I can step alongside her, two men block my path. They speak no words, but their firm stares tell me I'll have to get through them if I want to get to her.

Drastic times call for drastic measures. "We need to leave *right now*!" I shout. People murmur and look around, like they're unsure if they should listen to me. *Unbelievable.* A man grabs my arm to drag me away, but I don't care. "We aren't safe! We aren't—"

THUMP.

"Don't listen to him," Ellen counters. "He's scared and hysterical. Rest assured, we are in control. This building is robust and reinforced. Gerald, can we get this young man some water, please?"

HISSSS.

"I don't need water." I glance over at Dad, Dapo, Deja, and Mr. Merrick, who stand in a cluster. None of them speak. I need them to get it. That we aren't safe, no matter what Ellen's saying. She strides to the front of the room, backed by the drawn curtains and flanked by the two men. "Look, I hate that we are in this situation right now. More than anyone else, I wish for a quick resolution, but it is not looking likely. So, we have to stick together—do things correctly, calmly. That's the only way we're getting out of here. So please do remain—"

Loud static from Ellen's tablet device cuts her off.

"Hello?" she says. "Hello, who is this?"

"*Nowhere . . . safe . . . get . . . out . . . get . . .*" There's lots of rustling from the device. And then a chorus of screams.

CHAPTER 16

PANIC

ALL THE AIR IS SUCKED OUT OF THE ROOM, AND THEN everything happens in an instant.

Glass shatters from all sides, and the dragons rush in through the windows. The unlucky few who were near are sliced down and release gurgled shrieks that cut out abruptly as if they're—

Don'tlookdon'tlookdon'tlook.

The hissing and screaming are deafening. Staff and guests alike have no regard for one another: it's every person for themselves. A man is trampled by the hysteria as he cries out. I focus on finding the familiar—Dapo and Dad, Deja and Mr. Merrick. They're headed for the door. I take a step after them but stop when I hear Mui.

"Dad, wake up. *Please.* Dad." She shakes him, but he's limp. His chest is still.

I chew on the inside of my cheek. *He's gone.* Without thinking, I rush over and sweep her into my arms, then bolt for the door.

She struggles and kicks out. "Let me go. Get off me. Dad! *DAD!* HE'S SLEEPING!"

Sympathy, sturdy as a trowel, digs deep into my chest. Reaching for roots. Mui doesn't deserve this. I don't let her go, even when a stray foot clocks me on the chin. This is the least I can do for her dad. For her.

The path to safety means dodging a lunging glass dragon. My feet land on something firm and uneven. There's a terrifying yelp from below, and I snatch my foot away in an instant. Looking down, I realize the leg of an employee is bent in two places: at the knee and halfway down the shin.

I'm sorry, I mouth, moving on but feeling sick to my stomach. My shoes squelch on the carpet soaked in crimson. A wave of people rushes out the once-barricaded fire exit. A glimpse of Dapo and Dad is enough for me to follow suit down the hallway.

But soon I'm backpedaling as everyone reverses course all of a sudden. Their faces are colored with fear; their screams are forks against plates. Whatever the reason, we need another way out. I spin around and make it one step before we're pushed aside and swallowed by the crowd.

A stray elbow in my back sends me tumbling. I land on my shoulder and sharp pain spears through me. Mui spills out of my arms. On autopilot, I scramble after her. She's curled up with her hands over her ears and her eyes squeezed shut. My stomach knots. This is my fault. But if I hadn't gone after Mui, then...

Sounds muffle, giving way to the booming chorus flowing through my head. *I led the dragons in through the grate. Damn it. Damn it. Damn—*

A hand shakes my shoulder. All at once, sound snaps back into place. I glance behind me to see Mr. Merrick. "Pick up the girl and let's go," he urges. "This way, while they're still distracted."

"Everyone else?" I whisper, before scooping Mui into my arms again and following him.

"They're fine." He stops as a pair of glass dragons scurry across and pounce on the doctor—Whitley—trying to limp away. When Whitley drops to the floor with a whimper, I turn away in horror.

Once Mr. Merrick's content the dragons are too preoccupied pecking and munching to notice us, we creep past them and slip into a room on the left. Ellen paces around, muttering under her breath. Alberto sits with Dad, checking to see if he's all right, while Dapo and Deja are in conversation. In the middle of the room, a hatch in the floor is propped open.

All eyes turn toward us.

"Lock the door," Ellen orders. Mr. Merrick obliges.

I frown. "We can't do that. There are still people alive out there. If we can tell them where to go or help get them . . ." I look around at the blank faces. "We can't just . . ."

"I think we can," Ellen says flatly. "If you know what's good, you'll *listen*. Let me see if I can get ahold of someone."

She speaks into her tablet. "Hello? This is Ellen Trossard. Anyone there?" There's a long silence. "Hello? Hello?"

Further silence, and then a welcome burst of static. "Yes, go ahead." The voice belongs to Cuplow.

"This is Ellen. What are our next steps?"

"You need to make your way to the harbor."

Ellen scoffs. "Of course, we'll just make our way down there. Easy peasy. Do you understand that everything is going to shit?"

"I am well aware of the situation, Ellen. But I've been told to direct everyone to the harbor per our protocol. Please do that as a matter of urgency."

Thuds and screams seep in through the gaps around the doorframe. As much as I want to help everyone on the other side, opening the door is a death sentence. The smell of blood is so thick I can taste iron in the air. The room spins, and my clothes are suffocating. Sweat wicks along my back. I don't notice Mui until she grabs my hand. It's soothing and cool. And when I look down at Mui, wide-eyed concern on her face, I take a deep breath, feeling myself even out.

We are in a locked room, small and bare, and we are safe. *For now.*

"Don't be absurd," Ellen says. "The animals are rabid. We'll die before we make it. What about Richard's guard? Isn't anyone coming to get us? We must have some way to communicate with the outside world. Contingencies. *Something!*"

"Afraid not," comes the curt reply from Cuplow. "Connection with the outside world has been severed. Make your way to the harbor. I would suggest you stay belowground. Several others did and made it to the ferry safely. Once there—" The connection goes dead, and Ellen swears.

Alberto's already stepping down into the hatch, a small toolbox in hand, his mind made up.

One by one we follow without another word, descending into Backstage.

CHAPTER 17

DESOLATION

THE LIGHT IN THE TUNNELS IS REFUSING TO COME alive as we walk through. We have to rely on our phone flashlights, taking turns to preserve our batteries. Alberto leads the way in the echoing quiet. Mr. Merrick, who always lightens the mood, is silent.

The only noise is the soft pitter-patter of footsteps and the occasional slow drip of a leak. Tension fills the space like a blocked nose in the middle of summer. The walls, mottled with dark lichen, feel closer than they did before, as if they're closing in on us. It's impossible to avoid the smell that hangs in the air: iron.

Blood.

Last time I was down here I was struck by how muted the space was. Now I'm struck by how unnerving and haunting everything feels.

"Do you think we'll find Daddy awake again? And others?" Mui asks, her hands in mine and Deja's. "Are we okay?"

The screaming has stopped ringing in my ears, but my heart

breaks at Mui's questions. I choose the slightly easier one to address. "I think we're safe." *For now.*

Before she can respond, we come to a stop. Alberto pulls out some tools. Getting onto his knees, he plays with the padlock on the large metal door in front of us.

"Bingo," Alberto says as the padlock pops open. When he pulls open the door, the padlock drops from his hand, clattering against the stone floor.

"What the hell...is...is this?" Ellen's words stumble and trip over themselves.

The space beyond the door is littered with phones that are face down, flashlights beaming up; dead bodies are peppered with wet, gaping holes.

A huge moth is splayed out on the floor. Unmoving. Ant-like bugs are prowling around and crawling all over it. My skin breaks out into goose bumps.

"They're not moving," Mui mumbles, her grip tightening.

"Which way?" Dapo asks, knowing better than to keep looking. His gaze is fixed straight ahead.

Alberto kneels by a woman, caressing her hair. It's too dark to tell, but I think he's crying. *Friend? Girlfriend? Relative?* His grief is interrupted by Ellen saying his name several times. Shaking his head, he says, "Huh?"

"Which way? To the harbor?" she asks, her tone impatient.

Anger flares my nostrils.

"Oh, uh"—Alberto wipes his hands across his eyes and nose— "yes, we need to—"

"Ye!" Dad cries, and all eyes turn to him. His face is contorted in pain, and he drops to one knee. Dapo rushes to his side, and I do the same, letting go of Mui's hand. We ease Dad down against the nearest wall.

"Easy, Dad, easy," I say.

"Where does it hurt?" Dapo says at the same time, and we share a look. The fear is palpable on his face, and I wonder if I'm mirroring him.

Before I know it, Mui, Deja, and Alberto are here, too. Ellen's engaged in a debate with Mr. Merrick. The only thing that matters is relieving Dad's pain.

Gently, gently, we roll up his shirt. The bruising, like the doctor said, is serious. It's a deep, bluish purple, like there's a huge clump of blueberries hiding just beneath the surface of his skin.

Ellen huffs. Clears her throat. "We need to get going."

"Not now," I snap. "My dad needs help. Is there anywhere close we can—"

"Stay here if you want." She snaps her fingers. "Alberto. We need to get going. The ferry cannot leave without us. It can't."

A grimace twists Alberto's face, and I know his mind is made up. He wants out of this nightmare. He wants to live.

I get it, I do, but that doesn't stop anger—bitter as black coffee—staining my tongue. "Go, then. Don't worry about leaving us for dead."

Sorry, he mouths, getting to his feet. He's halfway to Ellen before he stops and turns. Stares.

"What?" I demand.

"There's an infirmary close by. Go right and follow the

medical symbol signs on the wall. Maybe there's someone still there to help you." He then tells us how to get to the ferry once we're sure Dad's okay. "Good luck."

I'm about to cuss Alberto out, but Dapo puts a hand on my shoulder, warm and understanding. He's angry, too, but he wears a patient smile.

"Thank you, Alberto," he says. "Good luck to you, too."

Moments later, it's the Fatonas and the Merricks and Mui.

"So, what now?" I glance down at Dad. His face is scrambled in pain that, in turn, scrambles my thoughts. *There's no way he's making it to the infirmary.* "We need to bring the infirmary to him."

"I'll go," Dapo states. "You just ... stay here and make sure he doesn't get any worse."

My eyes roll. "Yes, boss. Of course. With my many years of medical experience, I can do that."

Dapo sighs and leaves. Mui stands up then gives me a glare worth a thousand pinpricks. I bunch my eyebrows together. "What is it?"

"You're always rude to your brother," she says. "That's why you're always in super big trouble with him. *You* make him sad."

"As if—"

"La-la-la, I'm not listening." Mui heads after Dapo. "We're leaving so you ... you can elect on your actions. Bye, bye, bye."

"Us, too," Deja says, dragging her dad with her. She gives me a look that says *fix up.*

It's Dad. And me. And silence.

Until Dad's hand finds its way onto mine after several minutes. He squeezes. "S-son," he wheezes. "Son."

"Yeah?"

"Look at me, please." I do. His eyes are wet and weary. "My son," he says, mustering as much of a smile as possible. "It's going to be okay."

If only I believed you. "Yeah," I say instead.

"You don't sound convinced. I know my son." Dad attempts to chuckle, but it gets tangled in pained coughing.

"Because I know the situation is messed up right now. You don't need to keep treating me like a little kid."

After a few heavy breaths, he says, "I know. But no matter how big or old you get, you'll always be my *child*."

Dad says the word *child* with piercing emphasis. It's a kick drum at the end of his sentence. He wants me to feel the full weight of what he means.

"I have *only* ever wanted the best for you. I know you haven't always agreed with my … convictions. But the only reason I won't let go is because I don't want you to make the mistakes I made."

I won't. How, when my life is vastly different from yours?

"How are you so sure if you won't ever listen to what I'm *trying* to teach you?" Dad questions, somehow reading my mind. I catch his gaze, and he smiles. "Wow. It's like looking in a mirror. Son, life's too short. I'm sorry for getting it wrong more than I would have liked."

"Huh?" My lips move without thinking.

I clear my throat, reflecting on Dad's words for a while.

Something heavy sinks inside me. Something dense. Something jagged, sharp, and twisted. It cracks.

"We're back," Mui announces.

I compose myself. Dapo's armed with a multitude of medical supplies.

He kneels down by Dad and lowers the medical paraphernalia onto the floor. "In the end, I had no idea what I was doing, so I got everything that looked sensible." His head tilts, and an eyebrow raises. "Fems, you okay?"

"Yeah," I lie. "So many thoughts going on at once."

"Your brain's not used to thinking, take it easy," Deja says.

Shallow laughter spills out of all of us. "Right," I start, turning to Dad. "Let's get you sorted."

"How do you feel?" Dapo asks Dad for the tenth time as we continue through the seemingly endless, underground labyrinth that is Backstage. We managed to rub pain relief gel over Dad's bruises and bandage them up. There was some more ibuprofen, too. The good thing is that he's on his feet and seems to be moving much better.

A finger pokes me in my side, and I nearly fold in on myself. It's Mui.

"Do you think the ferry will wait for us?" she asks, lips pouting.

"Yeah," I say, trying to sound sure. "They have to."

"But what if they don't?"

"Then we'll find another way off the island."

"How?"

I draw a deep breath. "We'll figure it out."

"That doesn't sound very smart," Mui huffs, shaking her head. "This is the arcade all over again."

My jaw clenches. "Mui, honestly. Feel free to come up with a plan at *any* point."

"No thanks. Not if you're going to be rude."

Dapo clears his throat. "According to Alberto's instructions, we're almost there. I'll go on ahead and see what things are like. Hold tight. Dad, you should take another painkiller."

"I'm fine, son, really," Dad answers. "Besides, it's too early for another one."

"Yeah, but as long as it's a one-off, an extra pill or two is fine. I googled it once," Dapo says, holding out a couple of pink ibuprofens to Dad. I wonder if Dapo googled it because of his injury from last summer. He turns to me. "Make sure he takes them, please."

I nod, and Dapo heads off.

"Fems, honestly, I'm fine," Dad pleads.

"There's nothing *fine* about you." I hold out the pills. "If not for yourself, then do it for us. It'll make us feel better, all right? Please. We—*I*—can't lose you."

Dad swipes the pills. "Since you asked so nicely." He swallows them dry and goes *ahhh*. My eyes roll.

When Dapo returns, there's a grimace grooved into his face.

"What?" I ask.

"The situation is … complicated," comes Dapo's reply.

"Complicated? The ferry's gone?"

Dapo shakes his head. "No, it's still there, it's ..."

"The animals?" Deja questions.

Dapo nods, scratching the back of his neck. "Yes."

"How bad? I ask.

"Bad."

"I'm going to check it out."

To get out of the tunnels, I climb up a service ladder and push open a hatch. Emerging to the left of the pearl path, I find a vantage point of the harbor, far in the distance, and words fail me. *A handful of incidents*, they said. *It's under control*, they claimed. What I see confirms it was all a lie. Corpses litter the various paths, strewn in awkward positions, with chunks of flesh carved out of them.

A tasseled feline struts with its jaws around the neck of a woman whose body is being dragged along, before its jaws slacken and her body drops. I'm too far to see it in detail, but I'm convinced her hair is matted with blood. Her throat's a red mess, too, and the way she twitches and attempts to scramble away is more than enough to peel my insides like ripe mandarin skin. In that moment, the tasseled feline roars, pouncing on the woman before wrenching the body into the air and throwing it down with ridiculous force. Her head smacks against the path, and I flinch.

The woman doesn't move again after that.

A flock of golden raptors, feathers around their heads stained red, peck at a cluster of people writhing like worms. *They're still alive,* I realize with alarm. The raptors are forced to flee to safety when another tasseled feline approaches. They're clumsy, and a couple of golden raptors collide with each other in their escape. I have an idea.

When I return, Deja and Mui are playing rock-paper-scissors.
Dapo turns. "You look like you have a plan."

"I ... think I do."

"Go on," Dapo says. I break out into a smile that he mirrors.
Then he shakes his head. "Why do I get the feeling I'm not going
to like it?"

CHAPTER 18

IT IS WHAT IT IS

"Nope," Dapo says. "No way. Are you mad?"

"Who's mad?" Dad asks, craning his neck.

"Femi," Mui answers.

I sigh. "Hear me out. I think my plan can work if we move slowly and quietly. Mr. Merrick, when you helped me and Mui in the staff quarters, how did you do it?" Mr. Merrick shrugs. "There was madness going on. How come you didn't get caught up in that?"

"Oh, I was being careful. They didn't seem to look at me if I . . . kept to myself."

"Exactly! I've noticed something, too. Look, I think the animals have terrible eyesight. They're likely relying on a sharp sense of sound and smell." I recall how the glass dragons scurried after the fruit. "But they *can* be distracted and fooled."

Dapo scoffs. "You *think*. But are you certain? We can't just gamble and hope they don't notice us."

"Why don't we cover ourselves in the dirt of the island, too?" Mr. Merrick suggests. "Rambo-style."

It takes me a second to understand he's referencing the movie we all watched together the last time our families were on holiday with each other. Deja walked out halfway through because she found the whole plot silly. "Actually, yeah, that should work," I say. "To them, we'd be part of the scenery."

"Cover ourselves in the dirt of the island," Dapo repeats, his voice monotone. "Are you sure? We don't get to rewind the track. Respawn, or whatever terminology makes sense. If we get it wrong, we're dead." The last sentence he splutters out is quiet and higher in pitch.

"What other choice do we have? Dad needs help, and our only way off the island is getting to the ferry."

Dad grunts and struggles to his feet, helped up by Mr. Merrick. "I'm fine," Dad says for like the hundredth time.

"You're not," Dapo and I say in unison. In agreement for once.

There's a brief moment of silence before Dapo's shoulders slump. His eyes look weary. I want this whole thing to be over as much as he does. "Okay," Dapo concedes. "But let's think this through. What if there's no one to operate the ferry? What then? We all saw the ... bodies."

"Then we'll have to figure it out." I take a moment. "This is the only way. We haven't got any other options."

Mui appears by my side and clears her throat. "Dapo, you worry too much."

Dapo cracks half a smile. "I have to worry enough for the both of us," he says. "It's kind of my job."

I turn over Mui's words in the privacy of my skull. They're simple and yet they cut right through to the heart of the matter. "Let me put it this way. You believe Jesus is at the wheel, right?"

"Course," Dapo answers.

"Then why do you have to be the one to drive? Feels a lot like you're telling Jesus to sit back and relax while you try to drive in his place. Kò lè work."

Dapo clicks his tongue. "Touché, baby bro, touché."

"Yuck, don't ever call me baby bro again. But you're welcome."

I catch Dad's eye. He gives me a talk-to-your brother look, and I'm sure he beams his words *life's too short* into my head. I clear my throat.

"Before we go risk our lives," I start, "we should talk about the day I pushed you into the road. Because we haven't, and if not now…"

"Then when. I know."

"You know"—I smooth down my top—"not an excuse, but you hurt me that day. Your words, they ate me up. You suggested I didn't care about Mum."

Dapo's sigh could have anchored a suspension bridge. "They… weren't meant to. I'm sorry. I wanted you to see."

"See what exactly?"

"That you needed to get some perspective. That you needed to think about the risks."

"Questioning whether someone loves their own mum is not the way to do that, though." Anger creeps into my voice, but I compose myself quickly, needing to get the words out. "You… you made me feel alone."

"Alone?" His face wrinkles, hands wringing.

"Like I was useless and not worthy of being part of the family." My eyes close, and I breathe in the memory. The memory is broken by Dapo's arms wrapping around mine. *Huh?*

"I'm sorry. I'm sorry, Fems." He steps away from me, his eyes wet, lip wobbling. "You're my *brother*. And I love you. Facts. Always will be. There is nothing I wouldn't do for you. And I'm sorry I'd let you feel that way."

The silence lingering between us is light as a feather. It's broken by Mr. Merrick's fart—that sounds like a badly blown trumpet—and Mui's giggle.

"Oh, sorry," Mr. Merrick says, without remorse. "Carry on. Reconciliation is important."

Deja whacks him in the arm. "Dad, that's gross."

A smile cracks open across my face and reaches my eyes. Dapo and I shake our heads. I clear my throat. "And I'm sorry. Shouldn't have called you empty. I only said that because I wanted the words to hurt. I'm sorry. I shouldn't have pushed you. I didn't mean for you to get hurt. I didn't mean for you to miss your chance to—"

"I know. I made peace with it long ago," he assures me. "All right, enough feeling sorry for ourselves. You and Mr. Merrick win. Let's do it your way."

One by one we climb up and out from the tunnels into fresh air. It takes us longer than I expect to cover ourselves in dirt and leaves. Down to my right, Mui's got an eager smile on her dirt-covered face. Crumpled leaves are tangled in her wavy, jet-black hair. Her clothes look like they're made of dirt and stained with cotton fabric all over.

"Nice," I say, and Mui smiles wider. When I look at Dad and Dapo, they look ... lacking. Their faces contain a bit of dirt, and their clothes aren't ruined enough. "Seriously?"

Dapo huffs. "What?"

"Just ... Look, if you don't do it right, we might as well give up now."

"Fine."

Mr. Merrick and I inspect everyone else, and once we're satisfied we set out.

"All right, now remember," I say. "Balls of your feet, single file, everyone. Dad and Dapo, you go on ahead. Mui and I will be at your rear. Deja and Mr. Merrick, you stay at the front."

Nods from everyone indicate we are ready. Slowly, slowly, we make our way down the gentle slope in the direction of the harbor. Before long before we're on the redbrick path, in the thick of it, and Mui is stiff with fear.

I don't blame her.

To our right, the noses of four glass dragons nestle in the sliced-open abdomen of a staff member. To our left, there's a gurgled whimper as golden raptors burrow their beaks into the crown of a man's head. The sight is brutal.

I swallow down my fear as distant screams echo aloud.

There are slow-moving shapes between the trees, off the paths, and my heart lifts. A small amount of people are out there trying to get to the safety of the ferry, and it looks like they came to the same conclusion we did. I focus back on our group in time to grab hold of Mui's top and yank her back from stepping on a pair of blood-splattered glasses. Her head whips over her shoulder, and I glance down at where her foot was about to land. *Careful.* She gulps.

We continue, my heartbeat drumming loud in my ears. Yet, not my tinnitus.

"*NO, oh, oh—arghh-rghh—ghh,*" screams another person out of sight as we creep along the path now slick with blood.

Death is everywhere as we move around and over the many people who obstruct our way.

"*Cyril,*" moans Ms. Bedeau. She's off the path on her hands and knees, her back torn to shreds. With her arm outstretched she crawls forward on the dirt. I don't see her son. "*No . . . no, no, no.*"

She is overwhelmed by two glass dragons that drag her this way and that. She screams and bits of her flesh splatter over their snouts. I turn away, and we trudge on. Up ahead, Deja gags silently. I wish I could comfort her.

Every now and then a few animals seem to sense us, but they don't put the pieces together.

A few times, Dapo glances back, giving me a look I know too well. *You sure you wanna stick to this plan? It's not too late,* his eyes say.

I stare back and nod. *Yes. We need to keep going.* Even though the stench of blood-soaked stone and dirt turns my stomach inside out, the harbor is up ahead.

My hope for survival cranks higher and higher the closer we get. Stay focused. *Don't look, don't look, don't—*

Alberto's face stares up at me, mouth wide open.

His eyes, throat, and stomach have been gouged out. I stumble, catching myself at the last moment. My blood flash-curdles, and I bite down on the urge to vomit, shriek, and cry at the same time.

Close by, Ellen's limbs are in all the wrong places, at all the wrong angles. A tug on my shirt pulls me out of my trance.

Mui. Concern is etched all over her face. Swallowing, I plaster on a smile that says, *I'm okay.* When Mui keeps staring, I nod. "I promise." It's a lie and I feel guilty, but fear is contagious, and she doesn't need to worry more than she has to.

Our group stops moving. Up ahead, two people stand shrouded in shade. They step forward, one leading, until they're out the cover of shade. Enelle emerges, standing tall and broad and with a dynamism she didn't have before. Valoisa appears next to her. My first feeling is relief. *They're okay.* Then it's hope. If anyone can help us get to safety, it would be them. I'm about to step toward them.

Except Enelle is grinning.

Satisfied.

By her side, Valoisa stands, shoulders hunched and her gaze darting everywhere. It might be my eyes playing tricks, but it looks like she's trembling.

I look around at the bodies that lay still, then back to Enelle and Valoisa, who meet my stare. The pieces fit together, clamp on to my chest, and tighten. Nothing prepares me for the heat that burns through me and blurs my vision. Enelle holds out her arm and whistles. In moments, a golden raptor lands on her arm. Its beak is lathered in dripping blood.

My fists clench at my sides. There's a thickness in my throat, and my stomach churns.

Enelle turns to whisper in Valoisa's ear, before giving her a kiss on the top of her head and looking back at us.

"Esteemed guests of Richard Jenkins," Enelle purrs, still with the vicious bird on her arm. She's a far cry from the woman I met before. There's a strength to her now that she didn't have when she was coughing and had Valoisa feeding her medicine. Was she even sick? I notice, too, how the animals around don't stir at her voice. They don't try to tear her limb from limb. "We have a saying here," Enelle continues. "Ya osha oblisca, pan ye coldo remborda. It means 'the blade forgets, but the neck remembers.' Please know, this isn't personal. I have been in pain for so long." She smiles and looks at me. "I am sorry, but we can't let you leave. But the island thanks you." Then she pulls something from her pocket and throws it at me.

It falls short. It's a radio—*the* radio from their house that was playing the jazzy tune. My eyebrows bunch together, and when I look up, Enelle is walking away from us. Her arm is raised as the golden raptor flies off toward the canopy of the trees. Valoisa stays rooted to the spot, the distant traces of a frown on her face.

Static hums from the radio, and there's no time. I know what they plan to do.

The object on the ground is a death sentence.

CHAPTER 19

REMORSE

"GET BACK TO THE PLACE WHERE ELLEN AND ALBERTO left us," I say to everyone. The animals close by become alert, and I see understanding in Deja's eyes. "I'll lead them away, into the forest, then meet you back there." I don't wait for anyone's approval. My plan is a long shot, but it's better than nothing. I rush toward the radio.

I make it less than ten steps when the radio bursts into a screech so loud the air around me shudders. Seconds later, there are several thunderous sounds and the sudden displacement of water into the air. When I glance in the direction of the harbor, I see what looks like faint smoke. My lips wrinkle into a grimace. Did something happen to the ferry?

Some animals are lured away by the creaking metal. Most are drawn to the wailing radio. I pick it up and run in the opposite direction—away from the others. Once I cross the pearl path, I know the terrain is going to get worse. And it does. The ground in the forest is uneven, but my legs keep pumping. I swat away drooping branches from the direction of the harbor and step through clusters of untended flowers, pushing through the wilderness. Close behind, a glass dragon races at me, trying to close the gap between us. Golden raptors glide in and out of the trees. One gets close enough to peck at me, but I zig and zag; I'm rewarded with only a couple of scratches.

My head is on a swivel with each step, looking for escape. I need somewhere to hide before I get rid of the radio.

Up ahead I spy a run-down house with no front door and patch together a threadbare plan. As I approach, I crank the dial on the squealing radio as high as it goes and throw it off to the right. It's enough to send most of the animals the wrong way. I rush into the house and look for a hiding place. Hurrying into a dim room with its curtains drawn, I shuffle under the bed, kicking up dust, and wait.

And wait.

Moments later, the heads of several glass dragons stoop down into view. Their eyes are reddish and have a soft glow. They're too large to squeeze under the bed, but they still try. I'm reminded of Mui under the transport vehicle. My heart thuds all the way to my fingertips. I desperately need to take in air—my chest burns—but I know it's too risky.

One glass dragon sniffs, nostrils flaring as it lets out a low growl and stalks toward me. My spine crackles. It takes everything in me to keep still as I squeeze my eyes shut and dig my nails into the palms of my hands . . . *God, please. Pleasepleaseplease.*

Gnawing discomfort tickles the backs of my nostrils. I feel an itch grow in intensity until it's too late. I am sneezing and contorting my body in the most awkward way as claws and snouts try to reach me. They may not be able to crawl under here, but their limbs are long enough to do some serious damage.

My mind is a display of profanity as I kick out, making good contact with a snout. A glass dragon whimpers. But then jaws grab my foot and begin to squeeze. I ease my feet out of my Flu Game Jordans, and both shoes are quickly torn to shreds and flung aside by the glass dragons, who have no interest in rubber and leather. They want flesh. They want me.

As their snouts and limbs attempt to invade, I kick out again, and the wind is punched out of my chest. Pain engulfs my left foot like a blue flame, beyond hot and searing. A talon has sliced the sole of my foot. Blood drips from it. I swallow my scream and, trembling, I curl away from the glass dragons until I'm as far back as I can go, pressed against the dusty wall. I want to scream. *Need* to scream. But I'm not about to give them extra motivation to try to reach me. Eyes wet with tears, I breathe in and out slowly, clenching my fists tight.

There is stillness for a moment. Until a putrid smell invades. The glass dragons stop scratching at me, retreating and rushing out of the house. I give it a good few minutes before I let myself breathe and crawl out from under the bed.

The dragons' footprints have disrupted the settled dust. I exhale and, without warning, burst into tears.

Sitting on the bed, I wince in pain and take off my sock, examining the throbbing sole of my injured foot. It's all cut up and caked with blood. On the count of three, I hoist myself up to find the bathroom and stagger over to the bathtub.

When I run the tap, the water is a milky brown. I hesitate.

Screw it.

Whatever happens, happens. The pain is about to overtake the dregs of adrenaline I've got left. Slow and steady I take off my other sock and ease my feet into the tub to let the grimy water wash over them. As I use my fingers to cleanse the blood, I wince at the white-hot pain.

"This sucks," I whisper into the air, squeezing my eyes shut, cheeks burning with heat. I see my room at home. My bed. My TV. Comforts I could use right now. I see Mum's home cooking. I see moments from happier times. "This really sucks."

Once most of the mud and blood have been washed down the drain, I turn off the tap, clamber onto my feet, and head back to the bedroom to find a towel and something I can put on my feet. There's no towel, but in one of the drawers there are several pairs of moth-bitten socks. They'll do. I go for three on each foot. But when I take my first steps, the socks don't do much for the pain. But they do enough.

"Come on," I seethe to myself, limping toward the door. My stomach sinks with every step. I remember the smile on Enelle's face, and Valoisa right beside her. *The island thanks you,* Enelle had said to me.

She was talking about the device. *I thought I was helping.* Guilt and shame swell like a balloon. *I didn't know. They used me.*

The last couple of days, hours, minutes play in my head with beyond-perfect clarity as I cover myself once again in dirt. I draw in a deep breath in frustration. If only I hadn't argued with Dapo, I wouldn't have stormed off and crossed paths with Richard and gotten lost and within range for Valoisa to hack my watch. If only I hadn't plugged in the device, then all of this would not have happened. My nostrils flare and my nose burns as the tears break free. Again. Hot and slick. I sniff and wipe and sniff and wipe. *This is my fault.*

You need to tell them, the voice in my head says. It sounds a lot like Dapo. *I can't*, I reply with a soft shake of my head and a deep, shuddering breath. I need to find my way back and fix things.

I finally step into the blazing sun to find the group; as long as I take my time and tread lightly, the tasseled felines and glass dragons roaming around here ignore me. Some glance my way but move on. I take deep breaths as trembling invades my legs. A golden raptor screeches as it's chased by a tasseled feline. A huge glass dragon snores, its eyes open.

Crossing around an extra-wide tree, that's when I see her.

Valoisa.

Her eyes lock onto mine, and my heart plummets. Blood drains from my face. Moving one foot in front of the other suddenly feels impossible. She's standing there, a few yards away, and I wonder if this is it. A fitting end to the mistakes I've made.

Every nerve in my body screams at me to run. But then I see the panic in her eyes. I've been wrong a lot, but I know—deep in my bones—she's not here to kill me. Because if she were, she would have done it already. My fear turns into confusion.

"Why?" I splutter, almost breathless with anger.

"I—I didn't want any of this." She steps forward, then staggers backward. Dazed, she looks around. Then at me. "I'm sorry." Then away. "I'm so sorry. This is my fault. I'm sorry. I had no idea this would happen. I promise. I thought...I mean, I knew Enelle and my dad wanted to expose Mr. Jenkins. They said they were going to broadcast proof of his lies. I didn't think they'd do *this*."

"You knew," I spit. "You lied to me." She takes a breath but doesn't say anything. "Why me?"

"Wrong place, wrong time," she answers. "If not you, it would have been the next person to be wandering a bit too close to the boundary between our land and Richard's."

I shake my head. "If you're not here to kill me, then why are you here?"

"To...help you. I don't know their goal, but I know this island. I can help you and your—"

"Don't want to hear it." I brush past her and limp onward.

"Your friends and family will *die* without my help."

I stop with a frown but don't turn back. "Go on."

"You don't know Enelle like I do."

"You don't know her that well, if you had no idea she was plotting this."

A couple beats of silence. "I can keep your friends and family safe until it's all over. Please, let me help."

I take a deep breath, shake my head, and face her. "Why should I trust you?"

"You have to believe me, I *never* wanted this. I know I can't say anything to convince you, but let me show you I can be trusted."

"I need to get back to my family and friends," I say, walking away.

She ends up by my side. "You're hurt, Femi. Let me help you get to them in one piece."

I don't say a word. Instead I walk, her next to me. We have to stop every now and then because of the pain in my foot. There are no paths, just uneven terrain. Eventually I have no choice but to take a pair of shoes that will just about fit, from a corpse.

I swallow nausea when I slip into them, and we continue our journey.

There are more surprises on the walk. Every now and then, groups of casually dressed people with rich Black skin walk nearby. They move easily among the few tasseled felines prowling around. Like they know this area intimately. Bits of their conversations carry in a language that sounds like the one I've heard pieces of from Valoisa. Darlenian.

She makes sure we stay discreet and out of sight.

"The ones who stayed," I say.

Valoisa nods. "Yes. But hard to say how many follow Enelle."

Finally we make it down into the tunnel, where the air is cool. Before I head down the winding passages, Valoisa grabs my arm.

"I'll be right back," she says. "My family can't know I'm helping you. I also need to see if I can find out what their endgame is. Don't do anything stupid. You need to stay hidden." She climbs back up, and I move onward, hoping everyone made it back safe and sound.

Sure enough, they're all here in the underground space where Ellen and Alberto left us. Dad's snoring while Dapo and Mui feast on biscuits and water. Deja sits against the wall. A wave of relief smothers me. They're okay. But then I pause. There's no sign of Mr. Merrick, and my insides clench.

"You look awful," Dapo states when he notices me. "Glad you're all right."

"Yes," Mui adds, cracker crumbs tumbling out of her mouth. She looks me up and down, zeroing in on the new shoes. "You do look awful. And new shoes?"

I nod. "Lost my old pair. Then a glass dragon did a number on my left foot."

175

It's like talking about it makes it worse; pain has its own heartbeat as it pulses through my foot.

"Hmm. You should try a cracker. They're nice." She holds one out to me.

"I need some ibuprofen."

"I think the flavor is called smoked prikaprika." She thrusts the cracker out toward me again. Taking it, I shove it in my mouth and chew. It does taste good, but a jolt of pain from my foot reminds me of the ibuprofen I need. There's a packet by a snoring Dad.

Hobbling over, I ask Dapo, "How's Dad doing?"

"He's not great." A shrug. "The bruising and swelling have gotten worse."

"I know. Mr. Merrick?" I ask, swallowing a few painkillers.

"He—I—yeah." Dapo shakes his head softly.

I sway on my feet. Dapo's stammering is a punch to the gut. Pressure builds in my chest, and it's hard to breathe. I rub my hand over my eyes, trying to prevent the tears from forming. Mr. Merrick is…gone. The man who gave me my first driving lesson is—

I caused this.

Dapo puts a hand on my shoulder. "Deja hasn't said a word. She's still processing."

I take half a step toward Deja before turning to Dapo. "What do you think we should do now?" Dapo tilts his head and quirks his eyebrow. "Why you looking at me like I said something mad?"

His face ripples into a grim smile. "Because you asked me for my opinion. What happened to the version of you that only listened to himself?"

176

"Shut up, man. Just answer my question."

"Huh, baby steps, I guess. We'll fix your attitude later. We need to find a way off this island. How? I honestly have no idea. You saw the faint smoke and heard that sound, right? The groaning sounds. They probably sank the ferry."

I nod. *Probably.*

Dapo continues, "Those mad animals are everywhere. No phone signal or Wi-Fi to communicate with the outside world. If we could at least get the animals back under control, that could buy us time…"

My eyes go wide, and I start wringing my hands. *You need to tell them you know how.* But having that conversation scares me, even if it could solve everything. My temples start to hurt and I feel nauseous. If only I could teleport away from this mess…

"Uh, hold that thought." I make my way over to Deja.

"Deja?" Sitting against the wall, her head is bowed with her arms cradling her knees. I stand before her for a moment, unable to say anything. My heart wilts when I think about how useless I feel. I kneel. "Deja," I say again.

She looks up at me with shaking shoulders. Her wet eyes quiver; her upper lip trembles.

"Are you okay?" I ask.

There's silence for a moment, and then Deja goes still. "I'm fine," she mumbles.

"I see…I'm glad," I say, uncomfortable. I want to say so much more, but the words—the right words that would fix everything—don't come. I suck in a breath. Right or wrong, I go for it. Lowering my head, unable to look at her, I speak again. I—I'm sorry. This is my fault. If I hadn't—" I stop myself. Not the time or place. Deja bursts into tears, snot running from her nose. I put my hand on her shoulder. "Deja..." She looks up at me. Tears squeeze themselves from my eyes. "I...I can't imagine what you must be going through right now, but I'm here for you. *We're* here for you." I take her hands—they're warm, soft, like premium leather—and hold them in mine. My heart pounds. Deja looks at me, curious. I stare at her, before catching myself, and let go. "S-sorry."

Deja wipes away her tears and snot before standing up and looking down on me. She's blotting out a lightbulb above, and from down here the light colors the edges of her hair like a halo.

Dad's coughing interrupts the moment.

"Go be with your dad." I give her one final are-you-okay? look. "Femi, I'm cool, go on."

I stride across the room to Dad, who's still sleeping, and sit by him. Dapo's on the other side of him. Dad looks so peaceful. Regardless of our differences, I want so badly to keep him like this—safe from everything. But Dapo's right. Despite what Valoisa said, the only safe space is *off* this island. Then we can start to put this nightmare of a holiday behind us.

And if we want to do that, I need to come clean and tell them about the device. I get to my feet and take deep breaths, stretching out my neck. I'm scared to tell them what I know.

"Fems?" Dapo asks.

"I...I think..." Limping around the space, waiting for the ibuprofen to work, my mind enters double time, retracing every one of my mistakes from trusting Valoisa to planting the device. It's clear what I have to do. "Not I think. I *know* how to get the animals back under control," I say aloud so everyone can hear.

CHAPTER 20

MEA CULPA

"How?" Dapo asks.

I wait until Deja joins the rest of us. I can't stop wringing my hands and rubbing them on my shorts. Everyone looks at me expectantly. *I can't do this.*

"Femi?" Dapo asks. His voice is stern. "What do you mean you know how to get them under control?"

My mouth is dry. "Promise you'll let me finish what I need to say. No interruptions."

"I—fine, I promise. Fems, what is it?" When Dapo takes one look at me, understanding dawns. "What did you do?" He spits out the question.

Taking a deep breath, I explain everything. Right up to after I planted the device. There are a few seconds of silence before the deep frown already on Dapo's face deepens even more. Deja glares at me.

"I can't *believe* you," she exclaims, getting right in my face. Words fail me as she jabs a finger into my chest with force. "Why the hell didn't you tell me—or *someone*—when they wanted you to plug something in? Some machine you barely understood. Answer me."

"I…I didn't—I…" No matter how I try to respond I know nothing will be enough. My shoulders slump and I look away. "Sorry," I mumble.

"Sorry?" Deja laughs. "Don't be sorry, find a way to fix this. My dad is…" She sucks in air and storms off, knowing she doesn't need to finish her sentence. Mr. Merrick is dead because of me.

Mui goes off after Deja. Me and Dapo are left standing here.

"Say something," I urge, unable to take the silence.

"Bro." He puffs out a sigh and shrugs. "What do you want me to say?"

I look away. "I don't know. Something."

"I mean"—*here it comes*—"how are you holding up?"

"Huh?"

Dapo's eyebrows draw together. Somehow the look of concern he gives me is far worse than him losing it with me. "How are you holding up? I'm not going to shout at you. I think you're remorseful enough. Besides I don't blame you. They used you. You tried to do the right thing and help others." I don't answer. "Can I ask you another question?" I nod. "Why did you tell us? You could have kept quiet."

"Because I had to. You said it yourself; we need to get off the island, and no matter how I thought it through in my head, there was no way to get to the device without admitting I knew it existed."

"I see."

Deja returns, eyes puffy, with Mui in tow. I can't look either of them in the eye. I'll never be able to make up for what happened to their dads. Deja shakes her head. "I should have tried harder to get you to walk away when you told me about the batteries. We could have tried to figure something out for the blackmail. I thought that was bad enough. But this?" Her hands are in full swing, moving around with no rhyme or reason. "How could you be so *stupid*?"

Stupid? Anger flares. "I get it. But maybe I wouldn't have done something stupid if all of you hadn't been getting at me all the time."

Dapo tilts his head. "Getting at you?"

"What are you on about?" Deja says at the same time.

I shake my head, knowing how my words sound. "You guys don't understand. Look, I made a mistake, I'm sorry. Forget what I said."

"Don't annoy me." Deja's eyes narrow. "If you'd even bothered to think, we wouldn't be here right now."

"You think I don't know that?" My eyes sting. "It's all I can think about. I thought I was being helpful. I wish I could turn back time and undo everything."

"Too late for that now . . ." Deja closes her eyes and takes a few deep breaths. "Look, it's obvious you were used. You'll just have to fix it, yeah, no ifs or buts. You're going to take some responsibility for all the shit you've caused and get us off this hellhole, or I will haunt you forever and ever."

I nod.

As if to punctuate Deja's demand, Dad erupts into a coughing fit, and I rush to his side. His eyes flutter open and he smiles. "Did I miss something?"

"No," Dapo says, without skipping a beat. "You all right? You were coughing pretty hard."

"Thirsty," Dad says, sitting up.

I turn to go and find more water, but Dapo is already moving. "Don't," he says. "I'll get him some. You just...stay here." His voice is easy but the look on his face is firm and clear. Our conversation isn't over.

"Why the long face, son?" Dad asks. "Did you and Dapo fall out again?"

I gnaw on my thumbnail and shrug. "Not quite. We're working out how to get off the island."

"Oh?"

"Yeah. I'm...uh, I'm pretty sure there's this device that if we turn it off, then the animals will stop attacking. It must be interfering with the resort's control system."

"Are you sure because you were the one who put it there?"

"How did you—"

"Pretending to be asleep is a trick as old as time, son. Anyway, I won't lecture you. I think you know where your mess-up was. I am sorry though."

I'm confused. "About what?"

"Timothy Huxley. I'm sure you have questions for me."

I nod. *Plenty.* Timothy Huxley, the pig who left my aunt and stole from numerous charities, is terrible news.

"Why would you be paying him? Does he have something on you?" My mind races. "You're not...embezzling, are you?"

Dad scoffs. "Ah ah, of course not. I'm protecting my sister from some unsavory details coming to light. That's all I will say on the matter." Dad gives me a stern look, and I know not to ask for more details. I trust he's telling the truth, and that's all I care about. "Let me also say this before your brother gets back. He loves you so much."

"Yeah, I know." *He has an annoying way of showing it, though.*

"When you were little, there was a time we thought you got lost. We were on holiday at, funnily enough, another resort."

"Really? I don't remember that."

"Yep. And Dapo was the first one to put on his coat, grab a torch, and run out into the dark looking for you. When he couldn't find you, he wouldn't stop crying. Turns out you were hiding in a cupboard the whole time." Dad sighs and eases himself onto his feet and puts a hand on my shoulder. "Dapo has *always* worried about you. He's *always* wanted to protect you. So please, son, let him try, okay?"

Dad's words are like wearing a drenched hoodie on a humid summer's day. I don't know what to do with them. Dapo returns with a cup full of water, sparing me having to reply. He starts to say something, but I jump in first, addressing everyone.

"Right, I know I messed up big-time, and we can talk about it … once we get off this hellhole. The first thing we need to do is drive off the animals and, as you know, there's a device that must be messing with the resort's control system. We unplug it, then the part responsible for keeping the animals calm has to kick in." Mui's hand goes up. I'd forgotten she was standing right there. "Yeah?"

"When will we go back and get Daddy?"

I wince. "We … won't be doing that."

"Why?" Her face crumples into worry. "We need to wake him up. He's not safe alone."

It's like someone has pulled the plug on my ability to think. The words are swirling down the drain.

Mui looks from me to Dapo to Dad. "What's going on?"

"Your dad's dead," Deja says, not unkindly, finally saying the words we couldn't. "Like mine."

"No, no, that's not right. He was sleeping." Mui shakes her head and looks to me.

"I—I'm sorry," I offer.

"You're lying. He's asleep, not *dead*." She throws her crackers to the floor. "Stop lying. Ken, tell them to—Ken?" She spins around, lost and confused. "Ken?"

My heart splinters.

And while Dapo and I stand there looking useless, Dad steps past us and wraps Mui in the type of hug we know too well. She sobs into his shoulder.

"It's okay, it's okay. Hey, I didn't know your dad for long, but I knew him long enough to know he loved you so much. If he were here right now, what do you think he'd say?"

Mui sniffs, and in between gasps she says, "Daddy would want me to be brave."

"I bet he would. I know you must have a lot on your mind, and I'm sorry I can't answer many of your questions, but it is okay to feel what you're feeling." Mui manages a nod. "Can you do me a favor, though?"

"Depends," Mui answers. "What's the favor?"

I can't help but smile. She's too smart for her own good.

"I want you to remember something important: Weeping may remain for a night, but rejoicing comes in the morning."

Psalm 30:5, my mind recalls. I know it because Mum wouldn't stop saying it when Grandma passed away. I didn't understand it at the time, but now that Dad's echoing her words, I get it.

Mui tilts her head. "What do you mean by that?"

"I mean it's hard being sad, because sadness is like a dark cloud that can block out the sun. But even clouds have their limits. They don't last forever. So remember this, please, hmm?"

"O-okay. That makes sense. I'll remember."

Dad smiles and pinches her cheeks before making an absurd face. He sticks out his tongue, and Mui bursts into a fit of giggles.

"Ew," she says, before making the exact same face back. But she still looks a little lost.

"Okay, son," Dad says, turning to me. At that moment I swear he glows. He looks strong. "We need to turn off the device."

"That would be unwise," a voice says.

It's Valoisa.

Deja tenses and steps back. "Why are you here? You come to kill us?"

"I want to help you." Valoisa spreads out her arms to indicate she comes in peace. "Trust me, if I wanted you dead, you would be."

Dapo sighs.

"Don't go after the device," Valoisa says. "You need to stay hidden. Discreet. Knowing my dad and Enelle, and seeing what they've done already—it's better to stay *out* of the way. I'm starting to understand what they're trying to do."

"Do you now?" Deja asks in a snide tone.

"Yeah, I do. We're Darlenian and they're hurting after the way they—*we've*—been treated by Richard."

"Enough for innocent people to—"

"Yos myo." Valoisa sighs. "I didn't say they were right. I just said I understood. It's why you need to stay put. I can help you with supplies. Tell them you're dead. You aren't the ones being hunted. It's Richard they really want. That much hate in their heart is dangerous. I don't want to see how they wield it if you go after the device and start to interfere."

Valoisa makes a good point. But... "What about anyone still out there? I'd like nothing more than to disappear and sit tight, but we can't leave them to their fate. Not if there's a chance to fix things."

Not if there's a chance for me *to fix things.*

"This is not a good idea." Valoisa's voice is flat and her lips press together, stopping short of a grimace. Silence sits between all of us for a moment. "Fixing things won't be easy."

"I know. But we have to try, and it has to be easier with you on our side." I study Valoisa, trying to read her, but I get nothing back. "We're going to try with or without your help."

"Okay. I don't like it, but I'll help you. Except I have one condition."

CHAPTER 21

ON THE MOVE

THE CONDITION VALOISA HAS IS SIMPLE—THAT WE do things her way.

I don't blame her; if I were going to betray my family, I'd want to do it my way, too. Though it means taking a longer route to avoid suspicion. She leads us by memory, recalling the blueprints Enelle had of the underground network, which Valoisa says was used to funnel black market goods once upon a time.

We emerge from underground to stuffy warmth and the glare of the early afternoon sun.

"Are we there yet?" Mui asks in a hushed whisper fifteen minutes later.

I roll my eyes. "That question is getting old, Mui. We'll get there when we get there."

We're making slow progress along a dirt path that cuts through a glade of burnt orange flowers behind the resort's arcade. We're going a different route than the one I took to plant the device. I'm grateful there aren't as many dead bodies around, though. Silver linings.

Deja drops by my side and leans in. "How can you trust her? After everything."

"I know," I say. Deja stares, expectant. "But we don't have a choice. She said it best. If she wanted us dead, we would be."

"You don't just go against your family like that. Think about it." She glances in Valoisa's direction. "If someone told you right now to stab your family in the back for the greater good, would you do it?"

"Not a fair question, and you know it." Deja's eyebrows push upward. "Of course I couldn't do it." I look over at Valoisa; gears spin in my mind. I trust her, yes, but Deja's right. "But what choice do we have?"

"We should be approaching the river," Valoisa announces. The sound of rushing water becomes apparent, and soon after, a river with murky-brown water comes into view. "Ah."

"'Ah' what? Did we make a wrong turn or—"

"No, no. This is the right place. It's . . . There was supposed to be a crossing here." Two wooden poles at the edge of the riverbank mark where the crossing should start. All eyes turn to Valoisa. "Enelle must have done this. We'll have to wade across."

Deja glances at me and quirks an eyebrow. *See?*

Dapo edges closer. "Current isn't too fast," he says. He grabs a large stone nearby and hurls it into the middle of the river. "To see how safe it is," he explains.

Ripples emanate, but nothing stirs. Satisfied, Dapo nods.

"The river's not deep," Valoisa says. "Follow me." She looks at Deja. "You can swim, right?" When Deja nods with a stony look, Valoisa continues, "Femi, the little girl should get on your back." She looks at Dad, whose face is strained. Sweat drips from his forehead.

"Dad, you get on mine," Dapo suggests.

"Ready?" I ask Mui.

She draws a deep breath, still as a stone. "No. We're scared. I don't want to go in. I don't want to."

Ken's back?

"We have to. Do you remember what Dapo said?" She shakes her head. "Well, he said I'm a good swimmer. Don't worry. I've got you. Okay?"

"Us," she murmurs. "You've got us."

"Of course."

The water is lukewarm. It seeps through my clothes and slaps against my skin. Mui and Dad hold our phones so they don't get waterlogged. Valoisa has a different definition of *deep*. I'm on my tiptoes bouncing across, the water coming up under my armpits.

"You good?" Dapo asks.

"Yeah, you?" I respond.

Dapo gives me a thumbs-up. There's a moment of silence. And then he says, "Dad needs to lay off the pounded yam, though. He's killing my back."

I laugh out loud. River water sloshes and enters my open mouth. Immediately I'm spitting and spluttering.

"Shhh," Valoisa admonishes. I compose myself, remembering sound attracts the wild things. My head is on a swivel. But as water moves all around, nothing comes.

We're almost on the other side when a gentle bulge in the water appears on the right. An unnatural ripple heads toward us. I stiffen.

"Dapo…"

The bulge moves. Closer.

"Yeah?"

"There's something coming for us. Your three o'clock."

His head turns, and he mutters under his breath. Then he says to everyone, "Start swimming."

"Hold on, Mui," I say, jerking into a swimming motion and clawing to get to the other side.

I only make it a few strokes before I'm hit in my side. I try to back away, then realize I can't feel Mui's arms around my neck. Without thinking, I take a breath and sink into the river, searching for Mui through the murkiness.

Something slick and slender wraps around my ankle, and it's like I've been grabbed by a stinging nettle. I reach under to get free from the itching pain, but I'm yanked farther downward in a sudden motion. My eyes settle on a silhouette the shape of a squat eggplant with lots of stretching appendages. Must be some sort of octopus.

Tentacles sprout from its middle, and at each end there's a soft glow. The octopus-like creature pulls me into itself, toward a mouth. Alarm floods through me, and I feel my fear wring my insides. The itching pain is fading, giving way to lightheadedness. I can't hold my breath for much longer.

When I squeeze my eyes shut, there is no movie reel going off in my head showing all my regrets and fears. Only white-hot fear of what's on the other side.

In the depths of my heart, I ask God to look after everyone else. *PleasePleasePlea*—

Two more tentacles wrap around my wrists...

...and drag me up, then out of the water and onto the bank.

Not tentacles but arms: one from Dapo and Valoisa each. Their breaths are heavy as stone as they check me over.

"You all right?" they ask.

I'm too out of breath to answer. Too disoriented.

"Oh man, your ankle is all swollen." Dapo slaps me. "Hey?"

I try getting to my feet but buckle under my body weight. Intense pins and needles shoot up my left ankle. Not good. My head goes back and forth.

"Mui?" I gasp.

"Safe," Dapo says. He offers me his hand. "Let me help you up."

"Th-thank you," I mumble, taking it.

Dapo pauses before saying, "You're welcome."

"Son," Dad says when we make it over. He's propped up against a tree. "Nice of you to join us." Deja looks relieved too but says nothing.

Mui rushes up to me and wraps her arms around my waist. "You...came back? You came back." I break into a soft laugh as she hugs me tighter. When she pulls away, her face is scrunched up, and she struggles to contain her trembling lips and chin. "But you're hurt."

"Don't worry. I'll be okay. I promise," I say, answering the concern on her face. "How's Ken?"

"He's gone again. I—I can't find him." For a moment she looks lost. Her frown is deep and uncertain. Finally she lifts her head and holds my gaze. "He's...not coming back, is he?"

"I don't think so," I whsiper.

"The magic's worn off," Mui mutters, staring back at the river.

"Magic?"

She nods. "Magic brought him back, and now it's all run out. I think he let it run out so you could come back. Yeah, I bet that's it."

When I go to respond, there's an ache in my throat and a heaviness in my chest. I hug Mui tight and she squirms.

"You're suffocating me!" she says, bubbling into laughter.

Once most of the feeling returns to my left ankle, we set off, heading into a secluded part of the island still under development. There's a half-finished building with a sign that reads:

HELIPAD STATION

FLIGHTS TO AND FROM SURROUNDING ISLANDS

I scoff. There's no way the helipad or building gets finished after all of this.

As we zombie onward, I try to figure out Enelle and whether there's something more to all this—something we're missing.

A hand on my shoulder jolts me from my sluggish walking.

"Dapo, what's up?" I ask.

"I think we need to stop for a bit. Dad's flagging."

"But the sooner we—" I stop myself. Dad is lagging behind. "No, you're right. Let's stop." Between my own injuries and my exhaustion, I realize I could use a break, too.

Dad sets himself down by a tree, and Mui goes to sit next to him. We're in a part of the island I haven't been to before. It's populated by ruins and rocks, and I'm sure I smell the faint sea breeze. I wonder how far beyond the pearl path we are and why it's so quiet. If we are near the coast, as I suspect, maybe the animals aren't fans of seawater. When I look at the group again, Dad is rubbing Mui's back as she clings to him.

Dapo catches me watching. "What's happening on Planet Femi?"

"Nothing," I say. "Guess I'm realizing Dad isn't as annoying as I thought he was, you know?"

Dapo pats me on the back. "Nice of you to catch up. I could have told you that years ago, if you weren't so . . . you. But no, I get it. Took me a while to realize that, too."

"He can't walk much farther."

"I know."

"We should leave him behind." I nod. "Let the animals feast."

Dapo smirks. "Would be so easy. Cut our losses now. Who asked him to try to fight one of the beasts, right?" He sighs. "But . . ."

"But we love the old man to bits, don't we?"

"We do."

"So we need to find a way to make things easier for him." I rub at my temples trying to think.

Valoisa saunters by, heading in Deja's direction, and says over her shoulder, "Doesn't that fancy resort have those transports?"

Dapo and I look at each other.

"If we could find one of the vehicles—" Dapo starts.

"Then we could drive to where I planted the device and conserve Dad's energy," I finish.

"They don't make noise," Mui says, intruding on our conversation. "They're quiet, like mice."

"Of course," I say. Mui's right, noise won't be an issue. "Alberto talked about it. They, uh, they"—I snap my fingers—"use those batteries that mean they don't make a sound at lower speeds. Man, if we use clutch control, we might be able to make it without attracting mad amounts of attention."

Dapo grins. "Exactly! Question is: Where are we going to get one from?"

"There's got to be one around here somewhere. I'll go find it."

Dapo crosses his arms and scoffs. "You're in no shape to go."

"But I—" Again I cut myself off. Was I always this argumentative? "I need to fix this."

"Seriously, Fems? I know you want to make things right, but you can't do that if you end up dying."

"True, but—"

"No buts, baby bro."

"Don't call me that." I step toward Dapo and wince. A pulse of pain spears through my foot, enough to make my eyes water. As much as I want to make things right, it won't help if I heap on more misery. Or worse, get myself killed. "Fine. You win," I mumble. Dapo looks at me, confused. "Go, I'll wait here."

He pulls his lips into a wide smile. "Back in a bit."

Time sludges by. Mui, Dad, and Deja end up playing endless rounds of word association games. I watch from the outside. To my left, Valoisa paces, nervousness embodied, her head whipping around at every sound. She steps toward me after a moment.

"I still don't think this is a good idea," she says.

"We can't go into hiding, Valoisa." I sigh. "We don't know

what Enelle's plan is. What if the plan is to try to claim the island and make it so that no one can enter or leave, what then?" Valoisa says nothing. "Exactly. And I've been thinking about Enelle. She can command the animals, can't she?"

"Sort of. She understands the island and its animals incredibly well. She's not untouchable, but if she focuses, she is more like a tamer. It is why she was able to speak without them doing anything. They respect her."

"But you can't tame them?"

Valoisa nods. "I only know a fragment of what she knows and understands deeply." I gulp. "Now do you see why I am not keen to go after the device? But...I said I would help."

Ominous headlights cut our conversation short. Has Enelle found us?

But it's Dapo in one of the resort vehicles, a big grin on his face, and I'm grateful. The front of the transport is crumpled, the windshield fractured and blood-splattered. The car doors and windows are tinted and pristine.

"You couldn't find a nicer-looking vehicle?" I ask, limping up to the driver's side window.

He shrugs. "Only one with keys still in it."

Everyone squashes into the back, except me and Valoisa. There was space for me, but I still feel guilty so, despite my foot and ankle injuries and people imploring me to get in, sitting in the vehicle is a no. Dapo leans out the window and says to Valoisa, "Lead the way."

The blade forgets, but the neck remembers.

Each step causes unease to sink into my bones. Again, I think about what drove Enelle to stage this … I don't even know what to call it. Revolution? Coup?

No, those don't feel right. This whole situation right now feels too vengeful …

The blade forgets, but the neck remembers.

It's obvious something else happened. But what could Richard Jenkins have done to make this level of anarchy worth it?

What are they putting right?

Frustration bubbles within me.

It's not until I bump into Valoisa's back that I notice both she and the vehicle have come to a halt. Right in front of us stands Richard Jenkins himself and several armed men.

Whose guns are pointed at us.

INTERLUDE

RICHARD

On a summer evening twelve years ago, Richard Jenkins woke up in a cold sweat, energy crackling all the way to his tiptoes. He slipped out of bed, shivered into a silk robe, and made a call to his general counsel.

One picked up after the second ring.

"It's *three* in the morning."

"Ellen, listen, I've had a breakthrough," Richard stated, ignoring her. "Get me in touch with the Darlenian government. I want to make them an offer." Ellen sighed. He pressed on. "I've had … a redemptive awakening. Yes, let's call it that. The Grand Darlenia Resort."

"I don't think you can go and *buy* an island with a living population. Not to mention what happened when you—"

"Mr. Jenkins," intruded another voice. If there were legal hurdles, then Richard needed his lawyer on the call, too. "As I assured you last night, I will let you know once we conclude the acquisition of—"

"No, Spencer, it's not about that. I've had my next idea. Ellen seems to think I may have some roadblocks in trying to purchase Darlenia."

Silence settled on the line. After a short while, Spencer took a deep, rattling breath. "Well, Ellen's right. I don't see how—"

"I don't think you quite understand. I've had a *breakthrough*. This is it. The next child to be delivered from the womb of wonder." Richard put the phone on speaker while he lit a cigarette. After a long drag that soaked through his bones, he continued, "Can you get it done or do I need to look for assistance elsewhere?"

"I—I'll get it done," Spencer answered. "I'll find a way."

Richard smiled and inhaled. Power hummed through him. "Ellen?"

"Yes, sir?"

"How much are we talking?"

"Well," she started, "it would require a ridiculous amount of asset maneuvering. With that comes huge risks. You probably will pay a premium, too, for NDAs. Honestly, I don't see how—"

"*Ellen*," Richard said, not unkindly but rich with expectation.

"I'll see to it we have the required funds."

"Perfect." Richard hung up and strode over to the large floor-to-ceiling windows that overlooked the sea. On the horizon he saw the shape of the small town. This was his third-favorite house, but it had one thing his two most-favorite houses didn't—a helipad. The perfect place to come and go. As such, there were no roads leading to his house. Blobs of rain streaked in his periphery. The gnawing emptiness that had been eating away at him of late lightened and began to fade.

He reached for the pistol resting on the top shelf of his drinks cart, next to a half-finished bottle of Olderton whiskey that cost him over thirty thousand pounds. The gun was, for all intents and purposes, real—except it had been configured to fire blanks.

The prop gun had cost him over a hundred thousand dollars at an off-the-books auction. Richard had wanted it because, to him, it was a *concept realized*. He had always chased the impossible, and whenever Richard wanted to remind himself of his purpose, he would cling to the gun. Though there was also another reason.

One day, in its previous life, it *had* fired a real bullet. It happened, miraculously, when a collector was showing off his extensive collection of prop guns from various movies and TV shows. No one had been injured in the accident, but there were plenty of witnesses. Within a week, the collector was inundated with offers for the prop. When Richard heard the story, he knew he had to have the impossible gun. And Richard believed, one day, that prop gun would fire—just for him. Ever since making the collector an offer he couldn't refuse, he kept it close.

The impossible gun twirled around Richard's finger now. *The Grand Darlenia Resort*, he thought again. Yes, it had a nice ring to it. It was clear in his mind, too. It would be a place unlike any other. He would shape its troubled ecosystem to his will and make things right.

From footage his contacts had sent him, he had seen the beasts that lurked there. How beautifully savage and rare the animals were. They would need to be tamed, molded to cooperate. Whatever it took.

But more important was the narrative. In order for his idea

to work, he would need to seize the story. Darlenia would be an island he had *discovered*. Lost, but now found. Amateur research showed it was part of an uncontacted archipelago growing increasingly more contactable. He would wipe out any trace of Darlenia from the internet and ensure it remained that way. He would pay whatever he needed. No matter how delicate or drawn out, he knew everyone had a price. He'd made deals like this before.

Stretching himself out and yawning, he made a note to make a few calls in the morning. Tomorrow would be a big day full of his favorite thing: shaping dreams into reality.

Pointing the gun to the moon, Richard squeezed the trigger with a smile and said, "Bang."

CHAPTER 22

GUNFIRE

I PUT MY HANDS UP. IT SEEMS THE MOST LOGICAL thing to do when a multitude of guns are aimed at you. The others get out of the car with their hands up, too.

After a moment, Richard tells his small army of men, all muscle and sober frowns, to lower their weapons, then beckons us over, gun still in his hand. He tilts his head, narrows his eyes. "You're alive." I shrink back as he twirls his gun. "Alive and intact."

"What do you mean by that?" I ask.

Richard looks us up and down. "I'm surprised."

Dad puts a hand on my and Dapo's backs. "They figured out the best way to survive is to blend in. The animals have poor eyesight. My boys are smart." Dad then glances at Valoisa. "It's useful when you have a native who knows this island through and through."

"I see." There's a spark of fear. Richard must know we know the truth. In defiance, he looks past Valoisa as if she's nothing. "And why are you now coming this way? There's nothing here."

"There's a device," I say. "I...I put it in a structure around here, and if I unplug it, your security systems will power back up."

Richard frowns and murmurs something.

"Sorry?"

"Nothing," Richard says, louder. A tight smile is on his face. "Yes, let's get our systems back online. We need to salvage the situation. Where is it? This device."

"Valoisa is taking us there now." I bring my voice down so only Richard can hear. "I know the truth about the island—about you buying it and sending the natives away. You're a fraud."

Worry clouds Richard's face. "I don't know what you're talking about." Richard chews on his bottom lip and looks around as if he's being haunted. Looking past Valoisa, he says, "Show us where this device is."

Valoisa glares at him with clenched fists and, without a word, leads the way. I follow on foot, unable to take my eyes off Richard. His face is paler than it should be, and everything about him right now is tight. I get closer to him.

"You screwed the Darlenian people pretty badly, didn't you." There's no point phrasing it as a question.

Richard ignores me, his gaze fixed ahead. "With this resort I—I wanted to go beyond. Reach the impossible. Spare no expense, as the saying goes. What do you think?"

I frown. "About what?"

"The resort. Does it touch the impossible?"

He stares at me, searching my eyes for an answer. For validation.

And it's in this moment I realize his obsession with grandeur. After a moment longer, I say, "I don't know what impossible is, but I do know the resort feels like nothing else in existence."

"Hmm." His lips flash a shallow smile. "Absolutely. But, but, but, if all it took was a device to bring the resort to its knees, then it's clear I didn't touch the impossible. I see that now. Something to improve upon."

Improve? This isn't some beat that could do with more bass. There's no coming back from this. I offer him a forced smile before silence fills the space between us. Richard keeps running his hands through his hair and shaking his head. I take a breath. "Is there another way off the island?"

"Huh?"

"Another way off the island. Once the security system is online, we'll need to find a way off... since the ferry is likely not an option."

"No. We'll need to get the wider comms back online. Then we can call for help."

Something doesn't add up. "But wait, if comms are down, why hasn't anyone come? Wouldn't it be strange for there to be radio silence from you?"

After several heartbeats of silence, understanding flashes across his face. Stifling a laugh, he shakes his head. "Of course." He beckons one of his men over. "Tablet." A tablet appears, thrust in front of him. Taking it, he taps through a few options, then says, "Cuplow."

"Sir?"

"No one's coming for us, are they?"

Silence floats on top of the soft crackle of walkie-talkie static, and then: "No sir, they aren't."

"Enelle and Valoisa are your family."

My mouth falls open. When I glance at Valoisa, the resemblance is all too clear. Everything makes sense, especially the interaction Cuplow and I had in front of the painting on the ferry. *Melancholic.*

How did I not see this before?

"How much do you want?" Richard sighs. Color rushes to his face.

"Excuse me, sir?"

"In order for me to regain control of my island. How much do you want? Think big, but within reason. I can make you rich beyond your wildest dreams."

A pause. And then, "This was never about money."

"It's always about money. Tell me what you value, and I assure you it can be bought."

"You cling to wealth like it can keep you safe. Like it makes you above natural order. But the truth is, money has no *real* power. It cannot think. It cannot act . . . It is not alive. Do you see now? How useless it is, the thing you trust in?"

Richard clenches his fists. He doesn't say anything.

"This was never about the money," Cuplow repeats. Each word is sharp as a needle, laced with menace and resentment I hadn't noticed before. "It's about . . . sending a monster like you a message. You cannot take, take, take without consequences."

"Cuplow . . . I am not what you call me. I'm not."

"Sir?"

A beat of silence. "Yes, Cuplow?"

"Listen well."

The line goes dead with a short crackle. Moments later,

music blares all around us through the intercom system. I didn't realize it extended this far. An old Xavier song plays.

> *My pride may course through, but I still bleed red*
> *In a deep shade it runs like syrup does*
> *As the mortal wound forms a crown of dread . . .*

There's a chorus of squawking. A faint rumble beneath our feet. Appearing from the right is a tasseled feline. Its rib cage expands and falls with hypnotizing rhythm. Its sleek fur bristles over its lean muscle.

I turn back to Richard's men and bring a finger to my lips, but they already know to be sensible. The tasseled feline doesn't budge. It knows something is here.

It's listening. It's waiting.

For even the slightest.

Faintest.

Sou—

Dut.　　*Dut.*　　*D u t.*　　*d*　*u*　*t.*
　dut.　　*Dut.*　　*D*　*u*　*t.*

Gunfire punches through the air and kicks up the dirt by the tasseled feline's feet. Its roar splinters the air as it charges at the unlucky soul who shot at it. All bets are off as more tasseled felines emerge and more guns discharge, releasing pulsing flashes of light.

I weave away from the chaos and head straight for the vehicle.

One of Richard's men is entangled with a feline, holding it at bay with his gun. Another limps away, splattered in blood before being pounced upon.

Crap, crap, crap.

There's yelling...gunfire...screams...roars. Rinse and repeat. A thudding rhythm of violence. The vehicle is right there, but in the chaos it feels so far away.

In my periphery, I see a feline charging at me. It leaps, and I'm pushed out the way by Valoisa at the last moment.

"Go, I'll try and save who I can," she says. We share a fleeting nod as I watch her dash off. I scramble to the vehicle. Pull the passenger door open. Hop in. It's everyone sans Richard and Valoisa. "Go, go, go."

Dapo kicks the vehicle into gear and reverses before veering off the path and onto the grassland away from the madness.

THUD.

A bloody handprint slaps against the window by my seat before being pulled away. Mui squeals. A feline drags one of Richard's men, then tosses him to and fro, tearing its claws across the man's back.

His screams fade as Dapo wheels us away.

"You know the way?" Dapo asks.

I nod after looking around briefly and realizing the area is a little familiar. In all the chaos, I hadn't clocked how close we were.

After several minutes of frantic driving, we come to a stop in front of the box-like concrete structure with the white door. "This is it," I say, opening the vehicle door and stepping to the ground gently since my foot is still sore. However, it's guilt that shudders through me.

Dapo stands alongside me. "Let's do this."

I go to open the shed door, but it won't budge. I try again. Same result. It's—

"Locked," Dapo says.

"I was going to say it's stuck." But when the door doesn't budge for a third time, I stifle a laugh. "It's locked. They locked it."

Dapo smirks. He keeps the *told you so* to himself. "Maybe there's a window."

"Sounds like a plan."

We case the structure, and there *are* windows, but none are open. Until we come to the back, where a window is ajar. "Gimme a boost," I say. A flash of memory sizzles: After school, when Dapo and I used to forget our keys, we'd break into our back garden and have to find a way through the open kitchen window.

"Ready?" Dapo asks, lacing his hands together to provide a foothold.

"As I'll ever be," I answer, stepping up and pushing through the pain in my foot.

In one thrust I'm hanging from the window. Some deep breaths later, I've pulled myself up so I'm able to squeeze through the window. Controlling my descent doesn't work, and I end up toppling into a barren room with a *THUD*.

There's dust everywhere, forming thick layers on rows and rows of cabinets and cables and furniture. I step through the rooms to get to the device. And there it is. A beacon of pulsing light.

All that's left is to unplug it, but unease tugs at my stomach.

I've told everyone this was the way to get the animals to back down, but what if…

I don't want to make things worse, but what if…

Forget the what-if*s*, I tell myself. Like ripping off a Band-Aid, I unplug the device from the wall without any more thinking and pull out the batteries. This will work. It has to.

After several agonizing seconds of silence, an irritating, high-pitched humming blossoms. It's the sonic irritation, back now that the island's control system seems to be on here. The hum grows and expands and forces me to wilt and shudder as I stagger back to the window. And yet… and yet, this feeling has never felt so good. It crescendos into a chorus of nearby animals howling and screeching while Dapo helps make sure I don't end up in a crumpled heap climbing out of the shed.

CHAPTER 23

UNPLUGGED

"What now?" I ask.

"That…is a very good question," Dapo says as we walk back. He whips out his phone. "Still no signal. We need a way to communicate with the outside world, like Richard said." Dapo closes the door on the driver's side as I get in. "We need to send an SOS."

"What's an SOS?" Mui asks, against the backdrop of Dad's light snoring. His wounds have really taken a lot out of him.

"Distress signal," Deja answers without missing a beat. "Morse code. A way to say you're in trouble."

"And what does it stand for?" Mui leans into Deja.

Deja shrugs. "Nothing, actually. Well, people say it means 'Save Our Souls' or 'Save Our Ship,' but do a bit of reading and it actually doesn't mean any of those."

"Ah," Mui says, slumping backward and staring up at the vehicle's ceiling. "I don't like that. I'm going to pretend it means

'Shouting or Screaming.' Because, like, that's how you get attention, right?"

Dapo angles himself toward me, frowning.

"What are you thinking about?" I ask.

"About what Mui just said. We should try to signal nearby islands. I think there's maybe one or two islands not too far away."

"There are," Deja confirms, listing them out. "Hey, what if we set one of the big buildings on fire...or maybe the forest?" Deja suggests. "That ought to get their attention."

"I agree," I say. "Burning everything is like a supercharged alternative to a flare. Whoever's paying attention *will* see."

"Hmm," Dapo says. "But..."

"But?" I raise an eyebrow. Every fiber of my being is ready to push back. To make my point. Instead, I keep quiet. I've realized I have my own weaknesses.

"Let's take a step back. They've planned this all out so that we're stranded here with no way off," he says. "The moment we try something, I wouldn't be surprised if they're waiting. Almost counting on it. I think we need to think smarter. Sorry, not smarter, wrong word. More like, we need to think about this differently."

"Elaborate," I challenge.

"Think about it. They wanted something specific out of this. Like Richard says in his book, you don't go into any venture with no exit plan. Sooner or later, someone's gonna come checking in, yeah?"

"Yeah..."

"Ooh..." Deja interjects, forcing her eyebrows up, waiting for me to get it.

210

I frown. "Ooh what? I don't get it."

She breaks into a grin. "He's right. There's no way a plan like this is half-baked. There's got to be schematics, a timeline, maybe contingency plans... Femi, do you remember that movie we watched? The one where the detective thought he'd solved the case, but after speaking to the villain learned something bigger was in the works?"

"Okay, yeah, but it's not like we can talk to Enelle—"

Deja shakes her head. "No, no, remember what he did after speaking to the villain? He went to the villain's lair. Look, if we want to figure it out, then..."

I nod, getting it. "Then we need to find out what their end-game is." Enelle's cottage projects itself onto the wall of my mind. "I know where we need to go."

"Thought so," Dapo says, kicking the vehicle into gear. "Lead the way, bro."

Dapo drives us to the edge of the forest. It's too dense to get a vehicle through, so we all go the rest of the way on foot. Into the nostril of the forest. Familiarity seeps into the soles of my feet as the ground becomes riddled with rocks.

Fear takes hold when I realize we're in a part of the island the control system doesn't quite reach. The parts beyond the pearl path. "We need to be quiet."

"Why?" Mui asks at the same time as Dapo.

I point to my ears. "Security systems aren't operating here

because this isn't part of the resort. We're dead if we draw attention to ourselves."

Like before, tall rocky walls appear, closing off all other paths. There is no other way but forward, until we're in front of Enelle's small, crooked cottage.

Deja flinches and steps into me. "Jellyfish?"

One pulses through the air toward us and I laugh. "Yeah. Harmless. They'll return to the reefs by sunrise," I say. "Right now they're . . . It doesn't matter." I cut across the clearing to the house and wrap my hand around the doorknob. Before I can twist it, Mui is by my side, clutching my arm.

"What if it's bubble trapped?"

She means *booby*-trapped. I uncurl my fingers from the doorknob, because that's the sort of thing Enelle would think up. "Good point. Let's look around and check." Mui rushes off, and I call out after her quietly, "*Carefully.*"

Dad sits himself against a rock, grimacing. But he smiles when he catches me looking. Concern scrunches my face. *You okay?* I mouth.

Don't mind me, he gestures. Another smile, shallow and unable to hide his pain. Maybe there's some painkillers inside?

I join Dapo in examining part of the perimeter for anything that might point to a trap. Deja is checking out the other side.

Without looking up Dapo whispers, "You all right?"

"Depends."

"On?"

"What you mean by all right." I shrug and peer into the plants growing around the cottage. No signs of a trap. "This situation isn't all right, bro."

"Ha, for real. But I meant like, you know...how you feeling about everything?"

I take a deep breath. I'm scared. Angry. Frustrated... "Confused," I admit. "How did we get so bloody unlucky?" A strained laugh slips out. "Other than my mess-up, of course. All this because one man thought he could screw over an island and its people. Couldn't make it up."

"Yep. He—wait, what's that?" Dapo scrapes away at the soil, and in seconds I'm peering over his shoulder. He pauses and glances at me. "Bro. Space."

"Nah, keep scraping." With a shake of his head and a heavy sigh, Dapo keeps on until a wire reveals itself.

Carefully, carefully, we loosen the soil and follow the wire. It doesn't take long for Mui to join us, and soon the three of us are waiting to see what we'll find. It takes us around the back of the cottage—we pick up Deja along the way—to a speaker half-buried in the dirt.

Huh?

"Why would they bury this?" Mui asks.

"Because they knew we'd find our way here," Deja murmurs.

"Uh-huh." I remember the way they used the radio to draw the animals to us. "And if we came looking, they'd trigger this trap to play some kind of loud noise. And loud noise means creatures."

Think, think, think. If I were Enelle and I were to booby-trap the house, how would I do it?

By rigging all the entrances.

"Drop zone," Mui blurts.

"Huh?" Dapo and Deja say in unison. I smile because I get

The Guests reference. She's saying we should go in from above. When I look where she points, I see...

"Mui's right. The chimney's our way in." A smile builds on my face. "We can't risk the doors and windows. I doubt they rigged the chimney because let's be real—who the hell would think to get in that way?"

"Fair point," Dapo says. "We *all* can't get in through the chimney. Femi, you've been inside before. I'll give you a boost, and you can get what we need." He gets on one knee and clasps his hands together. I step onto the temporary foothold, pushing through the threads of pain. "On three."

"One."

I focus on where I need to grab on to—the roof gutter—and take a breath.

"Two."

As soon as I grab on, I'm going to need to hoist myself up onto the roof itself. I'm not sure—

"Three."

Dapo gives me a boost. All my focus is on springing upward and grabbing hold. But then the gutter groans and creaks, and I know I don't have time to linger. Or care about how I look as I claw my way onto the roof. Sprawled across the stony tiles, I take a few moments to catch my breath.

"You all right up there?" Mui calls.

I clamber to my feet and put a finger to my lips to let Mui know we need to be quiet before I give a thumbs-up. The roof is slanted with the chimney jutting out in its center. In about ten careful steps I'm looking down the chimney with my phone flashlight. Going down now seems like a stupid, stupid idea. I've got no harness, and if I lose my bearings, it's a straight drop.

Hang on. "Dapo?" I whisper as loudly as I dare.

"Yeah?"

"Hear me out." I scratch the back of my neck. "I go down the chimney."

"Yeah."

"Then I find out what's what."

"Uh-huh."

"What next?" I bow my head and laugh. "We did not think this through."

"Then you walk through the front door." He says this like it's that simple. "Hear me out because I know you're thinking, 'It's booby-trapped, why would I walk out the door' and all that."

"Firstly," I say with a laugh, "I do not sound like that. Why you always give me the highest pitch voice when you're imitating me? Not cool. Second, yes that is *exactly* what I'm thinking. Do you have a plan?"

"Yeah, we pray you can reach the vehicle before they reach you. We'll get Dad back to the vehicle now while you do what you need to do, all right? We'll be waiting for you, vehicle ready to make a fast getaway."

"Can't say I like it, bro."

"You got any better ideas?"

"Nope," I breathe. "In a bit."

I step into the chimney and press my hands and feet against the insides. Like a crab, I shuffle down. The occasional whistling of wind makes me feel like I'm sliding down the throat of some monster.

I make it to the bottom coated in dust but in one piece. Stumbling out of the fireplace, the inside of the cottage looks untouched, and like we thought, there are wires lining the windows and the doorframe. *Rigged.*

My first stop is the kitchen, where the device was, but rifling through the drawers and cupboards shows there's nothing. I try the living room. Zilch. The trash cans have nothing. I frown.

Where would they keep their plans?

A conversation with Valoisa blazes in my mind. Valoisa had said Enelle was the brains. Giving orders and uh…uh…writing in her notebooks. I go searching for them, finding a whole bunch in one of the bedrooms.

Most of what's written are lists, poems, and doodles. Useless stuff. I keep flipping through the pages impatiently. Who knows if Enelle will come back here.

Finally, three notebooks later, I strike gold:

Ya osha oblisca, pan ye coldo remborda.

Mr. Jenkins needs to feel the FULL weight of his decisions. He must know the true cost of exploitation. Through bloodshed comes change. We will give the showman a show. First we must throw the island into chaos and capture his castle. Cut off any hope of escape. He must stay alive until we have burdened him with failure and drive him to despair. Until the rhetoric he clings to leaves him. He will understand us and the island's pain.

He will know deep down this is because of his sins. Because of how he purposely poisoned our land with a chemical spill, covered it up, then used it as a means to buy the land from our leaders.

And once he understands, then we will put him out of his misery, and Darlenia will finally be ours again. Things can return to what once was.

My eyes widen. *That's* why they hate him. Not only because he bought their land, but also because of how he did it: By ruining it with a chemical spill and forcing the government's hand. I can't hate on how the Ruizes feel at knowing this. But, surely, they could have punished him in a more effective way without this much bloodshed.

As for their plan, there aren't specifics, but there's enough here to see what their endgame is. This whole thing is about vengeance but also about restoring things. If we'd stayed hidden, sooner or later, we would have been found out, and who knows what would have happened then.

Richard's "castle" must be his private residence. The control failure is the chaos, I'm guessing. I tear out the page and stuff it into my pocket.

Now…*Now* I need to leave through the front door. My scalp prickles and my stomach swirls when I reach the door. I've opened hundreds of doors in my life—maybe thousands—but this is the first time I'll open one knowing I'd be bringing the full weight of danger on my head.

Okayokayokay. I can do this. "Open the door," I mumble.

"That's all you need to do. Open the door and then run like hell for the vehicle."

I flex my ankle. Not too bad. Most of the soreness is gone. I plant my foot, and there's a jolt of pain, but I can take it.

One Mississippi.

Crank my neck.

Two Mississippi.

Crack my knuckles. Pull at the dry skin on my bottom lip.

Three Mississippi.

"Lord, give me strength."

In one breath I pull open the door. In two breaths, a riot of noise blares—a Xavier tune that sets off distant howls and squawks. *What is it with the constant Xavier?* My feet kick into gear, and I am sprinting.

CHAPTER 24

PURSUIT

My feet pound against the dirt as the sound of Xavier blares out from the speakers. Adrenaline and pain-killers drown whatever pain should be shooting through my foot. The squawks are close enough to send a shiver down my spine. The whole forest is rigged with unseen speakers, and soon enough it's going to be crawling with creatures.

The number of times I've stumbled is no joke. I leap across a small brook, weave through some rusted and discarded items, and duck through a chain-link fence big enough for me to fit through. As my feet come down, I take a look to my left—

I'm rooted to the spot. The blood drains from my face.

A flock of golden raptors peck at a body. One of Richard's men, it seems. *He's alive.* His legs writhe as the raptors tear at the flesh on his face. He doesn't scream because he no longer has a throat.

Bile turns my stomach inside out, and it rushes up my throat. I do my best to stifle any noise.

When I'm done retching, I empty from my mouth, let it slop onto the ground, and cover it with dirt.

The birds pecking at the man seem too hungry to notice me. One of them chokes on a pearl earring and coughs it out. I need to get by them. And the only way past is over a bed of dead leaves.

I start taking a step but pause as soon as the leaves crunch. The birds cock their heads. My heart motors in my mouth while the seconds drift by. They go back to feasting.

I need to rip the Band-Aid off. If I can reach the part where the island's system is back online and get to where the others are waiting, I'll be fine. I count down in my head.

... Three.

   ... Two.

      ... One.

I *RUN*, ignoring how the leaves sound like firecrackers beneath my feet. Ignoring the squawking and flapping of the birds who zero in on me. The fluttering of their wings is deafening.

Don'tlookdon'tlookdon't—

My breath hitches as I glance back, just as a bird dives toward me, talons first. It slices through the fabric of my shirt and scratches the flesh in my shoulder. Sharp pain stings its way down my arm and back. I stumble. Another bird whooshes past, missing the side of my face.

One lands square on my back, talons digging in and wings flapping. Pecking at me. My arms flail, fists balled up tight. I club its side and the talons loosen. I club it again and, with a squawk, the weight on my back lifts.

I make it to a tree and hide behind it, trying to control my breathing. The birds circle and squawk, but their poor eyesight means they can't see me. They know I'm close, though. My shoulder is bleeding. I swallow down the burning in my chest.

Calm down, Femi. Catch your breath.

I feel the tickle of sonic irritation. Up ahead, I spy the clearing in the woodland that means the pearl path is near. Energy rushes through me, and I look around. Yeah, I thought so. I'm close to the car. In fact, it's like fifty yards before I'm sure I'm in the arms of the island security. And yet it feels so, so far.

Fifty yards to survive the talons and beaks of the golden raptors. I can do this. Don't overthink, just *do*.

The moment I break into a run, the squawking starts back up again. Right on cue. They are baying for my blood, but there's a shallow smile on my face. Because with each step, my hope thickens and fear starts to fade. Adrenaline is well and truly pumping. The prickle of sonic irritation swirls, and while it's like someone's yanking the hairs on my arms, hard, the feeling has never felt more welcome. The squawks get more and more strained.

And then they stop, cut out like a short circuit. I hear a quick succession of thuds. My feet stop, and I turn to see the last of the golden raptors fall onto the pearl path.

The shallow smile on my face bursts into a full-on grin. "Ha! Let's goooo," I exclaim, pointing. "I know that's right!"

I bubble into laughter, and, without thinking, I say a prayer

221

of thanks in my head. Dapo would be proud of me. But for real, *thank God*. I made it.

Man, this feeling is similar to when I have a breakthrough with a beat I've been having trouble with. I want to hold on to it—revel in it—but a loud-as-hell growl snaps me back to my current reality, and I bolt for the vehicle.

"Took you long enough," Dapo says, leaned up against the vehicle next to Deja. "Knew you'd make it, though."

I offer an uneasy smile. "I didn't."

"Do you remember our handshake?"

"Course I remember it." I nod my head. "Who you take me for? Behave."

As if I'd forget our secret handshake. Even though we haven't done it since the incident last summer.

"Do you remember what you said when we made it up?" I ask Dapo.

He nods. "Of course. You were being a wimp about me leaving you in junior school and going to senior school. So, *I* said something like be strong and be courageous and—"

"You were quoting the Bible," I say, rolling my eyes. "Can't believe I didn't see it then. You were such a Bible basher, bro."

Dapo laughs, and it's his turn to roll his eyes. "Whatever. As if I ever bashed you with the Bible. Anyway, look, back to the point. I said something else. I told you that the handshake was more than just a few seconds of fun. It was our thing. It meant—"

"Connection."

Dapo holds out a hand, and I take it. We go through the rhythms of our secret handshake. And after a series of flourishes, we end up in a tight hug that lasts for an infinite second.

Dapo huffs. "Glad you're all right, bro."

"Yuck. What have I told you about being a melt?" He blows in my ears, and I push away and scowl. "You're such a prick."

"Yeah, yeah," Dapo says. "Now tell us. What did you find out?"

"They hate Richard's guts. And for good reason..."

"Where are we going?" Dad grumbles as the vehicle glides through the island.

I wind the window down because it's stuffy in here. "Richard's Residence on the resort," I reply.

"Why?"

"Dad, I told you already. It has to be the key to getting off this island. That's where they're holed up, controlling everything. If we can get there and take back control, we can put a stop to this nightmare."

"All right."

Dad starts whistling a tune that fills the vehicle. I glance over my shoulder, and he's got his eyes closed, the faintest trace of a smile on his face. Contagious enough to make me smile, too. As long as we're within range of the control system, we're safe.

"Why are you smiling?" Mui asks, tilting her head. "Are you thinking of something happy?"

"Something like that." I swivel back around and look out the window. For all the madness on the island, I can't ignore its beauty. We pass green flowers that look like poppies with two, large shimmering antennae then come by an animal that looks like a koala with droopy ears and has a squirrel's tail. It crawls along the ground like a newborn, stopping only to munch on flowers and fallen fruit. Integrated seamlessly into all this wildlife is the weight of the resort, almost like Richard said in his welcome speech. Was that really just days ago?

THUD.

The vehicle wobbles, and my insides knot. "What's that?" Dad asks.

THUD.

"It's getting closer," Mui adds. Vibrations buzz through the seats. My heart yo-yos in my chest.

THUD.

"Speed up," I tell Dapo. "I think it's a—"

In the passenger-side mirror, a glass dragon bursts from the greenery on the left. Bigger than any I've ever seen, and easily the size of a horse. Charging straight for us.

I frown. We're back in the security zone. It shouldn't be chasing us.

Mui swivels around and looks out the rear window. "Wow," she exclaims.

Dad coughs. "What's going on?"

"We're being chased," Deja answers.

"Dapo, put your foot down," I order. "Comeoncomeoncomeon!"

"I *am* putting my foot down, but the thing's at its limit, I think."

I stare at the hulking glass dragon.

"Blood," Deja says. "By the ears."

Blood. By the ears. Where I assume its ears are, there are dry rivers of blood. *It can't hear.* And if it can't hear, then the control system is useless.

I look at the path behind us, and see squashed fruit. If we've driven over that and it's all over the tires then no wonder.

This is not good.

Dapo fumbles around with the gears, and for a split second there's a surge of speed. We bounce around inside as the engine races and roars. The glass dragon lunges off its hind legs...

A claw scrapes the back end of the vehicle but can't grab hold. The glass dragon falls away and is left in the dust. The silence is overwhelming.

My toes and hands curl tight. I take a deep, deep breath and release the tension. Relief crashes into me like a hug from behind.

I shake my head and close my eyes and try not to dwell on how close we came to...I open my eyes and turn to Dapo, who glances at me with a smile on his face. Not the happy kind. More the holy-crap-that-was-close kind.

Giving him a smile back I say, "Fam, that was—whoa, whOA, WHOA!"

I see the squat ruin before Dapo does.

CHAPTER 25

ONWARD

The vehicle swerves too late . . .

RIDES UP THE RUIN AND LIFTS UP INTO THE AIR . . .

ROTATES . . .

. . . *AND CRASHES.*

TIME SNAPS BACK INTO PLACE. MUFFLED AND HAZY
sound now rushes back. The first thing I notice is the aching in
my chest from the seatbelt. Then the fact we're upside down.
Everywhere hurts. But I can still move. I unbuckle myself, and
gravity pulls me down. I look around the car.

Everyone seems okay, if shaken. I help Mui and Deja unbuckle
themselves. We crawl out of the wreckage. I look back at the
vehicle—wheels spinning and battered—with trembling legs.
We got lucky.

It could have been so much worse.

Dad sets himself up against a tree and is wheezing with his hands on his knees. "Dapo, I did not teach you to drive so you can be nearly killing everybody. *But* I am glad everybody is okay."

"Cheers," Dapo grumbles. "Sorry, everyone, I wasn't paying attention."

Mui has her hands on her head, a small cut on her forehead. I stride over and crouch down to her level. "You all right?" I glance at Deja, who stares at the wreckage with her hands on her head. "And you, too? You good?"

Deja nods, traces of shock still on her face.

"Uh-huh," Mui says. "Just a bit of a bump." She looks up. "Looks like it's going to rain."

I look up at the darkening sky and gathering clouds. They're a shade of gray that indicates it's going to rain soon. I remember from one of the loudspeaker announcements there was a storm that was supposed to be grazing the island. Looks like it'll do more than graze.

I shudder at the thought of getting drenched in rain. I hope the clouds hold long enough for us to get off this place.

In the not-so-far distance, the growling hiss of a glass dragon pierces through my thoughts. It could be the one we evaded, which would be bad news. "We need to head over," I say, standing up. "Things will get harder and more dangerous if we're caught up in the rain."

When Mum proposed we tag along with Dad for his conference, I was not envisioning so much walking. Yet here we are, trudging across the island yet again. This time in the general direction of Richard Jenkins's residence. I don't know how I'd have managed without those painkillers I took. It's almost like they're deadening me to all the horrors, not just the physical pain.

We follow the brick path until the pearl path intersects it. Then we follow it up an incline before we realize we need to go off the path if we want to get there quicker.

As we wade through manicured woodlands, we see luggage and smears of blood. Bodies are hard to find, which sends a chill through me. The monorail track is above us and I spy a carriage halted on the line, windows shattered and smothered in blood.

It's getting darker and darker, colder and colder. Mui's gotten fond of Dad and Deja, and she insists they both hold her hands while she walks, with all three of them behind Dapo and me.

"So when we get to the residence, what's the plan?" Dapo asks. "You've thought about that, right?"

"Not at all, bro. I'm winging it. It would help if Valoisa was with us." I recall what Deja said, and my stomach knots. *You don't just go against your family like that. So maybe not.* "They probably know we triggered the alarms at the cottage."

"True."

"They'll see us coming."

"Probably."

"So honestly, there's not much we can plan. I think we need to react. Freestyle it, so to speak."

Dapo sighs. "I'm scared, man."

"Same," I breathe. "You know what's mad about this whole thing?"

"What?"

I clear my throat. It's dry. "We shouldn't even be here."

"I know, but Mum—"

"Not quite. The week before we got on the ferry, Mum told me that if I didn't speak with you—sort things out—she'd be forced to do something drastic. I *may* have refused."

Dapo nods and without warning slaps me in the side of my head. "Dumbass. But good thing you did, or it could have been Dad out here dealing with this alone."

I roll my eyes. I'm about to respond when there's a scream nearby. The strangled sound digs into my skin. Moments later, distant gunfire punches through the air. The howls and squawks of animals can be heard, too. Richard's men must be in a firefight.

The noises carry on for a bit, and then silence settles in. *I wonder what happened.* Whatever, knowing the answer isn't going to help us. For a short while, the tension eases. Until the strong stench of blood is carried on a fresh breeze that has added a fresh chill to the air.

Soon, we step past the arcade, and it is uncomfortable to breathe in, let alone look at. I do my best, but it's hard to ignore the puddles of blood or chunks of flesh. *Keep looking straight ahead.* I turn around. "Dapo, I think you … never mind." He's already carrying Mui and making sure her eyes are covered.

We navigate through the corpses in silence. For some reason, the control system here is offline. The wind rustles the leaves of the trees. I frown. *Why?* Could the time it was offline have affected things? Did Enelle damage it but not enough to ruin it completely?

And then there's something else. Something moving. Greenery whips and bends as someone wades through. Richard stumbles out, drenched in blood and dirt, looking bewildered.

Shocked.

His eyes lock onto us and he marches in our direction. There is a fear in his eyes—and it's feral.

"Th-th-th-they're dead," Richard stutters. Each word raises in volume. "All of them are—"

Valoisa emerges. Pristine. She clamps her hand over Richard's mouth and glares at him. *Shut the hell up*, her glare says. At this, Richard seems to collect himself and calm down. He raises his hands, gun in one hand, as if to say, *Got it.*

Valoisa removes her hands, and Richard sinks to his knees. "They are all dead," he whispers.

"So why aren't you?" Mui asks. She's still in Dapo's arms. The way she says it is so matter-of-fact that we all burst into tired laughter.

"Well," Richard starts, scratching the barrel of his gun against his scalp. "I got lucky. I ducked and hid and covered myself in dirt. Played dead, too. *She* found me. And here I am. Here we are again."

"That we are," I say.

"So, where are you off to?" he asks as he glances between the four of us.

"Your residence," Valoisa answers. Richard raises an eyebrow. "Am I right?"

I nod. *You don't just go against your family like that.* "It's where Enelle and Cuplow are. But you knew that, didn't you?"

"Knew what?" Valoisa has an edge to her voice. "Say what you mean."

"Did you send that huge glass dragon after us? All for the sake of Darlenia's future?"

"What huge glass dragon? What future? What are you talking about?"

I pull out the page from Enelle's notebook and thrust it at Valoisa. "You keep disappearing," I state. "And every time you do, we have the worst luck. Tell me it's a coincidence."

Valoisa reads what's on the page before tilting her chin down at me. She frowns. "I told you already, I didn't know their plan, and I had no idea about any of this. I didn't know he'd done this."

I glare at her. I don't know what to believe.

She huffs. "I am a Ruiz, Femi. And despite what my family has done, we are proud people. I promise you, I had no idea. I don't know what else I can do, but I told you I was here to help, and that is what I'm doing. If I knew this, do you think I wouldn't have left Richard to die?"

Warmth floods my face. It does make sense. If she knew about Richard poisoning her home, I don't think she would have brought him back in one piece. "Okay."

"If you're both done, we cannot go to my residence." Richard's tone is terse and sharp. "We can't."

"Why not?" Deja asks.

Richard huffs. Tracing the butt of his gun in the dirt. "It's what they want. To make a spectacle of me. I will not give them the satisfaction. I refuse."

"That's all well and good, but we're going to go on ahead. It's

231

the only way we can get off the island. Unless you have any better ideas, Mr. Jenkins?" Deja asks.

The silence hangs until Richard sighs and shakes his head. "You can't get there by foot."

"Really?" Mui asks.

At this, Richard seems to perk up a bit. Color rushes to his face. "Indeed. I made it that way. You can only reach it by monorail."

CHAPTER 26

LAND ANEMONE

IT'S A LONG WALK TO THE NEAREST MONORAIL STATION. Valoisa keeps giving me the evil eye, and Richard won't stop talking about his residence. He doesn't need anyone but himself to feed his ego.

I can't put all the blame on him, though. Mui won't stop asking him questions. His addiction to wonder has infected her.

"No way! You actually own this land?"

Richard puffs out his chest and nods. "Yes."

Valoisa shakes her head and scoffs. A bit. Too. Loud.

"What was that?" Richard asks.

"Idiot," she mumbles.

"If you have something to say, then say it. I don't suffer cowards."

Her fists clench and she spins on Richard. "Coward? You stained my home with your chemicals and used that exact moment to buy it. Everyone calls you a genius, but you're not." Richard stiffens. "In any case, you're the coward and it's pathetic."

The words sit for a moment as Richard looks her up and down. There's an intensity in his stare that looks as if it's going to bubble into anger. But in an instant the tension in his face fades and he looks at Mui. "It was a mistake. Anyway, if things weren't so manic, I would have shown you phase two of the resort. Alas. But listen..."

I zone out, my jaw clenched, unable to listen to Richard drone on. Someone draws up alongside me, and I think it's Dapo, but when I look up, it's Dad, with a smile that cuts through the weariness invading my legs.

"Son," he says.

I notice how dry his lips are and how red his eyes are. He looks awful. I frown. "Dad... are you okay?"

Thunder rumbles. The heavens are going to open up soon.

"Something came to mind," he says, ignoring my question. "To say to you. A prompting of the spirit."

I draw a deep breath. He wants to talk about his faith *now*? Exhaling, I say, "Yeah?"

"We live in a world of pain. No one is excused from that. But everything that happens is according to God's purpose."

"What purpose could this"—I stretch my arms and gesture at the dead around us, at the dirt laced with blood—"have? I don't get it. At all."

Dad sighs. "I don't have any easy answers for you. Nothing I say will make a lightbulb go off in your head. But I have considerations. They help me make sense of this... this... what do you call it?"

"Madness."

"Yes, exactly." He sticks up his index finger. "One, horrible

234

things happen in this world, but it is not the end. There is more after, and that after will be *good*." Another finger goes up. "Two, I believe God is both sovereign and good in every sense of the word, and if that's true, then it means the purpose is good. Even if it is not understood."

I can't help the way my face scrunches up at consideration number two. "But isn't that frustrating? If God is who you say He is, then what is He doing? What you said feels convenient."

"Son." Dad's voice is firm, and safe, and full of warmth. "I did say I had no easy answers. And yes, it is frustrating . . . at times. But I would encourage you not to think I believe in God because it's convenient."

"Go on, then, encourage me," I say. I know I'm giving Dad a bit of a hard time, but we're talking freely, and I love it.

"Well, okay, then. Think like this. The ferry we got on left the UK and set out for Darlenia. Its destination had been fixed and agreed upon by the people in charge. Nothing could change it."

"A storm," I state.

Dad laughs. "Behave. It's an illustration for a point that is too big to understand. Anyway, assuming there is *nothing* that can change it, you could say that's an example of sovereignty. Now when we were on the ferry, we knew where we were going, right?" I nod. "We weren't being held hostage or reading a script. We ate, we slept, we watched movies, read, talked, et cetera. But still the ferry was taking us toward the island."

"Okay."

"That's exactly why it isn't *convenient*. Because I know in my bones where that final destination is. If I didn't, then I'd be lost. Then it would be convenient. Then what's happening would feel terrifyingly hopeless. But I know whatever happens is part of a bigger plan."

"Fair enough." It doesn't make sense to me, and yet it sort of does. But how he can get comfort from believing this is part of a bigger plan confuses me.

He places a hand on my back. "Love you, son."

Shrugging him off, I sigh, and say, "You too, Dad."

Satisfied, Dad goes to chat with Dapo, leaving me to walk with only my thoughts. They're all jumbled and pinball all over the place. I think of Mum. Does she wonder why we haven't been in touch? Or has she been having too much of a fun time with her girls that she's the one who's forgotten about us?

I walk into the back of Dad, who's stopped dead in his tracks. Everyone else, too. Their gazes are glued on something strange. A large colored... *thing*.

Sitting in front of the monorail entrance, the thing has a cylindrical body, with lots of flowy tentacles trapping a tasseled feline that makes no attempt to wrestle itself free.

"It's paralyzed," Dapo offers. There's a pulse of light that travels through one of the tentacles wrapped around the motionless feline. "Must have gotten stunned."

We watch the *thing* pull the feline apart limb by limb, blood and guts squirting, before shoveling the pieces toward a mouth in the middle. We all look to Valoisa—our resident expert.

She shrugs, closes her eyes, and starts speaking. "Not good. This is an ultra-anemone. If it touches you, you're dead." Her eyes open, and she gazes at it for a while. Then, "Follow me," she says only to me. We wade through shallow foliage and come to a stop in front of a large potted plant. *Why on earth is there a potted plant in the middle of the woods? Not important.* Picking up one side each, we shuffle back toward the group and anemone.

"On the count of three, we're gonna throw it, all right?" Valoisa must have seen the puzzled look clouding my face. "Trust me. This will work. Okay? One . . . two . . . *three.*"

With all our might, we throw the potted plant toward the anemone. It shatters on the brick path, and the creature begins to move, flexing and twisting its body toward the plant. Tentacles shoot outward like harpoons and pulse with light. They wrap themselves around the pieces of plant and clay, shoveling them into its mouth.

There's a moment of stillness before the anemone spits the bits of plant and dirt and clay back out. It retreats back to the monorail entrance, blotting out most of the glass structure behind it. As if that spot belongs to it.

"So what was the point of that?" Deja asks Valoisa, with a hint of annoyance.

Valoisa shrugs. "Simple. To learn. And we learned two things. First, we learned it reacts to sound and movement. Second, it's territorial. If we want to get past it and its tentacles, we need to distract it. That's the plan. Everyone, let's go find a few things that we can throw."

Deja nods with her eyebrows knit together.

"I'll, uh, wait here and stand guard." Richard waves his gun.

"Okay? Fine. Just . . . whatever." I can't deal with Richard's strange cowardice right now. We all take care to stay quiet as we survey the surrounding area looking for items to throw.

We end up with two items—another large potted plant and

a large glass coffee table. I have no idea where they got the table from, but it's perfect.

"Get ready to run for it when the table breaks," Valoisa whispers. On the count of three, Dapo and I send the glass table high into the air. And as it comes crashing down, Deja and Valoisa throw the potted plant.

The response from the anemone is instant. The tentacles twitch, and it grunts in this odd, warbled way as it flexes and twists toward the noise. Dad, Mui, and Richard rush toward the escalator leading up to the monorail.

Deja, Dapo, Valoisa, and I are close behind. We don't have long before the anemone pukes up the rubbish we've baited it with and returns.

uUuURGGG! the creature sounds, as if it's burping. A quick glance over my shoulder reveals it rushing toward us, then veering toward the escalator. It barrels into the side of it, sounding off another burping grunt.

The escalator shudders and groans and begins to eat its own steps. *Crapcrapcrap.*

Dapo inhales. "Oh shit, we pissed it off."

"You swear now?" I say, my eyes fixed on the grunting anemone.

"Only under extremely stressful circumstances."

"Well, we're going to need to find another way up to the—" There's movement in my periphery toward the creature. It's Mui. And she's hefting a large rock. "Hey, hey, Mui." I rush toward her. "No! Stop!"

Too late.

She flings it toward the creature and backs away. It lands on one of the long tentacles and pins it to the ground.

After a painful few seconds of agonizing silence, the creature makes a sound like a foghorn, and Mui shrieks. Tentacles harpoon toward her. She shrieks again and stumbles backward, bursting into sobbing tears, wailing like there's no tomorrow. Tentacles slip over her head and grab at nothing. Deja pulls her to safety and the tentacles curl back toward the anemone's body, ready to stretch outward again.

I run toward Mui and Deja, crouching down so I'm at Mui's eye level.

"You're okay, you're okay." The anemone grunts behind us, and I hear it move, drawn to Mui's tears. "We're fine, we're fine." I rise up and pull Deja into a hug. Our cheeks squish together, and I want to stay like this for a while longer. Pull back from her and say everything I've been thinking and feeling. But now is not the time.

Instead, I say, "Thank you."

I frown because Richard is standing still. There's a glossy look on his face. Hyperfocused. As if he's in a trance.

"Hey, Richard, what are you—"

Richard points his gun. "It will fire for me. Yes, it will."

He's lost it, babbling nonsense. I'm not even sure he believes himself, the way his arms and legs are trembling. "We need to go. Don't worry about being the hero."

"It will fire for me," Richard repeats again, still trembling. He's got blinders and ear mufflers on. "It will fire for me. It will—"

"Give me that." Dad appears and wrestles the gun away

from Richard, who struggles to take his gun back. The anemone grunts, and that's enough for Richard to flinch and lose the tug-of-war. He scrambles backward. "I'll deal with it. You lot go on; I'll be right behind," Dad says.

"Dad," I say, glancing at the incoming anemone. "We're not doing this again. Let's just all go."

"Son. Don't worry about me. I'm telling you. Go. I will catch up. You may not know this about your dad, but I know how to handle a gun."

I huff. "Dad, I swear—" Someone yanks my top. *Dapo.*

"Good, get your brother out of here." Dad nods at Dapo, smiling at us, wide and full of love. "I'm proud of you both. Now hurry. I have a bone to pick."

He turns his back on us and takes aim while we slink off to where Richard is trembling by a tree. I keep looking over my shoulder as Dad cocks the gun and waits.

He waits.

And waits.

And waits.

Click.

Dad looks down at the gun, points, and tries again.

Click.

Richard begins to giggle. I flash him a glare full of worry. "What's so funny?" I hear my heartbeat in my ears.

Click.

"I'm afraid the gun won't fire," Richard states.

My blood turns to slush. "What?"

Click.

Richard wears a wry smile. "It will only fire for me."

"Wh-what…?" Panic invades my very being. I turn from Richard to Dad, who looks at us. There is fear in his eyes.

But it morphs into resolve. He takes a deep breath.

Nonono.

"Sons," he shouts, letting the gun drop to the ground. The hulking mass of the creature isn't far away now. It looms large behind him. "Be good. I love you bo—"

A tentacle wraps around him. With a pulse of light, Dad goes limp. A shriek erupts from the depths of my soul. I don't think, rushing to get to my feet. But Dapo holds me back.

"Get *off* me." I struggle, my voice a storm of emotion. "L-let me go. We can't. We can't. We can't…"

My anger—grief—burns. I turn on Dapo. How can he do this when Dad's being torn apart? I try to break free, but he's stronger than me. I glance at Dapo, ready to cuss him out for stopping me. I don't. Tears fall as he sobs without a sound. I stop resisting. Deja and Mui look crushed. Even Valoisa has her hand over her mouth.

Richard coughs. "We need to get going. I don't feel comfortable staying here. We're sitting—"

"Shut up! Just shut up!" I scream, not caring how loud I am.

"If we stay here, we aren't safe."

"You *don't* get it. He is—was—my dad."

"Fems," Dapo whispers, through his own tears.

I glare at Richard. "This whole mess is your fault."

"My fault?" Richard seems offended. "None of this is my fault."

My mouth hangs open, and I laugh. "You stupid little man."

"Don't you dare. I have done nothing wrong. *Nothing.* I am the victim here."

"VICTIM?!" Noise warbles. "What are you talking about?! If you want to talk about a victim"—I point toward where the anemone got my dad—"*my dad* is a victim."

"Your dad was reckless."

My anger explodes.

III
HAVOC

"And when Alexander saw the breadth of his domain, he wept, for there were no more worlds to conquer."

—**Hans Gruber, *Die Hard***

"No one wants to hear our stories. What we've experienced. No one wants to look at despair. At what haunts them."

—**Former Darlenia resident**

"At first, I thought it was enough to be seen, but once that happened, I longed to be understood. Still, I want more. And when I ponder it, all that's left is to be remembered."

—**Richard Jenkins, *Vanity Fair* interview**

CHAPTER 27

REGROUP

I TURN ON RICHARD, WHOSE GAZE IS FIXED ON HIS gun now that the anemone has retreated back toward the monorail entrance. He steps toward the gun, but I block his path.

"You aren't a victim!" I scoff, jabbing a finger into his chest.

Richard swats away my finger. "You need to calm down."

"C-calm down?" I turn to Dapo. "Did he tell me to *calm down?*"

"Femi…" Dapo tries to reach for me, but I squirm away from him and fix my glare back on Richard, who's smoothing out his top, truly devoid of any sense of guilt or responsibility. I take a deep breath.

And then I lunge at him.

We go tumbling down into the dirt. I am *not* a fighter, but I know how to move my hands and arms with rhythm. They thrash and slap and thud against Richard.

"Get him off me! Get him *OFF*!" Richard cries.

He hits out and lands a punch into my chest that empties my

lungs of air and has me spluttering. I grit my teeth. Clench my jaw. Use my fist as a hammer and hit him right back in his chest. He kicks me off and we roll away from each other.

Both of us pant and gasp and stagger to our feet like we're about to go another round, and then Deja steps into the space between us and mouths, *Enough!*

I want to blank out. But the way Deja pleads with her eyes stops me. I don't want to disappoint her. I don't want to do something stupid that would cause more harm than good. I lift my hands in surrender. *I get it, I get it. We've got bigger problems.* Richard looks rattled. Like he isn't sure whether he should be more worried about me or the wildlife.

The answer is both.

"Let's all take a moment to calm down," Deja says. "Then we can get going again."

Everyone knows better than to come talk to me. Well, Mui doesn't, but she's pulled away by Deja. I rub my hands up and down my face, unable to make sense of anything. I want to cry, I want to scream, and I want... my dad back.

So, this is what it's like to hate someone, I think, looking over at Richard. Mum says hating someone means you're murdering them in your heart, and I've murdered him in so many ways.

"Hey," Deja says after I've sat in my hatred for several minutes.

She sits next to me and leans her head on my shoulder, and in that moment, something in me cracks and splinters. My eyes water.

"I'm sorry," I say. I don't dare look at her. I'll start crying if I do, and know it would take a while for me to stop. "I'm sorry... for my part in all of this."

"Look, I still think you could've handled things way better. And I can't pretend all is good between us. But I know you thought you were helping. And it's not how things start that matters. It's how they finish. We'll be okay."

Her words are everything and not enough. "Thank you."

We sit there for who knows how long. It's silent, but the moment keeps me from sinking into the nightmare. I lock eyes with Dapo.

He tilts his head. *You ready?*

I'm not, but I nod. I'm functional, and that'll have to do.

"Mr. Jenkins," Dapo starts. "Is there another way to your residence? Maybe another monorail stop we can walk to?"

"Yes. Not a monorail, though." Richard points toward a communications mast with the defective gun he's retrieved. It glints in the afternoon light. "I built a tunnel between it and my residence. For when I—"

"Okay, then, lead the way," Valoisa says, interrupting. There's a hint of a snarl on her face, and judging by the way her fists are clenched, I know she has had more than enough of Richard.

"C-certainly," Richard whispers.

The walk is silent, and we walk in single file, except for me and Deja. We're side by side. I don't mind lagging, and I definitely don't mind Deja.

She holds my hand and squeezes every now and then. Each squeeze helps me put one foot in front of the other. Each squeeze stops me shutting down. Each squeeze gives me the courage to tell her how I feel. "Deja, I—"

That's when the rain buckets down in drenching sheets and we seek shelter in the combination Harrods and Waitrose. I know things are dire when the dead bodies littering the front don't bother me.

"Don't look," I whisper to Deja as she trembles.

Richard slinks off to the drinks part of the shop and pours himself one. Mui says she's going to explore and drags Deja away with her.

If I were a drinker and I didn't hate Richard, I'd be right there with him. Instead, I spin around in one of those chairs they use to thread eyebrows, face scrunched while I—

"Femi." Dapo stops the chair from spinning and peers over me, casting a shadow on my face. "I'm not going to ask you if you're okay."

I laugh. "Cheers."

"I have an idea."

"Yeah?"

"A force field of sorts. We need an easier way to move. I've been thinking a lot, the control system before was all sonic, right? I noticed when you were warning us about when we were okay to talk and when we weren't. We need to find the right frequency—then we can make it so no creature wants to come anywhere near us."

"Uh-huh." I tilt my head. "How, though?"

"Frequency. Speakers." Dapo smiles. "And your ability to make sounds."

I sit up, energy zipping through my body as it dawns on me.

"If we know the frequency the security was emitting, then you can replicate it using one of your music apps," Dapo continues. "That's where speakers come in. So that it's audible and loud enough, we need a speaker. I've looked and there aren't any here, so we need to find some. Portable is best, which we can hook up to via Bluetooth. Put it all together, and we can create the force field on demand."

"That could work."

We gather Deja and Valoisa and lay out Dapo's idea.

For several seconds, they say nothing, and my excitement begins to fade. "Look, if you don't think it's a good idea, we can—"

"No, no, no." Deja waves her hands. "It's a *brilliant* idea. So brilliant I was letting it marinate. Like, wow. It's almost like this moment was made for you. But question: Where are we going to get the frequency from?"

At that moment Richard emerges, glass in one hand, bottle in the other.

Everything about him makes me sick. I point at him. "He might not know off the top of his head, but he'll know where we'll need to look."

Richard's face contorts as he takes a large gulp of whiskey. "What's this?"

"The frequency of the security system," Dapo answers. "My brother seems to think you'll know where we can find it."

"Your brother would be correct." It's slight, but the first signs of slurring are entering Richard's speech. "If we find one of the control panels you can see what the frequency is set to. Alberto explained it once. However, we'll need his access credentials. And, well, those are stored in one place..."

"Where's that?"

Richard brandishes his wrist, flashing his smartwatch.

Dapo gulps. "Are you saying what I think you're saying?"

Richard nods. "If you think that you need to find Alberto, then A-plus in the area of deduction." Richard coughs. "But why do you need the frequency?" Richard's gaze settles on me.

"We need a force field—a deterrent. We can't rely on stealth." I explain Dapo's plan, and Richard laughs. Deja takes my hand and squeezes. I compose myself. "What?"

"Nothing particularly." He shrugs. "Only that I wish I'd come up with that idea myself. It is ingenious. But there is the matter of Alberto's location. If I had access, I could locate him. Maybe if I . . . no, that wouldn't work . . ."

"We know where Alberto is," Dapo and I say in unison. Richard quirks an eyebrow that falls back in place when he understands the subtext.

"Oh."

"Yep," Dapo breathes. "So, here's what I think: me, Richard, and Valoisa—we go and get the watch and frequency. Femi, you, Mui, and Deja go get the chargers and speakers." Dapo strides to the nearest window and peers out. "Still raining, but it's a lot lighter. Let's agree to meet at the communications mast in about an hour?"

"Sounds like a plan," I offer.

At that moment, Mui appears out of breath with eyes wide like moons. "Everyone."

"Uh-huh?"

She swallows. "I found *the* coolest thing ever."

"What?"

"You're going to have to come and check it out." She grabs my hand and yanks. "Now, now, now. Everyone."

"Okay, okay. I'm coming."

Mui leads us behind the counter and points. "Look at that."

I crouch down.

Eggs.

All hatched, apart from one that wobbles and has a thin opening. It makes me jump. I pick up a fragment of the shell—and watch in amazement as the color changes in the light.

I turn to Mui. "Very cool."

The egg moves again, attempting to roll but never quite gaining any traction. Then a slick, translucent head sprouts, eyes gray and blinking. A baby glass dragon, it looks like. Its eyes close as it gulps in the air and struggles to wriggle out of the egg. It looks so adorable.

"Wah," Mui gasps. "I know the bigger ones are really scary, but how cute is that?"

"Very," Deja acknowledges.

Despite knowing the predator the glass dragon will become, I appreciate its beauty. And in a weird way, I don't blame them for being vicious. The animals turning on humans isn't surprising. They've been forced to be docile for so long, why wouldn't they descend into a frenzy?

The distant sound of thunder pulls me from my thoughts.

"We should get moving," Dapo states. He's pulling on a raincoat, plucked from one of the clothing racks. The rest of us do the same. "See you at the communications mast."

CHAPTER 28

LAND EEL

DEJA AND I WALK ON EITHER SIDE OF MUI, AN EMPTY backpack taken from a room slung over my shoulder. We're heading down the steep part of the pearl path toward the villas. Perched on the trees are golden raptors that pay us no mind as the rain falls. We take care where we step.

The way the wind blows and scuttles leaves helps, too. I look around. The island is a far cry from how it looked when we arrived. Gone is the awe, swept away by violence, and in its place is despair and nervousness.

I glance down at Mui—the source of my nervousness— whose gaze stays glued all around her. More than once I'm forced to tug on her top to make sure she doesn't go stumbling and give our position away.

This might be one of the *longest* walks of my life.

We come to the area that's home to the villas. The timer counts down on my phone. Ten minutes gone, fifty minutes to get what we need and reach the communications mast.

Mui pulls on my raincoat. "I think we're being followed," she whispers.

"Followed?" I hate the way my voice wobbles. "By who?"

Her only response is wide eyes and a finger pointing upward. My gaze slingshots in that direction. On top of one of the villas is the large shadow of a creature that turns my heart into a pulpy mess.

What nonsense is this one again?

Unlike the other animals on the island that have iridescent, translucent, or golden features, this animal has gray-red, mottled skin and eye sockets without any eyes. Its skin ripples.

And then I remember what Valoisa told me: *The Ghosts of Darlenia. They can't see, but they perceive. They are cunning creatures that come slithering out when there's rain—which isn't often. A kill here and there. It is enough for them for weeks.*

This must be a land eel.

Common sense jolts me into action, and I put myself between the creature and Mui and Deja. Without looking back, I say, "Stay behind me. We're going to start moving backward... slowly. When you're both close enough to climb through the nearest window, you do that."

"Femi... I'm scared," Mui says.

"I know, I know. But I need you to be brave. I need you to look for portable speakers and chargers with Deja. And when you get them, stay hidden; I'll come and find you. Remember what I told you, the speakers need to have the... what? Tell me, Mui."

"The, uh, the... uh... Bluetooth symbol."

"That's right," I soothe. "We're gonna start moving now, okay?"

"O-o-kay."

We start moving backward. The words Valoisa said cling to my mind. I leave several seconds between each step. I don't want the land eel to catch on. We reach the nearest window, and the girls climb their way in. Except Deja lingers in the window.

"What are you doing?"

"You're so annoying," Deja mumbles. There's a moment of silence before she leans in and gives me a peck on the cheek. "Be careful."

"I promise," I answer. Butterflies swarm my stomach, and it takes everything not to burst into a smile. The sound of their feet padding into the distance feels like a weight off my shoulders, and it's only then I smile, wondering if maybe my feelings could be reciprocated.

Concentrate.

The land eel in front of me hasn't moved an inch. A large wormy gargoyle.

I recall Valoisa's words. *But that's not even the most interesting thing about them. Their skin only ripples when they're hunting.*

I take the deepest of breaths and psych myself up.

And when they hunt, they want their prey to know it. In fact, they bank on it because that is their true face. That is when they act.

The creature rears up.

Waiting for even the

slightest sign of movement.

One final breath. A silent prayer. And then—

I run for it.

THE LAND EEL CLICKS.

CLUCLUCUG!

In my periphery, I see it slither down the front of the villa. Ready to hunt. Gooseflesh breaks out all over me. *What is the plan?* I scream at myself.

My heart thunders. Because right now I don't have a plan.

The clicking gets louder, and I pick up the pace. An idea hits. *Zigzag.* Isn't that like a universal truth, kinda?

I make a sharp turn to the left and slip by a water fountain. There's a loud *THUD*, and I take a quick glance. The eel has run over the water fountain. I zig right past a food cart stand before zagging back left.

My muscles burn.

Another *THUD*. Another glance. The eel has rammed right through the kiosk as if it wasn't there. And that gives me an idea. The eel isn't going to let up. So . . .

Let's see how you feel running through something a lot sturdier.

I keep zigzagging, looking for something to test the eel with. All the while, the clicks build in volume. The sounds fuse with my beating heart that rattles my rib cage. A shudder scuttles down my spine.

There!

Up ahead is a large glass revolving door. The entrance to the island's onsite bank. I curve my run right to chart a course through the archipelago of kiosks. Weaving in and out. Anything to slow the eel down a fraction and buy me enough time to make one final burst.

Every other step is a loud *BANG* and *CRASH*. A quick glance back confirms scattered kiosks and the eel is a bit closer. My heart clogs my throat. Swallowing it back down, I give everything to sprint for the revolving door. *Don't think. Don't look.*

CLUCLUCLUG!!

Run.

I focus on pumping my arms and driving my knees—lessons learned from summer PE in year nine, when we did one-hundred-meter sprints. At this point I'll try anything.

CLUCLUCLUGGG!

Almost there. A few more strides and then let's see this lumpy thing smash through several layers of glass.

CLUCLUCLUCLUCUGGG!

I push through the revolving door. Seconds later, there's a massive crash, and I flinch, falling to my knees as glass shatters. I curl up on the floor, covered in glass, and squeeze my eyes shut. If this is the end, I don't want to see it coming.

Except...

Everything is quiet. I open my eyes and roll over, taking care not to slice myself on the glass that's everywhere. Hanging halfway through the revolving door, the eel is limp. Dead still. I swallow and get to my feet. Taking deep breaths, I creep closer, panting, exhausted, and ready to bolt if I have to.

"Mad," I mumble, spotting syrupy-red rivers of blood oozing from the glass. "It's dead." I wheeze out a small laugh and break into a small dance consisting of multiple fists pumps. I exhale.

I hear glass crunching and my heart is ready to burst. But it's Deja and Mui walking toward me, Mui struggling to carry a bag of stuff. They stop outside the bank entrance, on one side of the dead eel.

"We got them," Mui says, smiling. "With the Bluetooth symbol just like you said."

"I told you to stay hidden," I answer. More to Deja than Mui.

"Yeah, well, it is what it is…plus, we're fine. Are you okay?"

"Eh, more or less." We stare at each other for a moment and then we burst into smiles. "Right, let's check what you—"

I take a sharp step back.

"What is that *smell*?" Mui exclaims.

"I…think it's the eel." The air smells rotten. Like bad fish.

"Because it's dead?"

"Probably. Anyhow, let's see what goodies you've brought me." I take the bag from Mui and rifle through. "Perfect."

Mui comes up alongside me. "So what now?"

"Now? Now we head to the communications mast, where everyone else should be waiting."

The journey to the communications mast, along the redbrick road is slow going. Every five minutes we're forced to pause or hide behind upturned kiosks as animals scavenge through garbage and the known predators prowl. For the other animals that have overrun the resort, there's no easy way to tell if they're carnivores or not. Better safe than sorry. Also, I am *starving*.

So naturally, we stop for food at one of the nearby combination shops—Liberty's and M&S Food. The lights flicker on and off, illuminating the blood smeared on the stone floors. And yet…there aren't any bodies to be seen.

My heart thuds—I'm on high alert. "Meet back here in five minutes," I say, handing Mui the phone so she can use it as a timer. "Be careful. I'm not sure what's lurking here."

I watch Mui step away toward the sweets and snack aisles.

"Of course," I mutter, smiling at her predictability. I head toward the sandwich section with Deja, and we rifle through the available selection. After a short bit of deliberation, I pick a few things out.

The sandwich and drink are lukewarm, but I don't care. It's edible. Food secured, we head back to the meeting spot, and I wolf down one sandwich, washing it down with a swig of Fanta. I'm halfway through the second sandwich when Mui appears. There's no food in her hands.

Instead, a panicked look flashes across her face, and she glances over her shoulder.

"What is it?" I ask, sitting up straighter, placing my sandwich back in its container and setting it down.

Mui wrings her hands. "We have a teensy-weensy problem."

"What kind of teensy-weensy problem?" Deja asks.

"Another one."

I frown. "Another what?"

Eel, Mui mouths. *It's following.*

My eyes close. After a deep breath, I open my eyes to scan the space. Sure enough, I spot a faint flicker of movement from an eel. As *if* I have the energy to deal with another one right now.

Maybe this is how it ends. Maybe I should—

A sharp finger prods my side, and I suppress a yelp. I glare at Mui, who has a speaker in her hand. I tilt my head at her. Confused.

"Ultra-flashbang grenade," she whispers with a smile on her face. "Like *The Guests*."

Understanding dawns on me. It will mean one less speaker to use, but I waste no time connecting my phone to the speaker and amping up the volume. "On three we need to walk out the front door calmly, okay? If we run, the eel will know. Got it?"

Mui nods.

"Got it," Deja whispers.

Scrolling through my downloaded songs, I look for the perfect one. A song that sounds like fear: "u" by Kendrick Lamar.

After using my fingers to signal a countdown, I slide the speaker as far away from us as I can down an aisle. Before it disappears out of sight, I press play, and Kendrick's vocals blare out.

"AhHhHhHhHhH."

There's crashing movement as the eel rushes after the sound. Mui, Deja, and I head toward the entrance at a slow pace. I snag a couple of bottles of water on the way.

Easing the door open, we slip outside and head for the nearest bed of dirt. Using one of the bottles, I pour so the dirt is easier to smear over ourselves.

"Yuck," Deja complains.

I shake my head. "Deja, you've barely covered yourself." I grab a clump of dirt—now mud—and fling it at her. It lands splat on her chest. "There, that's better."

There's rustling up above, and I spy another animal that isn't baying for blood—one I've never seen before. And with the watches having no service, I can't scan it in real time to identify it. I call it a tree rabbit. No different to regular rabbits, except here, their limbs enable them to climb. The longer I stare, the stranger the scene looks. This whole island is strange.

And to think a chemical spill spawned all of this.

"Hey, Femi," Deja calls, pulling me from my thoughts.

I glance down. "Ye—"

"Catch."

Mud slaps me in my face, and I take a few seconds to process what happened. My thoughts are interspersed with Mui's soft laughter. She proceeds to fling some more mud at me. Swiping the mud away, I shake my head and can't help but bubble into laughter, too. "Well, looks like we're all smothered now. We should get going."

Mui grabs my hand and squeezes. She grabs Deja's hand, too. "To the tower we go."

CHAPTER 29

AN APOLOGY

By the time we make it to the communications mast—it looks like a mini Eiffel Tower covered in satellites—the sun is lower in the sky, tinting it tangerine. Valoisa, Dapo, and Richard are waiting, and compared to us they look pristine.

"Took you long enough," Dapo says, looking us up and down. "Don't tell me . . . glass dragons?"

I shake my head. "Worse. Eels. Killed one, evaded the other."

"Huh, fair enough. Get what we needed?"

"Of course," I say with a nod. Mui presents the bag of chargers and speakers. "You?"

"Kinda. We got the watch, and after some tinkering, it led us to . . . this." Dapo hands me a thick-looking binder. "We know the answer's in here, but it's sort of"—he swipes a hand over his head—"a lot."

My eyebrow quirks. "All I'm hearing is that you're too lazy to figure it out yourself and so you're dumping it on the little bro."

"Yep. Spot on. Now figure it out."

Dapo places a hand on my shoulder and for a ground-trembling moment, it has the same weight as Dad's. My breath hitches and stomach twists. I can feel—*hear*—the thud, thud, thudding of my heart.

"...ems...Fems?"

And like that, the moment is broken. "Huh?"

"I said, let me know if you need me to help in any way, go on a supply run or something."

"Yeah, uh, of course. Give me a mo."

The binder is thick and heavy with a table of contents several pages long. *This is going to take ages.* I flick through, hopping between the contents page and the sections I think could have the answers. How is there nothing useful under the security section?

I'm in the lower half of the contents page now when I come across a section called Safety Protocols. This should have what we need. Scanning through the subsections I'm about to call it quits when I come across **SOLAR S4 48+**.

A quick scan ahead confirms it. I read through this section and it has everything...except for the frequency the resort uses to nullify the wildlife. "Crap."

"What is it?" Dapo asks.

"There's nothing here to do with the frequency we need." Dapo *hmm*s and says nothing. He knows as well as I do that we're stuck without that number. "There must be some way to work it out, right?"

Dapo closes his eyes and takes a deep breath. Thinking. He stays like this for a good while before his eyes open again. "I've got it," he says. "We experiment."

"Experiment?"

"Yeah, we can get a live sample—one of the many bugs milling around. I'm sure they were affected by the security system, too. I remember I saw them, but none of them could fly, even the ones with wings. They sort of crawled and hopped everywhere. We find one, and we start cycling through the frequencies till we find the right one."

"Okay, so all we need to do is—"

"Got one," Mui interrupts. "A bug. In my hands. Where can I put it?"

Glancing around the base of the communications mast, I see a discarded plastic cup. "In here," I say, placing the plastic cup upside down on a nearby trash can. On three. One, two . . . three."

In a couple of fluid motions, the bug Mui caught bounces off the inside of the cup. Black and hairy, it's also large and clumsy, with too-small wings and gangly legs. I have no idea how Mui felt okay catching it.

Without a word I get to work trying to synthesize the correct frequency the only way I know how—as if it's an element for a new beat.

I start with my mouth, latching onto my memories of what the control system sounds like. Before I know it, I'm using my app to record my high-pitch humming. My voice can't go any higher, but I don't need to since the app does the rest. As long as I'm in the right ballpark, that should be enough.

My humming loops, and as it plays I grimace. Perfect. I remember the security system being grating. Energy rushes into the tips of my toes and fingers.

I tinker, dialing up the frequency, compressing the sound to even things out, seeing if it's worth playing around with feedback effects to amplify sonic irritation. I'm using whatever tools I have at my disposal.

Until . . .

       Until . . .

              Until . . .

My eyes squeeze shut because the noise my phone is generating is beyond horrible. It fills my ears. I scrunch my toes. I hadn't missed this feeling. Like a small fly has gotten trapped in each ear and can't find its way out.

The bug trapped inside the plastic cup isn't buzzing around anymore. It's on the top of the trash can, barely moving. Docile.

"Voilà," I say aloud, and I put in the earplugs Dapo got me.

It takes us moments to hook up the speakers and have an irritable sound pulse around us. I wince. "We're in business." I turn in Richard's direction, my gaze slipping past him and never settling on his face. "You said there's a way into your residence from here—a tunnel?"

Richard nods. "Yes, yes," he says. "Follow me."

The entrance we're led to is unexpected. I thought it would be a discreet, secret-entrance type of thing. Instead, it's in plain sight with no frills. There are some steps down, and around the corner is an iron gate that has been warped by some hulking force.

"It seems our island friends got here first. Guess they didn't think to unlock the latch like civilized creatures," Richard says, chuckling at his own words.

Nah, he's taking the piss. So I stop and turn, making sure he sees me glaring. But before I can get my words out, Valoisa is one step ahead.

"And yet the supposed civilized creatures are the main reason we're in this mess."

"Touché," Richard grumbles. "This way."

The tunnel is dim, a little damp, and stuffy with humidity. Each step echoes off the walls. A chilling tune plays in my head. *We're off to see Ms. Enelle . . . the spiteful Darlenian girl.*

My throat is dry, and my heart hammers against my chest. Because what if I've made a mistake in my thinking? What if I'm missing something crucial? What if—

"It'll work," Dapo says, falling in step next to me. "And if it doesn't, we'll figure it out. Say it."

I blow air out my nostrils. "It'll work . . . and if it doesn't we'll figure it out."

"Good." He slings his arm over my shoulder, and for once the weight of his arm feels good—reassuring. "Mui, do you mind walking with everyone else? I want to speak to the little bro alone."

Mui scrunches up her face. "But then I have to be near Richard, and he's so crinnnnge."

"I know, but I need to speak to Fems. How about this—if you do me this favor, then I owe you a favor?"

"Fine. But I'm going to make sure it's the biggest, bestest favor ever." And with that, Mui stalks off toward everyone else.

"I thought you'd have shrugged me off by now, bro."

I roll my eyes. "Speak. I know you've got something lecture-y to say. So, speak. But if you're about to go war and peace on why I need to forgive Richard, then forget about it."

"You know me so well, little bro, but nah, I'm going to park that convo for now. Plus, it would be hypocritical of me if I told you that. I don't think you get how angry I am with him."

"So, what did you want to talk to me about?"

"Well, contingencies, really. In case only one of us … is there at the end, and what that might mean."

I swallow, because this type of conversation is so much worse than talking about forgiveness. "Why now?"

"Because … *look* at what happened to Dad, Femi." He looks away from me up ahead at everyone else. "Mui's just a child. And I don't trust Richard. Valoisa will hesitate. I can feel it—it's her family. And it doesn't feel fair to ask Deja to bear the responsibility for the worst-case scenario. It … just doesn't. So … that leaves us."

"Right."

"Before we get on with it, though, there's a few things I need to say to you. I've been writing them down in my notes app, actually." Dapo glances down, and in a few taps is reading from a screen. "When this is over you need to let him know that he means the world to you. That you've been harsh. Bruised him a bit too much. Words and conflict aren't your strong suit."

"Bro, it's okay, you don't—"

"I have to," Dapo says. He clears his throat. "When this is over you need to get the words out. But what am I going to say? And will he listen? God, you're gonna have to help me articulate. I guess 'sorry' is a good place to start. Sorry I was a drifting cloud; sorry for being cold metal; sorry for not hearing you; and sorry for being a 'colleague' and not a brother." He looks up from his phone. "Bro—I love you. And that's on everything. I know I can't pick you up myself. But I can show you there's still something to hope for."

The lump in my throat is dense and makes it hard to speak. I didn't realize I needed to hear him say any of that. But I manage to squeeze out two words. "Thank you."

Dapo doesn't dwell on the moment; instead, he removes his arm and carries on. "So, contingencies. Save yourself, Deja, and Mui. That's it. My lecture. No *ifs*, no *buts*. All right? If crap hits the fan, then you're the ones who need to survive."

"What?" I'm trying to process what Dapo is saying. "No? Why would I . . . leave you? That doesn't make any sense." I shake my head. "No."

"Unfortunately, this isn't a negotiation. I need you to promise me. Just like we were kids. Pinkie swear and whoever breaks it will be made to endure fifty dead legs."

"So silly," I say, locking my pinkie with his. "Fine, I pinkie swear, because it won't matter since we're both getting off this forsaken island, all right? Say it."

Dapo breaks out into a grin. "We're both getting off this—whoa."

I follow his gaze up ahead to the tasseled feline. It's frozen in place . . . snarling. No, as we get closer and closer, we notice it's trembling—shivering, almost.

It cowers, and I realize that our mobile security system is a success. I'm bloody relieved, but . . .

My chest tightens as I watch the animal grow more and more

agitated with each step we take. Its snarl loosens, eyes widen, and ears droop. I imagine sonic irritation building in strength and aggravating the feline's eardrums until I feel my arms break out into goose bumps.

The animal backs away.

> *Contorts.*
> *Limbs give way as it folds into a heap.*
> *Dazed and passive.*

All that's left is to go around it and press on.

We reach the end of the tunnel. The door into Richard's Residence looms large and undamaged. Unlike the gate at the other end of the tunnel, there is some sort of security measure—a keypad.

Richard steps up to key in the code and is met with an angry-sounding beep. He steps away and tilts his head.

"Looks like they've changed the codes." Richard laughs. A grating noise. "Cuplow, you ungrateful bas—"

"Is there another way?" Dapo interjects. "Tell us there's another way."

"No, I don't think there is. Maybe…"

Dapo and Richard go back and forth, and I rack my brains but can't think of anything. And then a question sparks in my head.

"Are there any buildings or anything like that close to the residence? I'm thinking if we can't go under, then maybe we can go over?" Deja asks.

"Yes, yes there is, actually," Richard says, catching on. "There's a roller-coaster ride, which goes over my residence. There are stairs we can use to climb onto the coaster, walk along the tracks, and drop onto the roof. There's a door we can enter from."

"Bingo," I say. "Then that's our plan."

Dapo catches my eye and nods. With a knowing smile, he claps to get everyone's attention. He's good at that. Being listened to.

"Right," Dapo starts. "Before we even *get* that far, we need to know what we're doing the moment we step through those doors. This is where the rubber hits the road—where push comes to shove. No more winging it. So, Richard, what can you tell us about your beloved residence?"

CHAPTER 30

REVELATION

WE SPEND A GOOD AMOUNT OF TIME FORMULATING A plan and come up with something passable. It involves us collecting a whole load of those plum-like fruits to use as a distraction once we get to the residence.

We emerge from the tunnel into gloomy darkness, spitting rain, and a strong breeze. Dapo's at the head of our group using a stray resort map to chart a course: into the woodlands to pick as many of those fruits as we can, through the intellectual property theme park, past the main street filled with all manner of merchandise, and then across the large, artificial pond.

It's a much longer way around, but in theory it should mean we encounter less creatures since we won't be cutting through as much woodland. According to Enelle's blog, they retreat back to the woodlands to rest—not sleep—at night. The island animals don't sleep. Not anymore.

And if they don't sleep, it means they are always ready. Our mobile security system doesn't make us invisible. It just means the animals can't get close to us, as long as the speakers are on. And since we're trying to preserve batteries by only using them when needed, we have to remain on high alert.

It's about light enough for us to see ahead of ourselves and navigate through the dim dark. Once we collect the plum-like fruit, we trek toward the intellectual property theme park, and I refuse to think about whether the squelching under our feet are puddles of rain or puddles of blood.

Lord knows I've stumbled over a few bodies. Each time I do, the knot in my gut tightens. I take deep, settling breaths.

Don'tlookdon'tlookdon'tlook.

Tripping over dead bodies aside, so far, so good. Any animals we've encountered have scurried off unawares. I think we've got this walking-as-quietly-as-possible thing down to a tee. We know when to stop. When to walk single file. When to offer up a distraction.

But there's nothing we can do when the PA system whines with feedback, and a voice—clear as starlight—booms: "We see you have found means to be resourceful."

Cuplow.

"Impressive," he drawls. Long gone is the politeness in his tone. Now he is himself. Anger and vengeance to his core. "I need you all to pay strict attention to what I say, because I will not repeat myself."

The voice goes silent for a few moments, and in that time, I hear Richard grumbling, "That. Spineless. Prick. Who does he think he is? If it weren't for me, then he'd still..."

I tune out Richard's complaints and wait for Cuplow to resume. Mui tugs at my raincoat. "Yeah?"

"They're coming." She points all around us, where silhouettes and dull, glowing eyes are starting to gather. "It's the sound, isn't it?"

I nod. "They can't see us, so we need to make sure we stay extra quiet. I don't want any of them trying to follow us."

The PA system squeals, and Cuplow is back again.

"My name is Cuplow Ruiz, my daughter is Valoisa Ruiz, and my niece is Enelle Ruiz. We aren't cursed. We aren't to blame. We aren't monsters. Judging by your movements, you know our plans for this island. We are at the end. Where we will wash our hands clean of the last stain of this island—Richard. He is also the 'why,' and I'm sure you've been thinking about this. What could he have done for us to hate him this much?"

Richard has his fists balled up and looks sulky. I guess he doesn't like being the target of a family's ire.

"Of course, you don't need to be a scientific expert to understand what happened fifteen years ago," Cuplow continues. "You just need to know this: *His* Vanildehyde spilled into the sea. It washed up on our shores. It polluted our water systems and, before we knew it, our plants, our animals, our very persons were altered—chemically.

"Now, let me tell you a story. Once upon a time, during the most recent worldwide recession, there was an American businessman working on his startup cargo business. He made a killing because he was able to alleviate the world's supply-chain issues. It goes without saying, this man's methods were less than transparent. He cut corners. Skimped on protocol. Et cetera, et cetera.

"*But* this was a period when those with low morals thrived.

Rather than own up to mistakes, I learned that this American and his business were responsible for scapegoating my family and my people? Well, then I had no choice but to take things personally, didn't I, Richard?"

All eyes swing to Richard, whose shoulders slump. Defeated.

"How dare you refuse to take responsibility for your mistake that cost us *everything*. How dare you bury us in legal shit and lawsuits when we tried to speak up. How dare you. Ah, yes, I can sense it in all of you. There's one thing you can't quite figure out. If I had such anger for this wretched man, why did I not act sooner?"

Cuplow's right. The hatred makes sense. But if they'd known *why* all this time, why did it take them so long?

"The answer is simple. It takes time to prepare, to build the tools, to scavenge. But also, you aren't the only person we hate. Those who have propped you up—your shareholders—and have turned my home into a spectacle. I hate them, too. Well... hated. They're no more."

A moment of silence.

"So," Cuplow announces. "Here is how I see it. Femi, Dapo, Deja, Mui: You are far too young and far too innocent to be caught up in the eye of this necessary storm. And as for my dear daughter, Valoisa—I forgive you. Now, here's my proposition, and it's very simple: Give Richard up to the creatures, and I will show you a way off the island. If you don't, well... then I cannot call you innocent. You have five minutes to decide."

The PA squawks, and then there is silence again.

"Please," Richard says. His voice is hollow. "You can't..."

There's no fight in him, and why would there be at this point?

He's the reason our dads are dead. He's the reason the Ruizes want to ruin him. He's the reason this island is terrifying.

And yet…we can't give him up to the creatures. Even though Richard is the most annoying person I have ever met and I would love nothing more, it's not something that feels *right*.

And it won't bring Dad back. It won't bring anyone back. We'd be no worse than Cuplow and Enelle if we did that. But I can't speak for everyone else. I exhale and laugh up at the night sky. *Damn it.* "Enough, you prick," I say, glaring at Richard. "We're going to vote."

"We are?" Mui asks.

"Yes." I lock eyes with Dapo, who makes it clear by his pursed lips and furrowed brows that he disagrees that we should vote. I know he's considering the possibility of the majority choosing to hand Richard over. "Majority wins. On the count of three, hands up to spare him. Keep your hand down if you feel otherwise. Whatever happens, we don't complain, and we commit to the result. Sound fair?" Everyone nods except Richard, who paces and mutters under his breath. "Okay, one, two…"

"Wait," Valoisa says. "I don't think we should leave this up to a vote. I think we should hand him over. *I* can hand him over and maybe talk them round? And then, Femi, you and your friends and family will be safe. I know my family. They will send everything at us if we refuse."

No one speaks for a moment before Deja pipes up and says, "But you didn't know them enough to think they might take things this far? You really think they'll let him live?" Valoisa's lips press together. "Exactly."

I clear my throat. "This is why we need to vote. Look, I get where you're coming from, but I agree with Deja. I don't think we can trust Enelle and Cuplow, no offense." Valoisa looks like she's offended, but I brush off her side-eye. "Hands up or down. One, two, three…"

Everyone's hand goes up, except Valoisa's. Valoisa shakes her head but says nothing.

The moment we start walking away as a group, the PA system starts blaring out some old-school Xavier. Again. I'm getting sick of hearing his voice. I knew he had a lot of fans, but all the way here on Darlenia? Next are bright lights, illuminating various buildings, and the electronic puppets and 3D billboards that move, slinging out various intellectual property catchphrases.

"Bet on it!"

"Who are you calling a monotone?"

"We're just two friends, trying to get the Guffin down into the valley."

It's a maddening amount of noise, which does the job. There's a flurry of movement as the creatures go into hysteria.

Birds, glass dragons, and tasseled felines flock toward the noise. They tear and pluck and claw. Outside of the space of about ten-ish meters all around us, the place is crawling with creatures.

Our mobile security system helps us carve a path through, but there's so much happening all at once, it's hard to navigate. Mui takes a tumble and scrapes her knee. She looks around, blinks, and then bursts into wailing tears that pierce through everything.

The creatures around us notice. Richard clamps a hand over Mui's mouth.

"Now's not the time," Richard hisses.

Deja shoves him away to free Mui's mouth. "What is *wrong* with you? She's a child."

"She's going to get me killed!" he shrieks.

The guy is unraveling. I look around, and the creatures are craning their necks and rushing in our direction, only to recoil at the barrier of sound. "No, you're the one who'll get us killed. You hear that? You see that?" I point up above us where the golden raptors hover. Some fall away and drift downward to the ground if they get too close. Nullified and docile for a few moments before regaining their senses. "They are here because *we* chose not to give you up. Don't forget that."

"Hmmph. Not all of you," he grumbles, glaring at Valoisa. "For all I know, she could still try to kill me when no one's paying enough attention."

Valoisa shrugs. "As much as I'd love to, I respect democratic processes." She flashes a cheeky grin. "But keep sulking like that, and I'll be glad to put you out of your misery."

Richard does this weird thing with his head and shoulders—a mini tantrum. *Muppet,* I think to myself.

"Mui," I say, "you all right?"

Her breaths snag, and after a few sniffs, she nods. "Y-yeah."

"Don't mind him. He's a bit lost and ignorant." I hold out a hand to help her up, which she takes. "And it's not good to be ignorant."

"Exactly," Mui replies with a smile. "But yes, it's not good." She glares at Richard, who glares back. But then he loses his nerve and looks away. When he does, she sticks out her tongue and whispers, "Idiot."

As we make our way toward the roller coaster, the good news is that we are untouchable. The less-than-good news is that the creatures are aware of our presence. They follow us at a distance. From all sides. Keeping out of range.

My phone battery is depleting with speed. I swear in my head. When I do a quick spot check on the speakers, I swear more. Some of them have died. I knew I wasn't imagining our sphere of protection shrinking.

"We need to move faster," Valoisa says aloud, a slight tremble in her voice. "I'm not sure how much longer our speakers or phones are gonna hold out."

Dapo grunts. "We have to jog."

"Jog?" Richard asks. "No, no, no, I won't jog."

"Yes, yes, yes, you will," Dapo states. "Otherwise, this is what will happen. We'll leave you behind, and before you know it, you won't be within the sphere of protection. Or do you think you can survive on your own?" Richard ignores the question. "No, I didn't think so."

After jogging for some time, we're dripping in sweat, and we're at the edge of the large, artificial pond by the base of the roller coaster. Ringed with trampled flowers and littered with floating bodies, the pond is still and reflects the structure on the other side: the roller coaster named Rich's Dream.

Admittedly, it's a mesmerizing mass of twisting metal that gets us close enough to the roof of Richard's Residence. That's where we need to get to.

"Before anyone complains," Dapo starts, for Richard's benefit, "we need to go across it. Time is of the essence."

One by one we step into the pond. It's shallow, and on Mui, the shortest of us, the water comes up to halfway between her waist and knees. The trudge through the water is slow and steady. The golden raptors circle above. The glass dragons swim after us.

We're almost on the other side, and we come to a high-up wall. I look left and right, but there don't seem to be any steps in sight. Which means there's no option but for us to climb out.

I stride forward and give Dapo a boost. He disappears for a moment over the wall before popping back into view and helping Deja and Valoisa out of the pond. Then he holds out a hand so he can help Mui. She strides forward. Hesitant.

"It's so high," she murmurs.

"You're safe," I reply. "Look, grab on to my shoulder and put your foot here." She stares at my hands hovering above the surface of the water. "On three, I'll push you up and then Dapo will pull you up."

"O-okay. I guess. But—"

SPLASH!

The sound is sudden. My shoulders tighten. Mui yelps. Richard swears, and before I know it, he's using my hands as a foothold. Next he's clambering over me, and I try to regain my balance.

But it's slipped away from me and I'm falling backward. My hands try to grab at something or someone. Judging by the shriek, I know I've grabbed ahold of Mui. Except she's a rubbish anchor. One moment we're above water; the next, we aren't. I thrash and rise above the surface.

My phone. The speakers. My heart thuds. I yank out my earplugs, shoving them in my pocket, and relief crashes over me when the sonic irritation invades my ears. When I look, Richard is peering down at us, his face flushed.

"Sorry," he mumbles. "I panicked. Here, let me."

He reaches out a hand to Mui. I give her a boost, and she is hoisted up and out.

I take Richard's hand, and I'm pulled out of the pond and over the wall. I take a step when a sudden, invisible pain wobbles my eardrums and I spasm into a heap onto my hands and knees. Shaking my head, I jump to my feet.

HissSsSsSSS.

"Crap," I say, looking over my shoulder. "The sound. We all need to *run*."

CHAPTER 31

COMEUPPANCE

WE RUN. HARD.

The good: The glass dragons are struggling to clear the wall and come after us.

The bad: The golden raptors don't have that problem, and they are all over us. It's an endless cycle of retreating and swooping.

The ugly: Richard's shrieking.

Not even Mui is making so much panicked noise. But I get it. Their talons are sharp, beaks firm. They lack the cutting edge the glass dragons have. We swat them away as we run. While the speakers no longer work, enclosed in a bag, they're a useful improvised weapon.

My forearms sting. I feel my flesh bruising in real time. But I push through with gritted teeth because I can't let them reach Mui.

"Stick close," I grunt, sending another bird veering away with a *thwack*. "You're okay, you're okay, you're okay."

The words are as much for me as they are for Mui.

I glance up ahead, and coming into view, at last, are the steps we'll need to climb the roller coaster.

HissSsSsSSS.

Ah, so the glass dragons found a way over the wall, then. The hissing sends a chill up my spine, frosting my nerves. "It's okay, we're okay, we're almost there."

I try to ignore the hissing. But like a Xavier chorus, it's the only thing I hear. And it is relentless as they get

LOUDER

LOUDER   *LOUDER*

LOUDER

Dapo reaches the steps first. Then Valoisa. Then Richard. Then Deja. Then Mui and me.

"Uh-uh," Mui says, shaking her head. "I'm scared."

HissSsSsSSS.

We don't have time for this. I lift her onto the steps. "We don't have a choice, I'm sorry. But look, I'm right behind you and I won't let anything happen to you. Let's take it one step at a time. Okay?"

Mui pauses. "O-okay."

Because I'm at the bottom of the climb, I get to deal with the smaller glass dragons who climb up after us. Turns out the bigger ones can't climb that well. One bites my ankle, and I shake it off. It hisses as it goes falling all the way down. I smash a speaker into a couple of our plum-like fruits and throw them in opposite directions. That seems to do the trick. Most of the glass dragons end up jumping into the air after the smell.

Only a few continue to follow us.

But we manage to make it onto the track in one piece. Walking along a roller-coaster track is not something I ever thought I'd do, but here we are. The breeze is stronger up here, and, *again*, the raptors are back.

Swooping.

               Pecking.

                           Scratching.

                           Retreating.

               Circling.

Squawking.

One wrong step and we'll go—
Don't look, I warn myself. "Don't look down."

"Too late," she says, trembling all over. She backs away and bumps into me. "I wanna come down."

"You can't, we're already here now. I need you to keep moving, please. If you don't, it makes it harder for me to stop the raptors from"—I swat away a brazen pair of raptors at the cost of a nasty cut across the palm of my hand—"hurting you."

Mui pouts but continues on in the direction of Dapo and Richard, who are in conversation. I wonder what about. Doesn't matter. What matters is—

There's a sudden burst of light all around us and the booming of a voice that belongs on radio:

"Welcome aboard Rich's Dream! I'm that *said* dream, and I

am delighted to have you scale these heights with me! So buckle up, eyes wide open, and remember, birds of a feather flock together!"

No prizes for guessing who's responsible for powering up the roller-coaster ride, soundtrack and all.

Their anger is understandable, and if this were a movie, I'd be on their side. *But* I'd still know, deep down, they were in the wrong.

Too many people have died because of their desire to punish one man. Tell me how that makes sense.

Whatever.

I glance to my left where the empty roller-coaster train moves forward, along the stretch of track before the highest point, with a dull mechanical clink. It's still got a fair way to travel, but I know how fast these roller-coaster trains go. We don't have as much time as we think. Still, we should just about make it.

Our task is made harder by the golden raptors everywhere…
Of course! I'm annoyed I didn't think of it sooner.

"Everyone," I call out. "When they retreat away again, I'm going to throw out a few of the speakers from the backpack and let them clank down the roller coaster to make as much noise as possible. That should confuse the raptors. When I do that we need to be as quiet as possible. Not a sound."

I get several thumbs up in response. *Good.* "Mui, remember, not a sound. Even if they come close, remember to be quiet."

The raptors swoop down, and, once again, we swat them away. Then I pull out as many speakers as I can. Mui helps me hold a couple of them. I look up at the raptors.

Circling.

Squawking.
Swooping.

That's my cue.

I hurl two speakers behind us so they skip along the track. Grabbing the two speakers Mui is holding, I do the same with those. I look up and, like a charm, the birds divert course and swoop toward the sound. Turning to Mui, I flash a smile before putting a finger to my lips and pointing forward.

Let's go.

We all walk to the curve that hangs over Richard's Residence. My eyes flick between where I walk and the latest position of the roller-coaster train, which has moved toward the highest peak.

The wind blows.

The roller-coaster track clicks and creaks.

It helps hide whatever noise we might be making. I find myself holding my breath in long stretches, focusing all my energy on not making a single sound. No doubt about it: This is *the* longest walk of my life.

The wind whistles.

The roller-coaster train reaches the highest point. It teeters, and I try to calm the way my heart pounds in my ears. Then it falls. And for a moment I am lost. A memory flashes in my mind.

"When you reach the front of the queue, go onto your tiptoes," Dad whispers. *"Ah ehn, just like that."*

"B-but isn't that lying?" I reply.

He winks at me. "I won't tell your mother if you don't." I nod at him, grinning ear to ear. "Good. Now then let's go and make memories. Remember when the roller coaster comes rushing down, that's when they get the pictures. So, make sure you make the bravest face you can make. Got it?"

"Got it," I reply.

I squeeze my eyes shut to stop the tears from falling. Dad's absence is like a lost tooth. The worst part about the whole thing is this mad island won't let me process it. It's one thing after another.

I take a deep, deep breath, steadying my thoughts.

Mum's words echo inside my skull. *There's a time for everything.* I put my grief on hold.

My focus returns to the track, as we are almost there.

We're about twenty meters away . . .

FIFTEEN METERS AWAY . . .

TEN . . .

"Hurry up," Richard hisses. Fed up, he attempts to squeeze by Dapo.

And slips.

Richard flails, a look of horror on his face, visible even under the dim starlight. He falls but manages to catch himself on the edge of the track. Dapo leans over and, with one hand, Richard grabs on. Straining. But I see it happening in real time.

Richard's grip is loosening.

First to go is the hand holding on to the track as he tries to heave himself up. It falls away like a leaf in autumn, hanging at his side. The strength in it is gone. And then the hand holding on to Dapo goes.

Richard is falling.

The morbid part of me watches him fall right until he slams into the track beneath us with a thunderous thud. There is a moment of silence and then Richard unravels. He screams and writhes and screams.

"AAAAAHHHHHHHHHH!"

His voice is a siren call for the golden raptors, who squawk and home in on him. I swear internally and put my earplugs into Mui's ears. "Idiot," I mumble.

Dapo shakes his head. "I tried to save him. That fool, he got spooked by the sounds of the roller-coaster train. It wasn't as close as he thought and we were nearly there."

As Richard is devoured alive by the flock of golden raptors, there is a flicker of light, and the sound of a single gunshot perforates the air. I squint, seeing Richard's defective gun plummeting downward, as we move to the drop point. The roller coaster still speeds toward us.

CHAPTER 32

JUDGMENT

THE ROLLER-COASTER TRACK FEELS COOL UNDER MY
feet. Below me, just a small jump forward, is the roof of Richard's Residence, where everyone is already waiting.

You can do this.

A quick glance to my right confirms what I already know—
it's now or never. The roller-coaster train is hurtling toward me.
The others have jumped.

So why are my legs refusing to move?

"Come on, come on, come on," I seethe, slapping and pinch-
ing my thighs.

If I don't go now, I'm finished. I won't grow up. If I don't
move, I won't do a lot of the things I want to. Like produce a
Grammy-winning album. Befriend a pet budgie. See the rest of
the world.

If I don't move, I won't get to do my dad proud.

The methodical click of the racing roller coaster is getting

CLOSER   *CLOSER*
CLOSER   *CLOSER*
CLOSER   *CLOSER*
CLOSER

"WE'RE GOING TO GET OFF THIS FORSAKEN ISLAND!"
Dapo shouts, snapping me back to my senses.

Without thinking any longer, I move to jump. Except the foot I push off with slips, and even though the distance is small, I'm short.

My chest lands on the edge of the roof, and the shock lances through me. My arms and hands struggle to grab on to something. Luckily, Dapo and Valoisa are there to pull me to safety.

I lie across the hot rooftop, trying to inhale, like a fish on the slick deck of a boat, but nothing happens.

"Are you okay?" Dapo asks, and I glare at him.

I can't speak, but I hope he can read my face and what I'm thinking: *What kind of stupid question is that? When you just saw me crash into the edge of the roof? Ask me that again and I will punch you.*

Finally, I'm able to take short, shallow breaths. But then, like clockwork:

Squawking…

Which means the raptors will be swooping toward us soon.

There's a large metal door in the middle of the roof like Richard said there'd be. We rush to open it, stream inside, and swing it shut behind us, leaving the golden raptors to angrily crash against the door. It holds.

I collapse on the stone steps in a heap, taking in this precious moment of calm. While I focus on getting my breathing back to normal, Dapo breaks the silence.

"According to Richard, there are two floors we need to get past in order to reach the control room: the viewing room and the showroom."

"And," I rasp, "they're large open-plan rooms. We estimated they were like eight regular-size glass dragons wide and eight regular-size glass dragons long."

Dapo nods. "Hallways narrow enough that only one could attack us at any given time. Knowing what we know about Cuplow and Enelle, they've probably placed glass dragons on each of the floors."

"That's why we have the fruits!" Mui jumps in, happy to have contributed. "Yep."

"Exactly," I say. "And we know they have bad eyesight, too. So assuming we run into them, then it's going to be like playing Granny's Footsteps. We need the fruit because there's no way for us to blend in, smell-wise, so we need to improvise."

"Everyone stick close, all right," Dapo orders. "We are almost to the end. But it's never about how we start or the middle bits, it's—"

"About how we finish," I say, with a wry smile. "All right, Mr. Unoriginal. Taking Deja's lines."

"Whatever. Now then, shall we?" With that, we get a move on.

As we make our way through the door at the bottom of the concrete steps toward the door leading to the viewing gallery, there is bone-splintering silence.

This is it.

I volunteer to open the door, because truth be told, opening a door without a sound is an art. Luckily, years of sneaking into the kitchen to steal meat in the middle of the night has prepared me.

I pull on the door handle...squeeze tight...and push

downward at what feels like a rate of a millimeter a second until the handle can't go any further. Now the hard bit: pushing open the door.

Deep breaths. Slowly, now...

The door is about a third of the way open when pushing gets harder. I signal at Dapo to take a look through the crack. When he does, he frowns.

What? I mouth.

Ned Potty.

My turn to frown. *Who's that?*

Dapo shakes his head. This time, with some pantomiming from him, it clicks. *Dead body.* Then he takes another look. *Lots.*

Unexpected. I guess that's it, then, for opening the door fully. One by one we squeeze through and step inside, me entering last.

And even though Dapo warned me, I'm shocked at what awaits us.

In the middle of the room, a glass dragon as large as a horse prowls. Every now and then it stoops to chew at the bodies strewn all over the large space. The uniforms mark them as Richard's armed men. The walls—floor-to-ceiling windows that peer out over the island from all angles—are splattered with blood.

But it's not just humans—there are glass dragons lying dead, too.

What the hell?

I scan the room. Several power sockets are dotted around, with devices plugged in to the them. Equipment identical to the one I unplugged earlier. They have pulsing green lights. I connect the dots—the pattern. They must be confining the glass dragon to this floor using those gadgets.

How is that possible?

But right now it doesn't matter. The whole situation is above me. I reach into the backpack to pull out a fruit. It's the one factor we can still control. The large glass dragon pauses and cranes its neck in our direction. With its full attention on us, my heart gets lodged in my throat. But then it turns away and goes in search of another nibble.

"It's huge," I murmur. I turn to Deja, who shakes her head. *Wild*, she mouths. Valoisa looks too awestruck. Meaning we can't rely on her to help us tame it.

I hurl the fruit as far away from us, and the door we need to pass through, as possible. It lands with a dull *THWIP*, bouncing off a wall and into the midst of some twisted limbs. The glass dragon hisses and plods in that direction.

The moment it does, we proceed. Quietly, we step around bodies, avoiding the pools of blood that have dried at the edges but are still wet in the middle. The faint whisper of a bird squawking startles the dragon, and it rushes toward us.

But then it stops.

We don't dare move as it slinks across our path to the other side of the room. Not until we hear the crunching of bone and chewing of flesh. I bring out another fruit. Halfway across the room, the glass dragon decides to let out a hissing bellow. Like a dentist's suction thingy at high volume.

Mui goes to plant her feet but steps on the tail of a glass dragon corpse, causing her to stumble forward. I reach out and grab hold of her top with my free hand. She gasps before clamping her hands over her mouth.

The glass dragon rears around and walks toward us. Its

tongue is flicking nonstop, sure there is something here. I swallow. Pools of sweat form in the pits of my arms. My heart *thud, thud, thud*s. I angle my arm holding the fruit.

On an internal count of three, I chuck the fruit behind the dragon.

THWIP-IP-IP.

With a loud hiss, the glass dragon charges toward the sound, the ground beneath our feet trembling. I yank Mui up with both hands, and all of us tiptoe the rest of the way, easing the door open and making it into the hallway.

Lub-dub, lub-dub, lub-dub. My heart refuses to settle. But there aren't any animals here, so our journey is easier. What makes it uneasy is how the walls are lined with photographs of Richard and prominent visitors to the resort. There's even a picture of him with Xavier. I forgot Xavier did a live concert here once upon a time.

I ease open the door to the showroom. I'm expecting priceless art and pretentious ornaments. Instead, the room is pristine and barren, except for a few chairs scattered all over. In the center of the room, one of them is occupied by none other than Cuplow. His arms are crossed, and a shallow smile is on his face.

How can he smile in the wake of murdering so many innocent people?

"Welcome, boys and girls. Mui, your dad and I weren't the closest, but we were amicable. And I always had a soft spot for you. Shame it had to come to this. Please, please, have a seat, let's talk." He stands and walks over to nearby chairs, dragging them across the polished wooden floor. The sound is grating. "You, too, Valoisa." Though he smiles when he speaks, there's something vicious about his words. I notice the way Valoisa trembles. She's the first to take a seat. And the rest of us obey.

"Are you here to tell us we are free to go home?" I ask. "Now that Richard's dead?"

"No, I'm not here to do that." Cuplow chuckles. "After the choice you all made, you aren't innocent. You have to take responsibility for your actions. The question now is, do you want to live?"

Deja frowns. "What a stupid question."

"A simple yes or no will suffice."

I snort. "Obviously we want to live."

"Then it's simple," Cuplow says. "Leave your old lives behind and stay here with us while we reopen the island. I can see Valoisa is quite fond of you. Perhaps you can be redeemed."

When he turns to Valoisa, she's quick to look away. A child scorned.

"Why can't we go home?" I press.

"Because it's not one of the options. And if you refuse the hand of mercy I am offering you, well..." Cuplow scrapes away some dirt from under the acrylic nail on his pinkie. "But if you remain here, then you will become protected citizens of Darlenia under our law. Given new names, of course."

"So basically be your prisoners forever and die to everyone we know, or die outright," Deja says. "Pretty rubbish options, Cuplow."

"'Prisoner' is a harsh word. But you are a threat to our immediate freedom. If you leave, they will ask how this all happened. You think they won't reframe the narrative and come for our land in force? When we have only just reclaimed it?"

"So your offer back there to show us a way off the island if we gave up Richard was a lie?" I ask.

"Well." Cuplow smiles. "The only way off this island would be to welcome death. Either metaphorical or physical."

I scoff. "People are going to come as soon as they realize no one on the island has contacted their families. You don't have as much time as you think you do."

Cuplow smiles. "We knew we wouldn't have much time. Right now, Richard's part of the island is being rigged with explosives by the Darlenians who stayed. It doesn't matter if the outsiders come—what they will find is a horrible mechanical failure leading to widespread fire and destruction and the death of everyone at the resort. A most fitting end to Richard's legacy. And the Darlenians who stayed, waiting on the fringes of the island, will pick up the pieces. If you leave, we can't control the way our story goes."

"Should have thought about that, then, before you decided to go and murder innocent people," Deja spits.

"Ah, but were they so innocent?"

Cuplow lets the question hang. He knows the answer isn't so simple, and I hate that on some level he is right. Still, I think of my dad and how—and how—and how…

"Dad," Valoisa begs. "Please. Don't do this. We can find another way. We can—"

"You ungrateful daughter of mine. All I have done is for you to know our home as it once was. And this is how you repay me? Yos myo. What did I do wrong with you? Hmm?"

Valoisa opens her mouth as if to say something but lowers her head instead. Deja was right. In the end, family is family.

Cuplow clears his throat. "We have a saying here." *Great, another saying.* He smirks and says the words in their language. "Translated, it means that while the moral tree of the world is tall, it surely leans toward the light of justice."

Deja rises. Though she stands still, I know something is off. Her head is bowed and her fists are all balled up. Then she erupts. "Fuck you!" she screams with everything in her. "My dad is *dead*. Because of *you*." She points a finger at Cuplow. "And you expect me to believe there's justice in that? No!" Deja takes a deep, heavy breath. "Who the hell are you to decide things? What about the families you've ruined? And *if* you get out of this alive, would you call it justice if those family members found you and decided they wanted an eye for an eye?"

Cuplow shakes his head. "I couldn't expect you to under- stand the—"

"The what? The pain? The hurt?"

"Exactly."

"Okay, yeah, I won't claim to understand that. But does that make it right? There is nothing moral about murdering those who never raised a finger against you. And even if they have, jus- tify to me how they deserve death. Show your work. You know what, I feel sorry for you." That wipes the smirk off Cuplow's face. "You and your family are hollow and lost."

"We're done here," Cuplow says, getting up and striding to the door that leads down to the next floor. "I can't stand the look of you."

"Y-you really don't have to do this," I call out, standing up and walking toward him. Because if he's done with us, it means he's decided we're dying here. And I can't let him get away.

"Please, you don't have to do this. We're all tired. We're all hurting— Hey! I'm talking to you."

But Cuplow ignores me. I see him reach into his pocket and pull out a handheld device. Memories of the radio Enelle used before play out in my head. My eyes dart around the room. Small devices are plugged into the some of the power sockets. But the lights are amber, not yet pulsing green.

Instinct takes over and I rush at Cuplow like this is a game of bulldog. My shoulder connects with his back, and before I know it, we both go tumbling to the ground with a *THUD*.

CHAPTER 33

FEMI

THE GADGET CUPLOW WAS HOLDING GOES SKIPPING along the floor. It looks like one of those old-style phones, but with all the circuitry exposed.

We can't let him activate this room. We can't have that hulking glass dragon come down here.

There's a flurry of movement. In the same breath, as Cuplow lunges for what he dropped, I pull his clawing hands back. Dapo appears, scrambling to grab the device. I can only imagine what we must look like, the three of us tangled on the floor.

"Get him!" Mui exclaims.

I struggle to put Cuplow in a headlock while Dapo tries to pry the gadget from his hands. There's an audible click from the device that freezes us all in place.

And then...

SPLAT.

A ripe fruit lands square in Cuplow's face. Then another. The device clatters from his hands, and all eyes turn to Mui, who, along with Deja, chucks more produce at Cuplow. He throws his hands up to protect himself. I roll away, and Dapo grabs the device.

We stand on either side of Mui and look down at Cuplow, who gets to his feet and brushes himself off. Gone is the beaming smile and puffed-out chest. For the first time, he looks frazzled. When he looks around the room, fear floods his face. His eyes go wide, and I realize why. The devices in the wall are now pulsing with green light.

Cuplow reaches out a hand. "You need to give that to me. Please." He turns to his daughter who looks visibly shaken, nothing like the bold girl I met just days go. "Valoisa, please. Don't let them kill us all. Tell them to give it back. If they don't we'll all die. Please. If you do, I'll forgive you." When Valoisa doesn't move, his face twists in anger. "You wretched little thing. You dishonor the Ruiz name. You'll kill us all."

"Dad, I'm sorry."

"Give it to him," I say. Dapo looks at me like I've forgotten who Cuplow is. "Trust me."

Dapo doesn't hesitate. He throws the device at Cuplow who frantically plays around with it. But even with several clicks the green lights continue to pulse.

"It's not working," Cuplow mumbles. "Why is it not—ah, it's missing a battery!" He rushes toward the door where a battery lies on the floor.

THUD.

The sound comes from behind Cuplow, from behind us, from behind the door we came through. He turns to face it and staggers backward. Fear and panic flood his eyes while he scrambles to slot the battery in.

The rest of us move to the edges of the room. Out of the way. Out of sight.

THUD.

"Almost—"

Bursting through the doors at breakneck speed is the huge glass dragon from before. Cuplow barely has time to look up and let out half a scream. He spins to the right as the glass dragon swings its talon and slashes across his chest, sending him sprawling to the ground. His gadget goes skittering across the floor and lands by my feet.

Valoisa clamps her hands over her mouth to stifle a shriek. Anguish is clear in her eyes. Deja covers Mui's eyes and holds her tight.

With no one paying attention, I pick up Cuplow's device before gesturing toward the door we need to pass through to get to the next floor. *We need to go.*

Not yet, Dapo expresses with a raised hand.

The dragon lets out a bellow before staggering toward Cuplow, who crawls away, leaving a trail of smeared blood in his wake. He's trying to keep quiet, but he can't muffle his whimpers enough. He glances back just as the animal is upon him. He kicks out, but it's futile.

The dragon tosses Cuplow across the room with a powerful swing. He lands with a resounding *SMACK.*

Dapo and I lock eyes. *Now.*

We move toward the door. Toward safety.

"Don't look," I whisper to Valoisa, as we leave Cuplow's cries behind.

It's hard to breathe. It's hard to think. Cuplow's death has me thinking about my dad. About unnecessary death. I want to scream, cry, *something*. The others look just as sick, especially Valoisa, who hasn't said a word. I take a steadying breath. Now's not the time to spiral. Not yet.

Focus.

All that's left is to walk down the hall and to the stairs. Then we come face-to-face with the final door—the one that leads to the control room. It's wooden with a metal handle. My mouth is dry.

"This is it," I mumble, squeezing down the handle, and I ease the door open.

The huge space is dim, full of screens and buttons and controls to our right. A table rests in the far corner on the left side. That's where Enelle sits, hunched over a plate and shoveling forkfuls of food into her mouth—looks like steak.

I laugh. It's absurd. Here I am, bruised and battered and beyond pissed. And one of the people responsible is busy eating.

"Oh," Enelle says, rising from her chair, keeping hold of the steak knife. "Where's Cuplow?" She searches our faces, and something breaks in her. She glowers at Valoisa, who whimpers. "I see." When Enelle smiles, it's empty.

"Why do all this?" Deja steps toward her. "This could have been bloodless."

"Why are you asking when none of it matters anymore? My home is free."

"You owe it to us at least," I reply. "You... you *used* me. You used your own cousin without a second thought. Innocent people died. I want to know why it had to be this way."

"Because ya osha oblisca, pan ye coldo remborda, Lost Boy." She walks over to the control panel and points with the knife. "Sometimes knowing is not enough. Sometimes you need to demonstrate."

"The world will find out you killed everyone. How are you going to get yourself out of that?"

Whatever Enelle was going to say is interrupted by a crackle from yet another radio. I hadn't noticed it perched on the table. A voice says, *"Enelle, everything's been planted as instructed. We are in the safe zone."*

Enelle smiles. "It was never about me. Besides, it's all over now. My home is free and soon the eyesore that is the Grand Darlenia Resort will be rubble. Go and find a way to safety if you can. Perhaps the fates of this world will smile upon you." She laughs, and her hand absently hovers over a black switch on the panel. This can't be happening.

Panicking, I look around the room, spying several of those same devices plugged in, with their lights glowing amber.

"I said go," Enelle says.

Valoisa sighs. Weary. "Eni, you don't—"

"You too, cousin. Go! I can't stand to look at you."

"Please," I press, trying to buy some time to get out of this somehow. My eyes flick from her hand to her face. I step toward her, but she keeps me back with the knife. "Enelle, I...I want to understand."

She looks me in the eye and sighs, irritable. "I told you, it's not enough to understand. Sometimes you just have to—"

I rush at Enelle and wrap her in a bear hug, trapping her arms. But I'm too late to stop the knife from plunging into my side.

At first, I feel nothing.

Then there's an avalanche of pain. I keep my grip tight around Enelle. Thousands of thoughts run through my head as I build up the courage to break my promise to Dapo.

I won't see Mum again.

I won't get to go to Dad's funer—

No.

I'm scared.

I'm scared.

I'm scared.

My mind stills. *If someone told you right now to stab your family in the back for the greater good, would you do it?* Deja once asked me. I thought the answer was no. But faced with the reality, I'm sickened at the realization that the answer is yes.

If someone doesn't do something, we all die.

"I'm sorry," I say, gasping each word. "I'm so sorry."

"Femi," Dapo says. His voice is barely above a whisper, face twisted by anguish. He must see the blood slowly soaking through my shirt. He must see I'm holding Cuplow's gadget. He must see my finger press the button. He looks at my hand and sees the pulsing green light. Panic blooms on his face, but it's too late.

THUD.

"Contingencies," I manage, pushing through the pain but still holding on to the button. "I'm sorry I broke our promise, big bro. Tell Mum we bonded in the end." I look to Mui. "Be good," I whisper. Then to Valoisa: "Rebuild your home the right way."

THUD.

"Lost Boy," Enelle growls. She tries to break free, tries clawing at me. We sway, but I'm not letting her go anywhere. "What have you done?"

This is it. The end.

I see Deja and the alarm on her face. "I never did tell you what I wanted to say." I smile.

THUD.

I take a deep, shuddering breath, making sure to say these words at the top of my voice, so the glass dragon will come straight for me and Enelle.

And so that the beautiful girl will finally hear me: *"Deja, I think you already know this. But I love—"*

POSTLUDE

MRS. FATONA SITS IN A BATHROOM STALL, SOBBING.
She texts her son.

> How far away are you?

> I'm on my way.

She's sitting in a bathroom stall in a television center. In about an hour, she will watch her son, and other survivors of the Darlenia Tragedy, as it was dubbed, be interviewed for the first time publicly. She will be reminded in new ways about just how much she has lost as a result of what has transpired, of which she knows little.

Dapo refuses to talk about what happened on that island where things went so very wrong. "A spectacular turn of events" was all the authorities had said, and it left news outlets confused. Mrs. Fatona has been told (not *knows*):

Those who survived had suffered considerable trauma, and thus, any account they gave was likely to be flawed. That is to say, when authorities had questioned them, they were dissatisfied with what they heard.

The authorities concluded that the events that unfolded on the island were the work of a terrorist group. Best guesses so far are: those who want to eat the rich, environmentalist groups, or an enemy of the "free" world. However, there are no substantial leads.

Lastly, Richard Jenkins, CEO of Jenkins & Children, and, at the time of the tragedy, owner of Darlenia, deserves better for his legacy—for everything he had built.

Unfortunately, because of the NDAs signed, none of the survivors have spoken out to refute the lies. And so many, like Mrs. Fatona, have been told, but do not *know*.

But things are about to change.

> Are you sure you want to do this?

I need to. Everyone should know the truth.

Sick and tired of the circus it's become.

There are moments where Dapo seems ready to talk, but those moments fade, and Mrs. Fatona knows better than to push him. After all, guilt at pushing her three men to bond gnaws at her.

After blowing her nose and wiping away her tears, Mrs. Fatona exits the stall and strides up to the bathroom mirror to fix her running mascara.

The entrance to the bathroom swings open, and Sophie

Bloom appears. She is a Black woman of similar height, wearing a no-nonsense pantsuit. Her heels click against the polished stone from the door to the sink next to Mrs. Fatona. Sophie catches Mrs. Fatona's eye in the mirror.

"You're the mother of one of the survivors, right?" Sophie's voice is clipped with northern intonations. Mrs. Fatona ignores her. Instead, she makes to leave, stopped when Sophie grabs her forearm. "I'm sorry for your loss."

"Th-thanks," Mrs. Fatona answers. With an uneven smile that does not reach her eyes, she eases herself out of Sophie's grip.

"I'm Sophie Bloom," Sophie offers. "I'm honored to have secured the rights to tell their story."

Mrs. Fatona nods. She knows who Sophie is. Everyone knows who Sophie is. She is the host of a popular talk show that examines those who have gone through some terrible ordeals. Or those looking to repair their public image. Some argue she does more harm than good, focused more on the story than the truth. Spectacle over reflection.

So why is Mrs. Fatona here with her son?

If it were her decision, they wouldn't be. Except Dapo had insisted, and how could she say no? Not when his grief is a tempest threatening to drown him. She refuses to lose any more, and when the opportunity arose it was as if her son broke through the surface and took a life-affirming gasp.

"Have you seen the memes?"

Mrs. Fatona shakes her head. She doesn't have social media, and the last thing she'd be doing is looking at memes that compound her tragedy. Sophie whips out her phone and slides it across the counter for Mrs. Fatona to inspect and scroll and scroll and scroll.

A bitter tang creeps into Mrs. Fatona's mouth, and she swallows hard. Hands shaking, Mrs. Fatona, unable to carry on, hands the phone back to Sophie.

"It's disgusting, isn't it?" Sophie sighs and adjusts her pantsuit. "They've just greenlit a film adaptation. It's got the working title of *Terror at the Grand Darlenia Resort*. Pay it no mind—the industry can be so gauche. Anyway, duty calls." Sophie flashes a smile and heads for one of the bathroom stalls.

Moments later, Mrs. Fatona's phone rings. It's Dapo.

Dapo waits for his mother in the cafeteria. He had insisted on being here for the interview, but as the time draws near, he is unsure he's making the right decision. He had told himself the world needed to know the truth. That much he believed.

But is this the right way?

He and Deja had debated it on a video call. The wounds of the island had barely scabbed over. They know the interview will be like scratching until the scab peels away and the wound reopens.

For the truth, they settled on.

Dapo gnaws on his bottom lip and peels the dead skin away. Spotting his mum arriving, he gets up to hug her tight. They take their seats.

"I'll be there," his mum starts, "a few rows back from the front. You know it's not too late . . ."

Dapo smiles at his mother, her concern warming his heart. "I know, but I"—*we*—"need to do this. For Dad and Femi"—*for everyone who was lost*—"I want everyone to know that they were heroes. That Richard Jenkins had a lot of problems…"

Mrs. Fatona zones out, not because she is disinterested, but because he is a furnace of energy and the determined expression on her son's face is one she hasn't seen in a long time. She wants to savor it. "Huh?"

"I asked if you think I'm doing the right thing?" Dapo says, his hand rubbing the back of his neck. "I want to do the right thing."

"We're here now," Mrs. Fatona says, taking hold of her son's hand. "Who knows. Listen to the promptings in your heart, yes? Say a little prayer, and follow through."

Dapo nods. "Thanks."

Under the glaring lights of the television studio, Dapo sits at the far end of the stage. Between himself and the talk show host, Sophie Bloom, is Deja. And on the other side of Sophie are Mui and Cyril with their guardians. They are all hardly keeping it together.

Four survivors in total, including himself. Cyril had been found later, curled up in a cupboard, looking faint as anything.

The truth is that there were five survivors.

When the glass dragon attacked Femi and Enelle, the rest had crept away. They scoured until they found a way off—a rusted boat that leaked. They didn't make it far, but they didn't need to. A local fisherman found them. He didn't speak a word of English, but the dialect was close enough to that of Darlenian that Valoisa could talk to him.

Once they arrived at the nearest island, Valoisa had said that was where they parted. And that was that.

Valoisa is out there somewhere. Dapo often wonders what she is up to. Does she know he is about to tell the truth about Darlenia?

Dapo's knee will not stop bouncing. He glances into the audience and finds the face that matters. His mother's. She smiles at him, but it does not reach her eyes. Still, it is enough to calm him down.

A light turns red to indicate the talk show is recording, and Sophie Bloom looks out on the audience.

Vultures, Dapo thinks.

"Thank you for tuning in to what is quite possibly the most anticipated interview I have ever held. I am joined by the miracles of Darlenia."

Dapo winces at that name but quickly schools his face as the audience bursts into thunderous clapping.

"To help set the context," Sophie declares, "I'm going to play a couple of audio clips."

The lights dim, and there is a soft click before the audio plays.

"It looked like something out of a fever dream. A liminal space where the dimensions on either side were paper thin. If that makes sense? And I think that sort of atmosphere was why up until, well ... up until you know ... it was a powerful place of wonder."

Memories come crawling back. That final moment of his brother with tears running down his face.

"What happened on Darlenia is nothing short of a tragedy that has left authorities confused," says a male voice. *"Many prominent men and women, including acclaimed entrepreneur Richard Jenkins, lost their lives in what is being described as a terrorist attack. Except the motive is unclear, and there are no credible suspects."*

Images flash in his mind's eye. Femi, Enelle, and the beast tumbling out of the windows. He doesn't remember if there was a spray of blood on impact.

"The survivors are described as the miracles of Darlenia. In a feat of extraordinary resilience, they are pictures of the improbable being made possible. While little is known about them directly, authorities have assured us they cooperated fully in their investigation . . . as well as could be expected after having experienced so much."

And then there is a voice that everyone knows.

"I'm Xavier, and, having been intimately aware of the island itself, I am deeply troubled by what transpired. Especially as one of the survivor's brothers was a promising prospect in the industry. We may not have collaborated in the end, but he was someone who had a bright future. I saw the sun on his shoulders."

More applause.

"Right. The first question I have is for all of you." Sophie beams. "It is this: How are you all okay? Let's start with you, Dapo."

All eyes land on him. Feral and hungry.

He clears his throat and focuses on Mum. On the life they now have.

The home they lived in had suddenly become a bit too big and a bit too quiet. So they'd moved. Downsized.

How are you all okay?

Looking his mum straight in her eyes, he says, "The answer is pretty simple: I'm not. Day by day I learn how to live. Day by day I learn how to be okay. That's all there is to it—I take it day by day. And there is one more thing." Dapo takes a deep breath. "Richard Jenkins was a fraud."

There is a collective gasp before the crowd erupts into a cacophony of noise.

ACKNOWLEDGMENTS

First and foremost, all glory to God.

Big thanks, and love, go to my family. Mumsi for getting me into reading, the Old Man for showing up in his own way, and my little brother, who will never fail to get me cracking up. All of your support has been immense.

Pete Knapp and Claire Wilson, my beloved agents. What can I say, except thank you sincerely. You are two titans who have been nothing but encouraging, open, and at the top of your games. Here's to many more stories, Lord willing.

Thanks must go to Safae El-Ouahabi and Stuti Telidevara for their diligence; and to the teams at Park & Fine, and RCW. I'm truly blessed.

Speaking of blessed: Cheers to another book with my editors, Emma Jones and Foyinsi Adegbonmire. We killed it with *We Are Hunted*. Thank you for walking alongside me for this one.

All my love to the teams at Feiwel and Friends and Macmillan UK who have been stellar in all areas from my debut up through now. Louisa, Beth, Charlie, Kelsey, Gaby, and Naheid, to call out a few.

People often ask me if I'm proud of my work. I am, but more

than anything I am grateful and humbled by those in my life who celebrate me, encourage me, and challenge me. There are too many to name but *I* know, that *you* know, that I know who you are. So, thank you. Yes, *you*.

BONUS SCENE

IF YOU MADE IT THIS FAR, THEN THIS IS FOR YOU:

DAYS, WEEKS, AND MONTHS HAVE GONE BY, AND THE world is a different place. It does not know what to do with Richard Jenkins's broken legacy. It does not know whether it wants to put it back together, or let it remain in pieces.

But to Valoisa it has all been one long moment she calls *now*.

Since the events on her homeland, she has mourned. Alone. These days, she can just about go a day without crying. That's new. So, too, are the moments of hope she feels as she wakes each morning.

This morning is no different.

Valoisa hides the wallet she stole yesterday and marches for the door. On the way, she passes a mirror and catches her reflection. "You look like dung," she murmurs.

The door groans as she pulls it open, and the chill of the early morning forces its way past her.

"Will you be back in time for dinner?" a woman's voice calls. Her accent has a good kind of roughness to it.

"Maybe," Valoisa lies. She doesn't want to overstay her welcome. She just needs to see about a boy.

Not bothering to hear what else the kind woman has to say, Valoisa leaves. She jumps as the door slams shut behind her.

She arrived in London deep into the evening, so she hasn't taken in this strange city properly. But as she steps through it now, she can see how Femi must have loved such a place. It is so full of charm. So full of hope. So full of character. One day, when Darlenia is done healing, she hopes others will think the same of the island she calls home.

She enters a secluded road with a renewed sense of purpose.

The moment is here.

Dapo walks down the street toward her. He hasn't changed much. He's taller and broader. Older in more ways than one. And suddenly Valoisa thinks this is not a good idea. That she shouldn't do this. That she has no right, but...but...she was strongly encouraged.

"It'll be okay," she says under her breath.

Yes. It will be okay.

Their eyes meet as their paths cross and...nothing. He does not recognize her. Valoisa is frozen. When he passes by, it occurs to her that maybe she should say something. *Hello?* No. *How are you?* No again.

"Dapo," she blurts, and Dapo stops and turns. He takes her in. Really takes her in. Surprise pushes his eyebrows up, opening his mouth wide enough that more than a few flies could enter.

"Dapo—he—uh—" This is a lot harder than she thought it was going to be. Valoisa tries again, ignoring the fact that her face is now wet with tears. "I'm sorry…about how everything turned out."

Dapo frowns. "Why are you here?"

She smiles weakly at him. "I'm not here to cause you any trouble. I just didn't want it to be a surprise."

"What?"

"We're going to be in the same program," she says at last. "Lelouch suggested I say hello before the internship starts. Since we had history and 'lest it get awkward.'"

Dapo says nothing for a few seconds that feel like forever. Grief dances in his eyes, and Valoisa sees a storm in his expression. Just as quickly, it disperses. "Well, then," he says with a smile. "I suppose I'll see you next week."

"Yes."

"Would you like to come for dinner? My mum's making homemade lasagna. It's to die for."

"I appreciate it, but I have to go." Another lie Valoisa tells. She cannot stomach the thought of looking Femi's mum in the eye. It feels wrong. "See you next week."

"Sure," Dapo replies. A broad smile is on his face.

They will not see each other next week.

You see, the day of the orientation, Valoisa will fall ill. A consequence of emptying a box of Celebrations chocolates in one sitting, while watching a documentary on some famous movie star with a tempestuous history.

And when she shows up the following day, the Ministry of Interdimensional Defense headquarters will be shrouded by an invisible barrier that will trap Dapo inside.

It's that simple. As one story ends another begins.

Thank you for reading this Feiwel & Friends book. The friends who made *We Are Hunted* possible are:

Jean Feiwel, Publisher
Liz Szabla, VP, Associate Publisher
Rich Deas, Senior Creative Director
Anna Roberto, Executive Editor
Holly West, Senior Editor
Kat Brzozowski, Senior Editor
Dawn Ryan, Executive Managing Editor
Jie Yang, Senior Production Manager
Emily Settle, Editor
Rachel Diebel, Editor
Foyinsi Adegbonmire, Editor
Brittany Groves, Assistant Editor
Michelle Gengaro-Kokmen, Designer
Helen Seachrist, Senior Production Editor

Follow us on Facebook or visit us online at mackids.com.
Our books are friends for life.